Steven Amsterdam is a palliative care nurse and the critically acclaimed author of the Guardian First Book Award-longlisted *Things We Didn't See Coming*, and *What the Family Needed*, which was longlisted for the IMPAC Prize and shortlisted for the Encore Award. Originally from New York City, he now lives in Melbourne.

Also by Steven Amsterdam

Things We Didn't See Coming
What the Family Needed

THE EASY
WAY OUT

Steven Amsterdam

riverrun

First published in 2016 by Hachette Australia
First published in Great Britain in 2016 by riverrun
This paperback edition published in 2017 by

riverrun

an imprint of
Quercus Publishing Ltd
Carmelite House
50 Victoria Embankment
London EC4Y 0DZ

An Hachette UK company

A CIP catalogue record for this book is available
from the British Library

ISBN 978 1 78648 084 2
EBOOK ISBN 978 1 78648 085 9

10 9 8 7 6 5 4 3 2 1

Typeset by CC Book Production
Printed and bound in Great Britain by Clays Ltd, St Ives plc

QUALITY OF LIFE

'HERE'S THE POISON we've been discussing.'

I hold the plastic cup out towards the assembled. Too eagerly maybe, because the wife lets out an existential, 'Oh.'

The trio of daughters at the bedside shift their stares between the cup and their emaciated dad. Horrified.

Unfortunately, this is what we're gathered here for today. Psychology and Social Work have signed off, Teddy's doctor has prescribed all we need, and has already left for the airport—an oncology conference. The anti-emetic has had a chance to kick in. It's just us now.

Oldest daughter makes two unconscious fists.

'Do you need more time?' I ask Teddy.

Again, the wife says, 'Oh.'

I'm blocking on her name. With all of them watching me so intensely, there's no natural moment to scroll back through his file.

'Teddo,' she says to him, sunken between the pillows of his hospital bed, 'I don't think we can do this today.'

Forty-one years old, a builder who didn't believe in sunscreen. Now he has small but insistent metastases everywhere but his teeth. Teddy stretches and winces, extending his bluish-white foot past the metal edge of his bed. He gives her a smirk suggesting that she's not the one making the call. There's a tinge of a too-late farewell to his face, like a ship that's already left the harbour.

'This is only going to get worse,' he tells her.

True.

The cancer ran through him like drain cleaner. First the disease, then the treatment, until he was reduced to the usual constellation of bony prominences, forehead and cheekbones around ashy eyes, all floating on a long and increasingly unresponsive body that's starting to go chalky at the edges. His right side is nearly paralysed. In his first interview with us two months ago, he could still watch his old rock band on weekends. That's long gone. Quality family time has been reduced to personal care. Increasing pain and decreasing consciousness are all that's on the horizon.

The oldest, whose graduation from hairstylist school her father will be unable to attend, proved she's been studying by dyeing his post-chemo chicken fuzz a bright blue and gelling it into a kind of mohawk, turning him into a frail, ageing rock star. The teenager's fingertips are still tinged the same blue. What a tender bathroom scene that would have been.

'We can do this,' Teddy tells his wife.

She confirms his decision with a deferential nod. What other, less weighty arguments between them have been resolved with this simple declaration?

His chin falls towards me: Continue.

I keep the cup held out between us, as specified, speaking clearly for the video camera in the corner and the one-way glass in the far wall. 'If you drink this, in a few minutes you will fall asleep and lose consciousness. A few minutes after that, your heart will stop. There will be no attempt to revive you. You will die. As that happens, your family will be here with you. I will be here too. We will do whatever we can to keep you comfortable as you die.' My pre-planned intake of air gives my next line the space it needs. 'Is this what you want?'

Despite the social worker's previous efforts and my open posture, there's a fresh round of gulping tears from the middle daughter. She collapses over the edge of the bed onto him, digging her head into his side, pressing against his spine. He squirms slightly to move away, even while resting the fingers of his working hand in her hair, tapping her head, *there, there.*

She straightens up again, trying to be good, plucking at the tuft on his head. He reaches up to catch her hand to stop her fiddling. 'Leave it.'

The wife grabs his hand, to keep Teddy from disciplining their daughter in his last minutes. Hand over hand over hand, the three of them are caught there in a tussle over a wisp of bright blue hair. This is the family picture: three hands and wrists woven together, each with a different purpose—the daughter grooming, the father pulling back in terminal retreat, the mother trying to protect them all.

I think the youngest is named Hannah, but I won't chance it. The longer they fret, the blanker my mind goes. She turns five next week. That I remember. They're going through with her party, to keep things normal.

The children's names I'm allowed to forget. They weren't supposed to even be here. After much processing, in fact, the wife had decided that Teddy's death would be too confronting for them. Instead, the grandparents would be with the girls today. But then, at nine-thirty this morning, without even a heads-up, the mother ushered them into Consulting Room B to wait for their father to be rolled in. I made a brave, more-the-merrier face. As they came through, Teddy's wife told me: 'They'll cope. This is better.' A short while later, each daughter signed some freshly generated paperwork so they could witness their father's death. Barely a sniffle then. No objections.

Originally, Teddy wanted his last drink to occur in the hospital room where he'd spent his last weeks—where he knew the nurses and where there is almost a view of the park. Yesterday at three, though, the ward (or someone several floors higher, more likely) decided that it wouldn't happen there. Management would rather confine our dirty business to the specialist wing and not have us skulking through the main wards with our Nembutal.

This room is less medical, I assured Teddy. His family would have more privacy down here. Pale pink walls, soft furniture and minimal ventilation give it the institutional comfort of a place where procedures are discussed, not performed. It also has three surveillance cameras, and a viewing room next door. Plus, it's closer to the morgue. These last were not mentioned as selling points.

The crux of the issue is that despite this being my first assist, I have skilfully adapted to unforeseen changes this morning and kept the patient on his desired track, but here we are with his family close to mutiny. Nettie will be watching me from somewhere in the building.

I make eye contact with Teddy, looking for an answer to my long-ago query. *Is this what you want?*

He knows and I know that it is. I relax my mouth and forehead to convey that, even now, after all the prep and diagnostics and psych support, he has time to say so out loud.

They have time. As the research shows, you don't do this alone.

He looks away, distracted by the middle daughter, saying, 'Don't, Dad.'

There, the wish to stop the administration has been seconded. As per guidelines, we may have to abort.

I allow an extra minute to let them each roam internally, consider the situation from one another's position—from the bed or bedside— or vacate the scene entirely and fly out over some long ago Christmas when the girls tore open the wrapping paper like they still believed in Santa. Or one afternoon they spent walking through strange streets looking for the dog. Or one of his band's last gigs, when the girls stood close to their mother in the front row, singing along, clapping for Dad. On return to the conversation, any response will be deepened by their brief meandering. Whatever the outcome, it will feel more real for having had the time.

I glance at the clock above the one-way mirror on the wall through which Nettie or anyone from upstairs who still has their doubts might be observing our progress. There we are, six white

6

people fine tuning a death. Anywhere else on the planet, Teddy would have withered from his disease months ago, no paperwork required. But his doctor was optimistic and pumped him up with six rounds of chemo. Since that didn't do the trick, here I am, sporting a pair of sweat stains under the arms of my best dress shirt, trying at least to get Teddy's last minutes right, to avoid the indignity of the inevitable.

'Let's get on with this,' Teddy says to me. His wife and children lower their heads in obedience. Dad decides. His primacy was hinted at in the interviews, but muddied by the social worker and the egalitarian fog that comes from passing around the talking stick.

The mirror offers no subtle glimmer to suggest we can or should move on.

'I need a spoken reply,' I tell him. With no perceptible second thoughts from the family. Untender, yes, but legally required.

He shifts, as if particularly humiliated at having to follow my orders at this late stage, but he knows we need to adhere. No doubt someone from Ethics will run a trace through this entire scene to make sure the words were said in the right order.

'Yes. I want to drink it.'

'Yes?' I say. Halfway there.

Blankness.

I'm going to have to be explicit.

My affect here must be perfectly flat, to avoid even the faintest tone of an assumption about where today will take us. Nettie admits it's helpful if we can limit the number of dropouts. We don't work on commission, but our program does need to justify its existence.

'And do you want to die today?' I ask.

The middle one gives me a filthy look that neither she nor I will ever forget. The wife chews her lip, resenting the whole wide world. The oldest, with her beaded cornrows, stares at the cup. Hannah, keeping her eyes on me, discovers the most healthy stance: her thumb has found its way into her mouth and she's sucking as hard as she can.

7

Teddy looks at them, at me, then closes his eyes.

I soften my posture further, keeping the fateful cup discreetly at my waist, and taking a step back to demonstrate all the space I'm willing to give them. I sure hope Nettie's watching.

Yesterday at four, she told me, 'Teddy should be uncomplicated. A good person for you to start with.' She was the one who conducted the preliminary discussions in his case, directed the family meetings, collected the medical reports, got the second and third opinions on his prognosis, and had the psychologist clear him of organic depression. All as per protocol. Last night, I replayed some of their conversations. He was clear at the start. *I'm done. Totally done.*

The guidelines for Measure 961 don't let anyone out that easily. *What does the idea of dying mean to you? How do you imagine your death? How do you feel when you think of the people in your world going about their lives without you?* The correct answer is *shitty*, naturally, but once you've spent a month in a hospital, you develop a sense for the responses that will get you what you want. Teddy found half a dozen different ways to say *Let me out.* Even then, the questions are reframed and circular, examining death from infinite angles until, by the third hour of viewing, you could believe that the suffering Teddy wanted to end was the evaluation itself.

And then there was the children's consultation. Nettie lassoed the widest-eyed, most child-safe social worker we have into the room to mediate. Festive blouse, clogs, greying fringe. She nodded like a primary school teacher throughout, no matter what was being said, listening listening listening to everyone until the notion of Dad's exit strategy had been explained and rationalised to the girls as one more unavoidable effect of big bad cancer.

I was present for those interviews, but in my earlier role, simply recording and making mental assessments, tallying up all the flickers of behaviour—Teddy's attitude (despairing or pragmatic?), his wife's (resigned or supportive?), and the visibly uneven adjustment of the daughters. When the social worker gave me the nod, I decamped to my desk to translate the variables into a report, with the relatively sterile goal of providing guidance for future interventions. Since everyone knows that suicides are like snowflakes, my reports don't really work as directives. Their true purpose is to demonstrate to Business Affairs—sixth floor, C wing—that one cup of Nembutal, with sufficient psychosocial support and bereavement follow-up as indicated, can be not only more in line with a patient's and a family's wishes, but also cheaper than a patient—against their will and comfort—occupying a hospital bed and draining morphine and nursing resources for three extra, extra-miserable months. Some hospitals have already shown this to be true by a factor of approximately one new MRI machine every three months. Again, not the selling point.

His wife pushes down the pillows to tell him, 'I want whatever you want.'

And it comes to me: her name is Geraldine.

I glance at the mirror. See, Nettie? I am so keenly attuned to room dynamics that my brain regains function as the family does.

The girls tighten ranks around the bed, but Teddy gives me nothing. I consider letting him know that if it's not today, he's likely to get rolled back to the ward and never make contact again. The few who tried waited until they had ten-out-of-ten pain, a week to live anyway, and zero capacity to endure our questions again. Death caught them first.

Like Nettie, Lena, who was originally lined up to do this assist, also thought Teddy would go quietly. He told her that part of his urgency was the painkillers, not the pain. They were giving him nightmares, mostly about Geraldine remarrying. He was being haunted by his replacement. This made the still-hazy mornings, when he would have to face his still-faithful wife, difficult.

Lena had been a solid assistant for nearly a year, so no one doubted her last week when she called in sick on the day of another patient's departure. Nettie pitched in enough so that the patient and carers were unruffled. Indeed, our model is to limit unnecessary attachment between staff and families. By lunchtime yesterday, though, Lena had made her intentions clear with the news of her reassignment to Renal. Not much pain there, and not many momentous decisions to be made as the patients slowly fatigue to death. She resigned via email. Nettie and I were walking back from the cafeteria when it came through. 'This work isn't for everyone, is it?' Nettie said, staring at her phone, not waiting for her researcher's response. Twenty seconds passed before she solved her staffing problem. 'Evan. It's not the job you applied for but you know you're appropriate. You're a registered nurse and you're on staff, which means I don't have to find or fundraise for a new hire. You know every one of the parameters. You've met Teddy and his family. It could be me in there with them tomorrow. It could be you.' Her eyebrows made a question mark.

Teddy looks towards me and grumbles distinctly, 'I understand that if I drink the poison I will die. That's what I want. Today. Now.'

Nobody listening or watching would detect coercion.

Geraldine bursts with encouragement. 'Yes, yes. That's what we're here for.' Even better.

'You come here.' He beckons me close, and I feel calmer. Happy, almost.

Every review of the literature confirms that the dying know the way better than all of us. I position myself next to his bed at the same latitude as his midsection. The family can hold the other side of him. There's an adversarial aspect to this grouping, but all I have to do is hand him a cup and step back.

It's what I told Nettie yesterday: I can do this.

'Wait, wait,' Geraldine says. 'I need a minute.'

Teddy tells her, 'Sure.' Like she's going back to the house for a jumper.

She turns to look out the window. It's tinted greenish brown to obscure the view of the Psychiatry Open Space (which is gated and locked). It doesn't matter. Geraldine's face is set as if she is gazing out to the horizon.

I keep my expression soft, really at ease, really present and so very open to whatever may come from Geraldine's minute.

Without looking down, she flattens the blue horn on Teddy's head, letting her palm rest against his forehead and slide down towards his neck. He doesn't move and doesn't object.

Once she's reviewed the recording, Nettie will tell me exactly how this went. She'll suggest a coffee, not tomorrow—the day after, *just to see where you're at*. We'll take a recessed corner of the cafeteria, away from the patients in their bandages and the staff with their lanyards. And I'll spin my cup on the table while she tells me precisely where I'm at.

She'll be sure to check in about Viv. *How's your mother?*

Every few weeks, Nettie has to take my temperature about Viv. Being in possession of a close family member with a degenerative condition made my hire into this program a bit of a squeaker with Human Resources. Nettie has taken it upon herself to be kept abreast of any changes in Viv's condition that might present me with conflict or mental anguish.

There are no changes and no problems. Parkinson's, atypical. It's the result, Viv's certain, of a toxic exposure when she was forcing the English language on poor islanders in her youth. The atypicality is a point of pride, though it also means erratic progression and fluctuating responsiveness to the more reliable meds, which is less fulfilling. Viv accentuates and embraces the uncertainty by switching neurologists with glee, maintaining perpetual enthusiasm for the new doctor, whoever it may be. She moved herself into a low-care facility near the Mercy, and applauded when I got the job. 'When it's my time, you'll get me the magic drink.' This was her idle suicide chat with no details, the kind of conversation we all have on long afternoons.

'You'd have to be terminal.'

She winked. 'You'll find a way.' Her wink, which was once so quick you weren't sure it had happened, has come to involve her whole face, from jaw to hairline, more of a grimace. None of it matters because Viv remains, sadly, stable, which is the only fact I ever report.

Still at Teddy's side, I exhale effusively, not to show growing exasperation with the unsmooth proceedings, but to provide a warm hum of support for whatever eventuates. Namaste, et cetera.

Geraldine tightens her grip on her husband's neck, as if to hold him away from me. 'No. I can't. Sorry, Teddo,' exhibiting enough conflict to sink the session. She straightens herself to face me. 'I think the family would be easier about it if this happened at home. That's doable, isn't it?'

I give a slow nod which means: Yes, people commit suicide at home. Carry him back to your master bedroom, source the drugs—online or near any major intersection. He'll be on his way and you'll have a few years of criminal inquiries to sort out. If you don't want to break the law all by yourself, there are services out there—not in the phone book exactly, but findable—that can help you score the necessary pharmaceuticals. I get the discomfort with this room. Familiar surroundings are cosy, with no legal guidelines to follow, no long prelude to the finale; and the outcome is a surer thing than for most medical proceedings, such as, say, a home birth. There's no chance of complications if the endgame is death and the players are committed. So the issue is not whether it can be done at home, but why she is coming up with this now. It doesn't look like an objection as much as what they call in the literature *bargaining*.

Teddy takes the wheel again, telling her, 'It's not later. It's now.'

'What about us?' Geraldine protests. 'What—'.

Teddy pushes out his lower lip at her, stopping that line of objection. She reaches for his good arm, lovingly, to squeeze him into changing his mind. He rotates his wrist against her grip until she takes her hand away.

Legal will adore this.

'If you need more time,' I say, 'or if you want me to contact the social worker . . . Nothing has to happen—'

'No. Today it is,' Geraldine says. She and her daughters look down at Teddy's legs, splayed under the sheets as if they aren't his. At least she tried.

Hannah twists an edge of the sheet around her non-sucked thumb, pulling and pulling at it until Teddy reaches out to stop her. The kid needs hugging before she'll settle. She pushes his lame arm over towards me. I guard the cup with my hand.

'Please,' Teddy says to me. 'Just sit with me. We'll get there.'

I provide gentle eye contact for the family to see, for any observers in the adjacent room or watching through closed circuit from the ceiling. 'If you are all in agreement, we can go forward. There's no urgency.'

'We are together on this,' Geraldine tells me. 'We know that today is the day.'

Teddy wastes no time. 'I want to drink the poison. I want to die. Today. Now.'

After a few seconds of sober assessment, I continue through the final litany of disclaimers. Hannah gives me stink eye worse than the other one, disconcerting from such a rosy-cheeked cherub.

Through the stiffest officiating—*we respect and acknowledge*; *you understand and absolve*—I try to keep my easy vibe aimed at her.

Teddy says his last *yes*, then looks to me, following my arm down to the bed. 'Hey, what're you doing?'

At some point during the to-ing and fro-ing, my cup-holding hand has tilted, dripping an oblong stain of poison wetness onto the bed.

His cup runneth over. It's half-empty. Half-full, depending on your perspective, but that's not mine.

In the dizzying instant that we each gather the meaning of this new show-stopping impediment, which is pooling on top of the barely absorbent hospital sheet, the puddle punctuates the scene by overflowing, trickling onto the grey-green linoleum. With a whiplike response, I overcorrect, and jerk—jerk being the operative word—a seemingly equal amount of the Nembutal onto my shirt and pants.

My stunned, 'Shit,' seems insubstantial.

Primum non nocere. I have done harm.

13

Nettie is going to review the hell out of this, and she won't wait for the day after tomorrow. I remain seated, grasping for an expression of undisturbed tranquillity, suggesting forgiveness for everyone in the room—myself included.

Teddy, who has been opening and closing his mouth in fishlike distress, throws his head back. 'You were all against me. All of you.' His voice breaks. 'This one thing I asked for. This one thing.'

The daughters stand back, accused, and look to Geraldine, who can't look at all. She's covering her eyes with her fingertips.

'I am so sorry,' I say. 'I can fix this. I can get to the pharmacy and have a replacement dose ordered. I'll bring it back as soon as it's processed. It can be accomplished in minutes. I am so sorry.'

Teddy's not ready for negotiating. 'One blessed mercy,' he chants to himself. 'That was all.'

Hannah, bewildered, hides her face against her mother's hip.

The family draws in, assuring him, no, they were with him all along.

Impossible promises keep spouting from my lips. 'We won't need to go through the questions again. We can skip them. I can be back in ten minutes. Fifteen at the most.'

In truth, a mistake of this magnitude has to be documented throughout the system, which involves my working through at least twenty screens before any more Nembutal can be dispensed. Five to ten minutes right there. For the replacement order to be made, which could take the pharmacist any amount of time, depending on who is working now, I'll need Nettie's signature. If she's not watching this disaster unfold from next door, I'll have to find her. She'll take my call, wherever she is, but what will my story be? Was the spill a novice's nerves? A manifestation of my own deeply buried judgment? Did my hand act on behalf of the daughters, as some sort of proxy? Or was it nothing so Freudian, simply the first, poorly timed announcement of my very own Parkinson's?

The excuse doesn't matter. Even if I found Nettie, performed the necessary administrative penance, and worked a miracle with the pharmacist, all with serendipitous time flow, it would be half an hour before the job could be done, and by then those assembled here would surely be in open rebellion. Abort.

Geraldine stabs her fingers into her forehead and tells me, 'Just take yourself out of here.'

'Understood: I'll give you time alone and then—'

'Get out!'

The teenager with the blue fingertips pities me. I certainly do.

'Going.' Standing causes my pants to drizzle Nembutal onto my shoes and the floor, leaving behind a slip hazard which itself should be reported—not to mention the unattended family in the consulting room, which is another breach.

My plan is to pose out in the hallway as a relative in deep grief until the family in deep grief tell me what they want. I close the door behind me and slide down the glossy white wall, letting my body fold into a squat, so that the passing crowd won't see the dark stains on my pants.

At least the air is cooler down here.

A gurney wheels past, carrying an occupied body bag, sealed and on its way to the morgue. The jiggling mass inside seems to mock me, letting me know that somewhere in the hospital someone knows how to produce a corpse.

Let's regroup: in the Golden Book of Drug Errors, failing to kill a patient doesn't have to be a career ender. If Nettie's feeling kindly, she'll shunt me back to research. If not, I can always put in for a transfer to Psychiatry, where the complaints come so thick and fast that this little blip wouldn't matter at all. If it's decided that my ineptitude has been too awesome, even for the Mercy, I can always go private, work in a house on the west side, and double my income. All good options.

Viv would not be impressed with me going private, since anything that pays well must be ethically flawed (assisting deaths or drawing a royal flush excepted). In the end, she'll stop complaining. My salary contributes to her mortgage and keeps her in stewed peaches at Willow Wood.

The glittering possibilities are all spreading out in front of me when Nettie appears, her too-good-for-hospital shoes announcing her. The finest calves a fifty-year-old could hope for, and she always keeps them on display. Her lanyard and badge are rakishly beached over her left breast. Most encouraging of all, she's carrying a plastic cup of something.

I slide back up the wall to attention. With her free hand, she blesses the top of my head with a kindly pat. I am still employed.

She holds out the cup. 'Same drug, same dose.'

'Is that for me?' I ask.

'No. Are you ready to go back in?'

'Do they need more time?'

'Do you?' She hands me the cup. 'Trust me. This will be fine. You flinched. You all took turns flinching. You've seen this before.'

She takes my other hand in hers. At first I think it's for solidarity, but she tightens her fingers over mine and forces them into a fist, which she lifts and uses to knock on the door.

The oldest daughter opens it. I brace for impact and enter. The atmosphere in the room remains foul. Nettie steps in after me and shuts the door behind us. Despite wearing a shirt that seems to be perspiring on its own, I proceed with confidence, keeping the cup stable and in front of me.

Nettie leads. 'Hello, Geraldine. Hayley, Ruby, Hannah.' Looking at me as she names them. 'I've been made aware of what's been going on in here, and . . .' She raises her shoulders at the helplessness of mortals, exonerating each of us. 'Teddy, I was able to replace the Nembutal for you, if this is what you want.' She points to the cup in my hand.

'I do,' he says, cocking his head towards his wife and the girls. 'Please?' It's his first time asking them, rather than telling, and maybe this is what we've been working towards for the last hour.

They acquiesce.

'Then we'll continue from where we were,' I say, setting off an outbreak of hugs among the family.

For my ears only, Nettie lets out a satisfied cluck.

Teddy gives the replacement Nembutal a fuck-you look and says, 'Bring it here.'

A quick glance at Nettie tells me that's consent enough. I put the cup in his good hand and he downs it in one long drink.

Apparently the stuff tastes like it could kill you, but as he drinks— whether to protect the others from any more of his discomfort or because he's tasted worse in his day—he doesn't react. He drops the cup onto the sheets. His good hand idly finds its way up to massage his throat, milking it all down.

Nettie taps my wrist and choreographs us into the background. Hands clasped in front of me like a funeral director, I indicate that I will remain respectfully withdrawn and still available. In the event, for example, that he upchucks.

The daughters cocoon around him, desperate for the last traces that he'll be leaving. They're not even trying not to cry. The *I love you*s commence, with a couple of *We'll miss you*s thrown in. Geraldine stands behind them, overseeing. The family will be all hers now.

Teddy comforts them, switching between their faces every few seconds as greedily as he can. 'I'm going to miss you girls so much.'

After all the interviews and fuck-ups, this is what finally gets me.

Assistants are advised to allow themselves to express sadness. Silent tearing up is permitted, even encouraged, as it demonstrates empathy. Weeping, not so much. But *he's going to miss them*.

To steel myself, I tally the *I love you*s exchanged (twenty-one, and counting). The tiniest choke escapes from my throat.

Teddy tells them, 'You're going to be okay—better than okay: you're going to be wonderful.'

Geraldine smiles as best she can, adding to her daughters, 'You'll be okay, because I'm going to be okay.' She includes Teddy in their huddle. 'We're going to be okay.'

All I can think of while steadying my breath so as not to make another sound is that nobody's going to be okay for a while.

Teddy is pushing the bright side too. 'You can get back to school and—' He trips on whatever was next, and for a long moment he can't even speak. 'Let's just be together,' he says. In another minute, his eyes droop. In another, he's out. He went down fast.

Geraldine tenses with the urge to do something. She stuffs another pillow behind his head, accentuating his shallow breathing.

'Is he dead?' Hayley asks me.

'Not yet.'

'Then can he hear us?' asks Ruby.

'Some part of him can,' I say.

Hannah shouts, 'We love you, Daddy!' into his face. What is she even making of this whole event?

Nettie dabs her eyes with her knuckle.

Hayley asks, 'How long does it take for him to totally be—?'

'A few more minutes.'

With this information, their trauma turns to curiosity as they study each inhalation, waiting for death to take over his body.

A sudden deep breath comes, as if he's been startled, followed by a wet gurgle. Hayley looks to me for guidance. Nettie notices. Big win.

'I don't think he's conscious now,' I assure Hayley. 'It's more of a reflex.'

The noise increases, gets closer to a drowning gag. I tell them how to let his head rest back to modify the acoustics in his throat. Not for him so much, but for them. This moist sound is the last audio they'll have of him.

Last week Nettie performed an assist, which went off without any interruptions. I watched it again last night as an instructional. A youngish woman. Advanced motor neurone disease, still able to lift the cup. No witnesses present to shower her in *I love yous*, just a quiet 'Thank you' to Nettie as she shut her eyes, and waited. Nettie rubbed the woman's hand for five minutes more, emanating well-trained warmth until the neck relaxed and the face fell slack. A few minutes of weak raspiness, then silence. At that instant, I caught a rare glimpse of uncertainty in my supervisor. Alone with the body, her eyes searched around the room in controlled panic, as if the woman might have played a trick, hid in the closet or under the bed. The moment passed, but the uncanniness of death was briefly evident.

A final bubble bubbles up from Teddy's throat and he comes to a halt. Anywhere else in the hospital, this is an emergency. Here, it means a good outcome.

Geraldine is a single parent.

I lead the family through this moment by telegraphing wise and respectful thoughts, to the best of my ability. Geraldine, unforgiving of the gods that brought her to this, shepherds her daughters into her arms. Her expression falters, as if the real flood is about to begin. Then the smell reaches us. A fart or worse from Dad. Hannah isn't too upset to acknowledge it by pinching her nose. This distinct mood-breaker is my cue. I reach past the tangle of embraces to pull a blanket from the foot of the bed up to Teddy's chest to limit the smell's range.

Breathing through my mouth, I check pulses, radial and carotid. The family seems willing to step away from him for this, as I keep my fingers on his dull warm blood, waiting for the requisite minute.

Geraldine watches me as I count out exactly nil pulses of blood moving beneath his skin. 'Dad is dead now,' she tells the kids.

I confirm with a doctorly nod. 'Do you want time alone with him?'

'No, I don't,' she says with the most certainty she's shown all morning. 'He's not here.'

Away from the main stage I notice Nettie drop a paper towel onto the puddle of Nembutal and deftly foot-mop it under the bed. She then leads the daughters, who have opted to skip this part, down the hall to the bereavement room, Consulting Room C.

Geraldine and I stay behind to wash the body. I fill the basins, bring in the towels from the bathroom and pull down the sheets. Gaunt and sallow flesh. Still, more lifelike than it will be in an hour.

I wash one arm while she does the other, her eyes examining every fold of his skin.

'This isn't how I'll remember him,' she tells me.

I let her wash his face. She pokes at the body-length bruise developing where his body meets the mattress. When the heart stops pumping, blood obeys gravity.

We stand on either side of the bed and strip him to his half-full diaper, which I remove and bag. I start washing around his torso. His legs. 'He told me this morning he dreamed about dying last night, except it wasn't here. We were in a rowboat on a lake we took the girls to. That's where he really would have wanted to go, right in the middle of the lake. You were there, he said. We only found out yesterday it would be you but you made it into the dream. Be flattered. I didn't sleep last night. He had the morphine on his side. I don't think he really dreamed all that, but it's sweet he wanted me to think so. It was like him to tell me that to keep me going. He said everything in the dream went well.'

Rather than address the unwellness of today's intervention, or wonder if he really had a nightmare about Geraldine's next husband, or if this is simply a gloss that the new widow wants to tell herself, I silently squeeze out my washer over the basin. Working together, we bring up the pale knee closest to me so that he can be turned toward Geraldine and I can start on his back.

She leans into his shoulder to take one last sniff of his skin. 'Doesn't even smell like him anymore.'

'Hospitals,' I say.

She gives me a patient smile. 'At the end of the day, he's where he wants to be. In the last part of the dream, he said, we slipped him naked into the water.'

———

After Teddy has made the short trip to the morgue and the family has left, I send a fearful text to Nettie suggesting an early debrief. It gets an immediate reply.

Oh yes.

I wait for her in our office. There are two enormous desks here, leftovers from the last renovation of this wing. Like the old computers and monitors we were given, they are too large for the room. They have been pushed to opposite walls. One for her and one for a floater, who has mostly been me.

Teddy's death gets replayed from all available angles on my monitor. I watch with Zapruderian intensity. Here's the frame where my too-open posture made them squirm. Here's where I squint into the one-way glass for rescue, the salesman of death. There's the middle daughter giving me disgusted side-eye as I stick to protocol.

Teddy's sheets obscure the precise moment of my spill, so I can't focus on the embarrassing mechanics of that. The only relief, as far as Ethics might note, is that for the minutes when I'm out of the room, the assembled loved ones linger in bewilderment and frustration but never come close to abandoning the mission.

I remember Lena's performances. They seemed to be driven by self-regard. Among my previous duties was to judge the outward expression of a family's contentment post-intervention, and correlate it with, if available, the assistant's reflective reporting of their experience during. Lena's focus on her internal circumstances betrayed, on several occasions, an inability to achieve professional presence. Either she'd be looking overwrought as she handed over the cup, tears welling too early behind her eyeliner, or there'd be a bland stare throughout, as if she was waiting for a hamburger to finish on a grill. The reason for the variability was inevitably revealed in her written reflections: the patient reminded her of a family member, or of herself. It also depended on how she felt the patient saw her: as a great humanitarian, an activist, a gun-for-hire, or a devil. She was hit hardest if she'd had a big night the night before. Her orphan status figured in, too. Her mother had a heart attack when she was ten and her father fell off his bike and died two years later. Lena took this to indicate that, organic or accidental, her death would come suddenly, which meant that she was nothing like our pitiable patients. I added a margin note to more than a few of her write-ups: *I question the appropriateness of this assistant for this role.*

So, how does my performance compare?

I watch the snuff film again, but as a researcher this time, documenting each transaction in the room, counting the tears, and so on. It's a hedge against whichever job I'll have left at the end of the day. As I watch the family, I look beyond my foolishness to where I find the usual anxious peaks (the assistant enters with the cup, recites the depressing but necessary words) and the grim troughs (Teddy's insistence that this is happening today). The tiny exchanges between people are turned into paragraphs, highlighting our deep consideration of our clients and underlining the seriousness of our efforts to do right by them. Mostly the verbiage pleases Nettie, whose aim is to suffocate the head of the hospital with qualitative data.

She doesn't come back to her desk, likely detained elsewhere, leaving me with the sense that I'll be allowed to do another assist.

I read up on the next case.

Uma, a dentist, enjoying her retirement. Walked the Camino last year, Mount Fuji the year before that, then two months ago a tumour started gnawing its way through her soft palate. By the time it was diagnosed, during the week of her sixty-second birthday, she didn't need to be told how the story would end. There isn't even a drug trial to dream about, and even if there was, she's already too sick for it. The psychologists deem her sound, ready to go. Two hiking buddies and her partner will be present.

The reflection window suddenly blooms onto my screen from Teddy's still-open file. The window is timed to pop up for whoever assisted, prompting them to record how it all felt. The process is optional but pushy and, research has shown, therapeutic.

I drag the cursor across to the little red dot in the corner and opt out.

I escape the hospital at 5 pm through the sliding doors, wondering what soon-to-be-five-year-old Hannah's formulation of this afternoon will be. *Death is something that happens when a stranger makes you drink from a plastic cup.* How will she cope the first time a dental assistant offers her mouthwash and tells her to rinse?

Not that I would commit anything to the official record, but this assistant's own childhood experience with death may be relevant: I'm six and drinking a box of something orange. Viv is standing in the hall, shakily attempting to place the cordless phone back in its seat. The handset drops and skitters across the wooden floor. This is not a symptom. She picks it up slowly, then places it back in the cradle. Her mother-in-law has just called to tell her that my father died. Our forest-green Volkswagen missed a tight switchback in the national park. It rammed into a tree then spun down a cliffside, landing right-side up on a rise in a shallow creek bed and turning into a fireball. Broken neck, burns, asphyxiation. Those words came later.

The long view on this missed switchback of his is also relevant. After an auspicious young adulthood that included top-of-the-class honours and a national scholarship to design a vaccination program for impoverished populations in the same do-good outpost where he met my mother, my father, in his twenties, peaked. There was the wedding, followed by the idealistic relocations that kept not working out. The locals weren't equipped, weren't engaged, weren't appreciative. White guilt, an embarrassed move back to the mainland and a short résumé of ineffective attempts to improve the lots of others. So they had a kid. All this, and seven-plus years without real work, in the context of his undertreated depression, managed only with daily use of marijuana, sourced straight from a lab. He refused to try a different approach; say, to see a therapist.

Picture my mother's increasingly withering patience.

The completion of his failure to fulfil early promise came the day before he died. Viv suggested he move in with his parents for a while. Her thinking, she told me when I was eleven and old enough to understand, was that it might induce him to smoke less. 'I had to save us,' she said. If she feels responsible for what happened next, she's never said. The more pressing questions for me have always been about how much a dead father can miss his kid and why he didn't anticipate it the way Teddy did.

At the moment, though, I'm only six.

'There's no sugar-coating this one,' she says, instantly ruining a whole species of donut for me forever. 'Dad is dead. It happened last night. He drove off the road and died. Someone driving by saw the smoke.'

I remember saying, 'What?'

'It was where we camped last summer, where you fed the ducks. Around there, it sounds like. Near the river. They only found the car today. It would have been quick for him, the whole accident.'

I also asked, 'Can I talk to him?'

'No. We won't talk to him again. That's all we get of him.'

I grabbed the phone and handed it to her, thinking this was simply another strategy of hers in the ongoing Mum-versus-Dad battle. Apparently I also said, endearingly, 'Don't be obstinate.'

'I wish that's what it was. He wanted to be gone.'

Death was still an abstract, but *gone* I understood. There had been a grim succession of turtles in the previous year. 'Like Molly and Milly?'

'Like Molly and Milly.'

This process of *going* had been outlined to me each time we buried one in the grass between our building and the car park behind the bank, but I needed more. 'Does it hurt?'

'It's different for everyone. For Dad, I imagine it hurt some. But it would have been over fast.' Only then did she make the motherly move of pulling me close. 'He hurts less now than he did before. I know that.'

'How do you know?'

'When you're gone you don't feel anything anymore. No breathing, no sleeping, no hunger. No brain. There's nothing.'

'Even nothing feels like something.'

'Nice try, but death trumps.'

'That means death wins?'

'Every single game.'

I pulled away from her. 'So why do we play?'

Viv didn't answer. Instead, she crushed me and my juice box against her and shook. She was still crying when she called back my grandmother to report the adorable thing I'd said and report that I'd taken the news well, all things considered.

That's how she told me the conversation went. Over the years she's elaborated, especially with new friends, turning me and my reasonable quandary into the sparkle that kept her going. The thrust was that because of me she didn't have the option of falling apart.

We were sustained by more than my adorable precocity, however. My father had had the forethought to take out a generous life insurance policy, and had then waited past the exclusion period and—with a last flash of the old college smarts—chose a sufficiently isolated road to drive off; this, in the absence of a documented psychiatric history (his resistance to treatment may have been his last stab at genius), meant that his death happened within the acceptable guidelines for full payout. Viv thinks the fact that this synced up with her eviction of him was possibly not an accident either. 'He knew where he was going for a while.'

My mother and grandparents decided that, for the benefit of helpless me—the apple of everyone's eye as well as the eye of the resulting storm—marital discord would be left out of the discussion with the claims adjusters. When the time came, his joblessness was minimised too, with loved ones instead citing his devotion to raising me while my mother worked her taxing hours. This was interesting spin, as he had a steady record of forgetting to pick me up from school and she was a part-time guidance counsellor working on her thesis. To anyone who asked, though—and few were brave enough to harass poor me—I was coached to describe Dad making dinner every night with Mum coming home late and exhausted.

They gave us the money. Viv bought herself a new bed, queen, and us a new Volkswagen, brown. It wasn't until the next year that we really got to try out the car. There was a dispute at her work over a student who was failing to thrive. The administration didn't budge and she didn't either. Instead, with the confidence lent by her bank account, she decided it was change time for us. With one week's notice to her school and mine, and the same to my father's parents who had been picking me up every day, we moved across the state. 'Start again,' she said.

We could have gone to live with her parents, but they were mean know-nothings with zip to offer us of the world. No way was she going home in these circumstances and no way would she let them get their claws into me. Alternatively, she could have afforded to go back to her thesis (early childhood education as linked to adolescent mental health stats) and might have even done well, but no. The subject no longer captivated her.

The best moves were to new school systems in places where she knew no one. Making it all work was a challenge. Fun. Fresh. Every time.

In the earliest days after his death, the ones before the funeral, I worked out what had gone wrong with Dad. The summer before he died, driving that same road, I was in the back seat by myself. There had been talk of a sibling but they got a miscarriage instead. (Information also filled in later.) I remember being centrifugally shoved against the red-orange plastic cooler as we rounded each bend. The cooler—weighing the same as me though it only held sandwiches and some lemonade—would slide across the seat to crush me pleasantly against the other door or swing me to the centre of the seat. The cooler and I, you see, were crucial for keeping the car balanced. My theory went that when Dad tried to make those turns alone, without Mum at his side or the cooler and me as ballast in the back, the car took flight. I waited until people were back at the house after the funeral to explain what the problem had been. They were kind, I'm sure.

In my memories Dad always has five days of stubble and the smell of bedroom on him. The rest I know comes to me from photographs. Or stories from Viv. I see him most clearly when he's driving that car by himself, with more energy in his eyes than there's been in a long time as he enjoys the thrill of the ride, taking the turns harder and harder, then finally deciding this is the one, *here*, and sailing out into freedom. The joy lasts the eternity of the few seconds until the car slows and the Wile E. Coyote recognition sets in. His body suspended for a second above the seats, his thick brows tilt outward and he considers what he's leaving behind. That hesitation is for my sake, not his. There's nothing left for him but the all too terrestrial plunge down the ravine, to the broken neck and burning and the hot last breaths of air.

The whole concept, that a momentary respite from gravity would be instantly punishable by death, imprinted itself on me. It keeps me off planes. When my turn came to climb onto the trampoline at school, it gave me shivers. My pause was too long for the other kids waiting. All I knew was that being weightless was terrifying. It seemed to be a prime way to tease this gravity/death character. I channelled my mother as I explained to the PE teacher in my most adult voice, 'I'm afraid that I can't do this exercise today.' I assured him, 'Maybe tomorrow,' which for both Viv and me means never.

We moved from that school district within the year.

Ultimately, we embraced our winnings, not as the shameful fruits of an insurance scam but as a consolation prize that actually consoled and paid for some practical healing. When I first asked if Dad had committed suicide, my suspicion was confirmed and then shushed. *He was sick. But you and I are okay.* That's been the bargain all along: we ignore his past misery in favour of our most excellent and frenetic evolution. As if we might outrun him.

The arrangement has been such a key part of self-preservation that, twenty-five years later, in my application to work at the Mercy, when asked to declare if there was any history of suicide in my immediate family, without a pause I checked the box *No*.

The most recent revamp of the hospital grounds aimed for imitation Roman ruin, with faux-eroded columns and a not very mystical circle of concrete benches. The plaza is also dotted with bombproof rubbish receptacles. Still, in the late afternoon sun, with clusters of smokers fingering their ID tags, drinking coffees, and pacing like senators, it's almost convincing.

A few steps further and the protective chill of the lobby air-conditioning has evaporated. The summer heat wraps both its legs around me and begins to hump. It doesn't even pretend to be gentle.

Shiftwork typically dumps nurses out early, amid the 3 pm rabble of teenagers snaking home—or after dinner, when darkness gives cover to the reckless and their vices. I used to require a few minutes to adjust to the plethora of the Oblivious Healthy all around me. A thousand emergencies just inside the hospital, and these fools are stealing each other's backpacks and making out in the bushes, carrying on with their lives. Since I've been keeping business hours at the Mercy, I've discovered that 5 pm humanity is just as clueless. People lifting fat-free muffins to their fat faces and barely listening to each other in their afternoon drowse towards home. Oblivious. Healthy.

Even Hannah has probably shifted her focus to the theme of her upcoming birthday.

I look around. Two construction workers are sharing a joint on the ledge of a drought-friendly fountain that maintains a thin shimmering puddle. They're shoeless, dangling their toes in the water.

I seem to have exited the building along with a staggered trio of orderlies wheeling out a trio of new mothers, attended by a matching trio of attentive fathers gently swinging their newborns in their new car seats, all sleepy and sticky and full of oblivious and healthy promise. Never mind the babies left behind who couldn't be discharged today, taped and tubed, ninety-nine percent lifeless, laid out under heat lamps upstairs, with their parents hovering right outside their plastic tents, optimistically calculating probabilities and outcomes; these women out here are flushed, not from the weather, but from their own successfully executed hormonal purpose. The scene is effervescently straight. Even the senior citizens being wheeled into the hospital against the current can't help but strain their arthritic necks and bonded teeth back towards the babies with a kind of animal wonder at the sight of silky-smooth youth. The final touch would be for a big band to kick in with a tune while an overhead security drone captures the synchronised swings of each new mother's wheelchair rolling up to each new father's waiting car.

Despite the irrepressible flow of life, no musical number bursts forth. One by one, the babies are buckled into position and whisked home to be inculcated with the first falsehood of life (*you will be given all the sustenance you need*), while the old folks, still looking behind for a last glimpse, get rolled inside to fail their tests, endure their complications and, amid the solitude of never enough visitors, discover the last truth (*sorry, we're out of options*).

A more enlightened assistant would transcend this dark, adolescent impatience with the young innocents and support the enjoyment of any available good health that may blossom along this mortal and endlessly diverting coil. And, look, I would. But these are the same fools who demand that every illness be cured or managed or banished, as if death is some rogue entity and not a dependable yang to the lovely yin that delivers those babies out onto the promenade. On behalf of Teddy, who endured our checklists, and Geraldine, who is wondering how she's going to describe this morning's procedure to the neighbours, I refuse.

Nettie would encourage me to take this out on the reflection screen. After such a rickety debut, wouldn't I benefit from selecting the shade of a nearby tree, sitting down deep in it and recording my rant in full? Within a few paragraphs I could burn through my noble rage. Here she would bat her eyes: *Who knows? Maybe find something closer to the truth?*

Never mind. My parents didn't raise a softie.

Once I'm two minutes free of the forum forecourt, my daily indignation dissipates and slips into the same crassness as the rest of this 5 pm demographic. In short order, I forgive myself for the spill, calculate my improved hourly rate for assisting instead of observing, and crave only the most basic physical comforts.

Air-conditioning, a meal.

Mother.

———

For those making the journey from the Mercy Hospital to Willow Wood—and not travelling by ambulance and stretcher—there's a grey footbridge, exactly wide enough for one pedestrian and one cyclist, that leads you over six lanes of freeway. It's fully caged, to prevent throwing stones—or selves—onto the cars below. If the direction of the commute doesn't trigger thoughts of mortality, the view certainly does. Canny city planners should have gone further and taken full advantage of the deathiness of the zone they were creating by annexing the football oval on the far side of the hospital grounds for a cemetery.

Viv managed her slow-burning decline for years, limping through the last laps to her pension, doling out wisdom from a windowless office adjacent to the school gym. She's certain that the soundtrack—the tribal cheers of teenagers and the steady tap of basketballs on polished floor—slowed her deterioration. What really helped, though, was poker. Taught to her by my father when they were still occupying tented housing in hurricane zones and playing for nothing, it had always provided a pleasant background hum of strategy and luck. After retirement she went big, using every trick twenty-two years of high school students had taught her, allowing her to bluff and chop and spot the weakest players. If anything, the Parkinson's flattened her game face which, when she could still get herself to tournaments out at the casino, improved her overall take and made her pension livable. Blessedly, she was free enough from the gambling gene to walk away when she was up. Usually. There have been some sudden dips that I've known about and others I'm sure I haven't, but by the time she gave me power of attorney, she was solvent and then some.

That was eight months ago, when her illness shifted up a gear. She was dragging a trove of *National Geographics* up the stairs from the recycling pile to her apartment with the intention of making a collage and woke up on the bottom step, her chin wet with blood, her two front teeth lying by the lobby door. The next day, after I'd found cover for a week of shifts and travelled the four hours to get here, she showed me the ivory trophies. 'Like they were shot out of my mouth.' That episode, and the consequent dental surgery, suggested that change time was again upon us.

'I've come to a conclusion,' she lisped, once the anaesthetic had worn off. 'Quit your job, stay with me. You'll find better work here. Save some money, see what happens.' Imagine these words spoken by your toothless mother, with two bandaged wrists, a splinted forefinger, two black eyes and stitches down one cheek. Was it so hard to ask me to move closer?

This was right after 961 passed, and it wasn't hard to decipher the ad on the Mercy's careers page. *Wanted: a nurse to fill a new position with a pilot program.* The job involved psychiatric assessment, patient advocacy, writing skills and an ability to liaise with other hospital departments, including Ethics and all medical wards. I had recently witnessed one spectacularly bad death on the psych ward where I had been working. A woman in her forties with that burnt-out kind of schizophrenia that imparts few delusions anymore but limits daily function to drinking coffee, smoking cigarettes and taking every drug except the ones prescribed. The lung cancer was an occupational hazard for her and it had gone to the bones before it was caught. Poorly managed schizophrenia led to poorly controlled pain—because no one wants to give an addict too many opiates, even if it is her last month alive. In the end, they put her in a room away from the meal area, so her screaming wouldn't distress the other patients. My memories of the sound of her pain, along with the lingering question of my father's consciousness as his car burned around him, led me to apply. Who doesn't like the idea of a comfortable death?

Eight months before, I had been on a cardiac ward. Before that, on a cruise ship. Before that—God help me, a general ward. And so on, all the way back to my mother's knee. When Nettie called to schedule my interview she told me that my spotty résumé showed a broad exposure to physical and mental suffering as well as a capacity for adapting to new environments and systems. Giulia, who I'd been living with for all of a year and a half and who is familiar with my tendency to wander, thought Nettie's enthusiasm about my history suggested we would be a good match. I was hired and Giulia gave her blessing.

My mother said, 'This is the real deal. You've spent enough time with the sickness end of the business. Death is where life gets really interesting.'

She leapt past the idea of my renting an apartment. 'I've decided: why pretend I'm going anywhere besides a nursing home? I'm a social animal and I need help during the day. Smarter to do it now, while the brain's still plastic. You stay here. I'll go.'

She was no doubt jealous of my move and wanted to pull a geographical of her own.

At first she was thrilled with Willow Wood. Since the decision to move had been hers, the entire experience was supposed to yield non-stop benefits. Surprise, surprise—to no one who has ever set foot inside a nursing home—the place accelerated her losses. The meds that had once kept her stable never regained their set point of effectiveness. Her appetite and energy dwindled, as did, finally, her previous interests. Lunches with her favourite students passing through; political protests against any dispossession taking place in any distant location; poker; or even random trivia related to the stone or colour turquoise (there's an extensive online community): none of them could compete with the goings-on in her single rectangular room and maybe the dining room. An admirably urgent hunger for the world was reduced to asking anyone who would slow down long enough: *Why on earth do they have to lock up Mylanta?*

Willow Wood greets you with a long wooden pergola, the kind that looks as though it should lead up to the stepped garden of a manor, only here it ends at a keypad and a pair of glass sliding doors. In front, on the hot, breezeless breezeway, residents are scattered in clusters, tilting their visors and amber sunglasses away from the sun. These are not the oblivious healthy people that clutter up the streets. These folks have a prime view of the ticking clock. More residents are congregated inside, on washable furniture, watching the doors slide open and shut, experiencing competing blasts of air-conditioning and heatwave while they wait.

I keep up the efficient gait of a staff member, smiling blandly and not inhaling deeply. Despite possessing the unfortunate gift of being able to diagnose a urinary tract infection at five paces, I am not at work and don't want to know.

The whiteboard tells me that Lon isn't nursing this shift. He is a distinct benefit of this experience. When we first toured the place, Lon was behind the drug counter upstairs, explaining a blood pressure medication to a patient who appeared to be hearing about it for the first time. He was in the act of being kind. More to the point, he had the just-washed crumpledness thing happening, rare in nurses, plus slow camel eyes, which managed to give the patient full respectful attention while keeping an equally attentive gaze on me. Viv saw me notice and poked her forefinger at my spleen to underline. Five minutes later, he and I geolocated each other. I was outside on the breezeway, ready. He told me he was about to give someone a shower, but I might have a chance later. We hooked up that night.

When I gave Viv the expurgated version, she said, 'Careful not to make an enemy there. I'll need an inside man.' In that, as well as in other domains, he has served admirably.

The safety doors at the end of the parlour lead to the stairwell, which leads up to the second floor corridor, the Elm Wing. Viv's door is open, a rarity in itself, and, more disturbing, she isn't in her room. The light is on in her bathroom. Her good blouses, the ones she worried would be stolen by other residents, are on her single bed, folded into a tidy pile by the pillow. She has abandoned her walker. It is facing the corner of the room, as if it is being punished.

I check the corridor, expecting to see her hand inching along the tan bannister, her feet slowly moving in tandem. No one's there. Just carpeted silence and a dent in the plaster wall at the height of a stretcher making a turn into or out of the room next door.

I do a complete loop of the ward until I find Trish near the laundry. Her otherwise dull silver hair has been finessed with a thin stripe of glam purple. The colour matches her fingernails, visible through latex gloves, which are holding a bundle of sheets a safe distance in front of her. This task is two levels beneath her station. She must have run out of work in the office.

I get a firm nod of greeting. 'Evan! Have you been to see your mother yet?'

'She's not in her room.'

'That's no shock. When did you talk to her last?'

'I was in on Monday.'

'There've been some changes. Let me dump this first.'

I swing open the laundry door for her.

'Thank you. My bet is she's in the activities centre. There's a class. It'll be done soon.'

'She left her room to socialise?'

'About that.' Trish degloves, works antibacterial gel from her fingertips to her wrists, and reassumes the royalty of her position. 'You know I adore your mother, don't you? Her whole *way*.'

'The feeling is mutual.'

'Well, about *that*: her capability has changed in the past two or three days, significantly. So has her perception of it. I assume this is the implant, finally working. Which is wonderful.' She hangs onto the last syllable, stopping short of *but*.

Being professional colleagues of sorts lets us bypass some of the usual formality. It's not hard to imagine how my mother might bring unwelcome challenges to an otherwise peaceful shift. 'Tell me,' I say. 'I can take it.'

Trish tilts her head, as if perhaps I can't. 'She and I had a disagreement this afternoon over where I feel she can safely go on her own.'

'Can she go anywhere on her own?'

'You're in for a treat. That's the main point. But I want you to know, from my perspective, I have to protect my residents. The conversation got heated. Now I want to apologise to you, as I already apologised to her.' She lowers her voice to confess, 'I called her the B-word.'

This kindly, competent, vanilla-scented administrator? 'Bitch?'

She nods, shamefaced.

'That's not a word usually chosen by the enlightened.'

Trish looks stunned. 'That's exactly what she said!'

'It's what I was raised on.'

She smiles, still falling for this vexing resident. 'There are so many reasons I shouldn't have said it, but it came out. It's because she and I have developed such an intimate rapport, but that is no excuse. I am profoundly sorry.'

I have a few clues about Trish, courtesy of the aforementioned rapport. Middle-aged, divorced, with full custody of two under-parented girls, both already shoplifting. Add to that a few work emergencies—say, that sweet old man in room 12 falls in the shower, and a dementing grandmother experiences an episode of double incontinence in the dining room just as the main course arrives. See if you can manage all of that and not resort to name-calling.

'It happens,' I say.

'That's good of you.'

'It's up to her to accept the apology though.'

'She's not there yet,' Trish says.

'Give her a day,' I tell her. 'She doesn't hold grudges. I have a question though: the activities centre?'

'Singing group.'

'Are you telling me she's settling in?'

'I wouldn't go that far.'

'Participating though?'

'Her head off. Why do you think she copped it from me? She's been right in my line of vision for the past few days.'

———

I'm dousing my face at Viv's basin, searching my eyes in the mirror for the person who helped Teddy die this morning, when a fist pounds on the bathroom door.

'Who's in there?' Viv yells, before opening up and hurling herself in, bracing for a two-handed stop against the counter. She's plastered with makeup, wearing a harlequin blouse I've never seen before, with gold buttons across the top of one shoulder. Her lips are freshly coated with Lady Danger, a lipstick from her more functional past. She's puffing from the effort but not looking remotely disabled. It's more like she's ducked in for a cocktail before going back on stage.

'Here you are,' she coos. 'Everly.'

My commune name. It was chosen by me at age ten. I answered to it for nine months out of a lifetime, but she still whips it out now and then.

She rights herself, standing up straighter than she has in nearly a year, grinning.

'How are you?' I ask.

More panting and intense staring. Since her incarceration, she's neglected her hair ('I'm not trooping out to the hairdresser every Tuesday to try to con this crowd into thinking I'm still Medium Ash'), but today it has been blow-dried to a two-tone wave, with a top layer of silver.

I try again. 'I'm not just being conversational. How are you feeling?'

She stretches her arms out and up, hour by hour, up to twelve o'clock, grazing the tiled walls with her fingers. 'Vital.'

'Trish says you've been singing.'

'She speaks the truth. The man they bring in, with the guitar, has the smokiest voice, ideal for the standards. And he's stuck with the crowd here and their greatest-hits mindset. No room to grow. This is the only paying gig he has right now, he told me, a complete injustice, but that's music. He should be anywhere but this place. We both should.'

Perspective: on Monday, as I cut up her dinner for her, conversation was limited to a soft yes, no or brief, philosophical commentary on her current level of debility.

She goes on, 'I only came back to use the bathroom. The one in the activities centre is for both sexes and the men here have no better aim than you do.'

At this, she turns and lifts the toilet cover, backs up to the seat, pushes down the elastic of her black slacks and lowers herself down. A noisy stream starts as soon as her knees bend.

We weren't at this point the other day either.

I reach for the door so I can leave and preserve dignity all round. She slides a foot across the tiles to block my path. 'Stay.'

Save for toilet training, there exists no history of us hanging out in the bathroom.

'Grow up,' she says. 'It's pee.' She settles back on the seat, satisfied that she has made me hold still. It's not her foot against the door or the blue eye shadow that's mesmerising. It's the movement, the deft angling of her foot against the door, the sentences coming so easily—and she's still peeing. It's a dazzling show of coordination and also offers a far more intimate view than even the most devoted son requires.

'Do you remember a tall woman here, named Evie? Five doors down, across from the elevator? We've barely spoken. Turns out she's a human being.' Viv had pointed her out once, handing down a harsh sentence: 'More wallpaper than wall.' That verdict has apparently been revised. She tells me, 'The pearls, the closet full of dresses—turns out it's bluster. Now that I'm lively enough for her

37

to converse with she invites me to the sunroom. Out of the blue. When I get there, she pulls out a deck of cards and asks if I care for a friendly game. How did she know?'

'Your lipstick?'

'After seven months of looking up her nose, do I want a friendly game? Five-card draw, low aces to sevens, she offers me. "As a matter of fact, I would."' Viv shrugs her shoulders and tilts her head, movements that in themselves are amazing. 'My reputation must have snuck out,' she says, tearing off a few squares of toilet paper and wiping.

Some questions of responsibility emerge: if my mother is my patient, do I remain unflapped and stay by her side, hands ready to catch her when she attempts to stand, should she miscalculate her strength, dislodge another tooth or, almost inevitably, a hip? Or, if she is merely my mother, can I flee the scene of her semi-clad body, press the call button for a staff member to come make her decent again, and send a message to the right technician so they can adjust the implant that's shooting a bit too haphazardly at her dopamine receptors?

I stay where I am by the basin, doing neither. I revert to my role as researcher, observing and taking notes, so I can report it all to Dr Marais, her current specialist/saviour.

She covers up, slightly, and leans back against the toilet cistern, settling in between the silver bars on either side as if it's an easy chair. 'Evie's okay. She's never been pro. After a few rounds yesterday, just the two of us playing for packets of salt, we hunted around for a third. That's when, as I like to say, we found Jesus.' Even if she's laughing at her own joke, it is such a fine sound to hear. 'A Spaniard, here two months. Says he's been in one small game or another since he was a teenager. And he knows plenty.'

With her hands on the rails, she abruptly thrusts herself to standing, skilfully—and thankfully—bringing her slacks up with her. After a wobble, she adjusts her blouse over her slacks, then pushes past me to the basin.

At the sight of her face in the mirror, she says, 'Holy smokes.'
The vision sends her hunting through the drawers for her Pond's.
She applies it with as much gusto as she put on the makeup before.

'Should you go slowly with Evie?'

Through her creamy mask, there is irritation.

I prod. 'Can I quote you to you? "A friendly game is reconnaissance. The term implies another game in the future that will be otherwise."'

She leans towards the mirror to scold my reflection. 'Before you get yourself excited, Nurse Fink, the cards are Evie's, not mine.'

The Pond's is wiped off with a tissue and her sixty-two-year-old face is revealed to be pale and moist. The view is distractingly youthful, even to her, and she takes advantage of her regained ability to make faces. A tough, a vamp, a clown, all in easy succession.

She sprays her entire self with Chanel No. 19 and returns to the topic. 'I'll own up: there was discussion today about putting up our eight o'clock pudding cups to add some heat to the game.' She gives me her old wink. Three days ago it took all of her concentration to get one hand to steady the other so she could tear the foil top off one of those pudding cups.

'Trish says she called you a bitch.'

'She did.' The subject is already old. With an unthinking stretch of her arm she reaches back to flush the toilet. 'Let's blow.'

As we walk through her room, her movements falter a little—a calf muscle not quite strong enough to glide her forward. Still, we pass by the walker, keeping its lonely vigil in the corner.

In the hallway, she reaches for the handrail, but then pulls back as if it's hot, resting her hand on my wrist instead. 'They're raising the prices for guest meals next month. Eleven-seventy.'

'They've told me.'

'Don't let's worry,' she says, waving her other hand at the wall. 'If these bits of me keep coming back online, I should be able to pick up a real game before long.'

At the first assessment, Marais warned us about hope. 'Whenever you reach a plateau with this, I advise you to enjoy it but to remain realistic.' In other words, sooner or later it's going to fall out from under you like sand. He kept his eyes on my mother's quivering right hand while he said this. If she went ahead with the implant we could look for a slowing of deterioration or, at best, a temporary halt, but the direction was not negotiable. Right before we made the first payment on it, he warned us again, to be sure we weren't expecting too much. 'Hope is the most addictive narcotic that modern medicine offers. All I can offer you is science.' That additional bit of rational poetry won her over completely, confirming her good feeling about this one. After that, we were handed over to his juniors for the prep and didn't see him again until after the surgery three weeks ago, when he beckoned me to an unoccupied, unlit corner of a waiting room to tell me, no irony, 'All we do now is hope.'

But the procedure didn't work. The next Monday, she sat in a booth, the shaved patch at the back of her head wired up to a console while they tested her executive function and adjusted the device. Viv smiled as she followed Marais's commands, sitting down and standing up, with marginally fewer freezes. Twenty percent improvement, we were told.

'Don't give me the odds,' she said. 'Let me see what I can do.'

Despite her best efforts to engage the placebo effect, she froze in the hallways and on the steps and during meals. I made the last payment on the procedure without mentioning it to her, because there really hadn't been much in the way of gains. Until three days ago, it seems.

She stops walking so she can rub her fingers across my smooth cheek. 'Ooh. Job interview?'

'Wrong.'

'If I were your boss, that's what I'd think.'

'It was a regular day.'

'Bull,' she says. 'Did you put on a PowerPoint for the bigwigs?'

'Are we allowed to discuss your current condition?'

She picks at my collar. 'Not until you tell me why you look like this.'

'All right. I assisted today.'

'Hah!' she says, too loud. 'My son the suicide assistant!'

'Dying assistant.'

'Have it your way. Their way. The effect is the same. On your own?'

'Yes.'

'Training wheels off. And?'

'I was nervous, but we got there.'

'You did it?'

'The patient did.'

'Not without you there. You'll get past nervous,' she says, clapping her hands together, almost missing. 'Why were you going to keep this from me?'

'Your news is better. I didn't want to steal your thunder.'

'My news? My thunder is intact.' She looks down, surveying her body, wiggling her hands and feet with showy ease. 'I wish we had some champagne in here. We could throw a party.'

'Are we calling the implant a success?'

Viv shudders away the thought of an outside contributor to her wellness. Her faith in her body has always hovered in the higher bandwidth of positive thinking without actually embracing anything so vulgar. When a treatment doesn't do what it says on the box, the problem is false advertising or the limits of technology. When it does, the victory belongs to her unique self.

'Some muscle groups have been neglected in recent times. They're coming back. With effort, they'll come back. *All* of them.'

'And the voluntary socialising?'

'What can I tell you? The salmon-coloured walls here have weakened my resistance.' She fingers the tablet-sized lump on the side of her stomach that's sending a regular tickle up to her basal ganglia. 'It *has* been a blissful few days.'

'I'll let Marais know in the morning,' I say.

'Why?'

'There's been a big change. I can see it. So can you. It's worth following up. Trish sees it too.'

'Nothing slips by that one. Do you know how good that felt, just to spar with her?' She punches her hands upwards towards the ceiling. 'I feel lucky, like I'm letting go of—'

'Inhibitions? Marais would want to know what's up.'

'None of his business.'

'What if I'm thinking of your safety?'

She folds her arms. 'Name your concern.'

'You seem up.'

'I'm happy,' she says, not smiling. 'More than I've been.'

'Have you been eating?'

'Better than ever.'

'Sleeping?'

'Yes. My bowels are soft and regular. Any more?'

Her readiness to fight is a joy to witness, but she's firing with even more than her previous vigour. I'm sure Marais would want to fine-tune the device. Trish would want the same.

'You've never kept me in the bathroom with you,' I say. 'What was that?'

'A trauma, apparently. Stay here for a week and get back to me on your sense of privacy.'

'Have you been into any other residents' rooms? Any male residents? I'm just asking.'

'And I'm just telling you to fuck right off!'

'There: you've never said that to me.'

'I've thought it.' Suddenly, consciously, she puts herself at ease, rolling her shoulders and turning her folded arms into a soothing self-embrace. 'New topic. When was the last time we went camping?'

'It's been years. We got soaked.' A cruise I was booked to work on was delayed because a big storm was predicted, but she didn't

42

see that affecting us. She wanted to play the long odds. 'We lasted one night.'

'That's your memory. The great outdoors is on my mind,' Viv says. 'That's how I'm feeling. Almost strong enough to think about getting back out. Almost. You see? I am realistic. Today, with Trish, I only wanted to venture past the front doors. She had the gall to keep me from going to the park by myself because no staff were available. It was too hot. I might fall. Of course I might fall. Who cares?'

'I'm sure Trish was just being cautious. It's her job. I understand how she feels.'

'That I'm a bitch?'

I take her hand. 'I've missed your speed. I'm glad it's here.'

'Me too,' she says.

I'm about to suggest she shows herself off to Dr Marais when she pulls her hand away. I give up. 'Let's move on to the chicken tetrazzini.'

This earns me an embrace. She reaches up, pulling me in. Her perfume, which has been competing with the air freshener and metallic smells of the institutional dining room, assaults my nostrils, blinding them with citrus and rose and triggering an image of the dark wooden beams in the bungalow we lived in on LaPlaca Boulevard for my last year of high school.

Viv locks an arm around me chummily and directs us past the salad bar towards the seating area. We pass one of the more established pairs here, two sisters, each dressed smartly for this dining room, each with a plate of soft food in front of them. Neat scoops of brown, orange and green. There are two cans of Ensure on the table as well, chocolate and vanilla, in case they don't eat their veggies. They probably settled that one a long time ago. I'm thinking that at least they have each other for company here, when Viv annotates: 'Poor sad souls. That's not going to be me.'

She spies an empty table for two and speeds up until we reach it. 'There,' she says, staking her hands down on either side of a setting.

'Quite an accomplishment, given your peak velocity three days ago,' I say.

She smiles a sneer. I've patronised her. 'You know, they did a big study. *Scientific American* is where I saw this, I think. Universities on six continents participated. You know what they discovered?'

'What?'

'They concluded that bitches are usually right.' Straight face. Not frozen, just deadpan, with a barely detectable glint. 'Disproportionately to the rest of the population, they are. You should look it up. Informative reading.' With her fingers tight around my elbow, she puts me in a chair. 'No one calls Marais. Not behind my back. Not in front of it either.'

I repeat after her, 'No one calls Marais.'

At that, she gives me a slap on the arm and says, 'Best boy.'

———

The lobby where Viv lost her front teeth is a century old and bordered with alternating navy blue and pink tiles. With the ambient humidity and a whiff of old human piss, heated, you can almost imagine you're near the ocean.

Before I moved here, Giulia and I had a good thing going. For a few months at the commune, we had shared a bunk bed; aside from Viv, she's my only remnant from that time. Twenty years later, she made contact, told me to visit the next time I was nearby. This was when I was on the cruise ship and she was living a mile from the port. We met for cheap pizza. We remembered the bottomless raisin jar and the chore wheel that breached child labour laws. We remembered the house debate about the leaky roof (should the group expand their carpentry skills or pay roofers? They did the former and then the latter). We drank tea. She was sober now.

Having confirmation from Giulia that that whole experience really happened was gratifying. Viv had a different focus back then. She doesn't remember the raisin jar, the chore wheel or why we left.

Giulia was renting a first-floor deco apartment that backed onto a roast chicken place. I had two nights between jobs, so I crashed in her study. On the first morning, she copped to the fact that she'd looked me up because even though she'd been fifteen, she remembered a cute ten-year-old and wondered if I might have become suitor material. We agreed that this was suspect but forgivable. She assured me she was glad to reconnect anyway. Did I want to stay longer than two nights? I travelled light, so I wasn't going to crowd her. She had the necessary belongings, so I didn't need to buy any. We could save money for some better future. I inserted myself in the nursing pool at St Vincent's, lurching between departments when the mood hit, resisting the inevitable offers for white male advancement in an off-white female industry. Within a month the gig in cardiac came up. What followed was an age of communal living for two people who had been trained for it. A nurse and an environmental compliance officer, we kept the place far cleaner than the commune ever was and we never ran out of toilet paper. Occasionally, our respective internet searches would yield a skirmish for me or a romance for her. If the candidates didn't fulfil any deeper needs, at least they were entertaining. Mostly, Giulia and I ate dinner and went to movies. The roast chicken place changed its fuel to something more acrid, but the domesticity, the scalding heat through the bathroom pipes in cold weather—it was all worth staying for. That is, until Viv fell.

Giulia stood by while I packed to leave. 'Back to the funhouse.'

'She sort of needs me.'

'Whatever. It's time for us to break up anyway. We're one bad winter away from buying a home entertainment system. And this way we get to find out what we've been saving up for.'

So now I cohabit with my mother's stuff. Decay is abundant in here, starting with the bananas browning on the kitchen counter, continuing with the planter of good intentions on the windowsill, which despite twice-weekly watering is giving up. I open all the windows and turn on the fan, stopping in the middle of the room to let the air blow past me. Above the bricked-in fireplace is one of Viv's favourite things, a picture she did in her early days in the Pacific. A charred Cessna in the jungle, being reclaimed by vines, painted from life. 'As soon as we found it, your father told me I had to come back with my oils. The passengers had rotted, but you could feel that they had been alive, strapped in, ready to enjoy their affordable getaway.' The painting is florid. This was when she first bonded with the colour teal. It was the eighties. A thick green vine wraps its way through the cockpit and bursts into bright tropical bloom. Representing the triumph of nature over modernity, see? A bright blue parrot sits on top of the fuselage, its head cocked sternly at the viewer to make sure the point is made.

This is Viv's story of how they met: idealistic young do-gooder biking into town to buy art supplies for her English students finds herself the first on the scene of a car accident. There is Dad in his premier mishap, hanging upside down in a LandCruiser; a turn of his head and he sees her, beyond the box of plastic syringes scattered all over the ceiling of the car beneath him, love at first sight. Their first time, Viv was boundaryless enough to tell me, happened in a poorly staffed hospital with only curtains for privacy. He was in two leg casts, she said, giving me a clear picture of the prehistoric scene. Hot, right?

Cut to: her son the suicide assistant, living in her apartment with her dried-up oils and broken easel, supplementing her bills with his nest egg. Turns out this is the future I've been saving for.

I leave my clothes on the growing pile behind the couch and hit the bathroom, soaping my way through a profoundly unerotic shower. The deaths I've been present for have usually been followed up with a late afternoon wank, as has every other workday I can remember, so this flaccidity makes me wonder if Teddy's dispatch has softened things tonight.

Consternation hovers as I dry myself. Not that I want to mix my Eros with someone else's Thanatos, but I do enjoy my victimless habit.

Lena, who assisted many individuals to their last drink before she bailed, wrote that for days after each one, she couldn't shake the sense that a key detail had been forgotten during the procedure. The unease reminded her of leaving a pot on a lit stove. Not a pot in the next room, but one that was so far away she couldn't possibly get back in time to turn it off. Her extensive reflections never covered masturbation.

Wrapped in a towel and already sweating again, I fall onto the sofa.

When Viv started to lose range, she decided she ought to have a decent place to sit. Some genius talked her into buying the most enveloping couch ever created, difficult for even the abled to get out of. He let her buy on credit. We're paying this off too, twenty-one dollars a month. My head sinks back into the fake brown suede. If it weren't for the merlot stain on the arm that's shaped uncannily like Africa, I could get something for it. I slide my fingers into the deep crevices between the cushions. It's mine now, all mine.

I think about Lena's unease. I feel like an undotted *i*.

There's one solution. I find my phone and take a picture of my open mouth, apply a lush filter, and send it to Lon.

A few minutes later, he replies. *We already ate. Stir-fry. Leftovers are yours if you want.*

I clarify: *Had the chicken at Willow Wood. Dinner isn't what I'm after.*

A quicker turnaround this time. *Come.*

———

Even after a few dozen nights with Lon and Simon, I start out like a guest, sitting on a stool by the kitchen counter, watching them in their natural habitat. Lon has his face in the refrigerator, looking for what he can offer me. 'I'm not seeing beer,' he calls to Simon.

Simon is in the corner of the living room, amid a wall of plants—where a television would go if they were that sort. He's weeding a giant globe terrarium with leaves pushing up against its domed roof. 'It's there,' he calls back. 'Think happier thoughts.' He's culling leaves off one that looks like lettuce and putting them on his knee. 'My father promised this would be a slow grower.'

'Found it!' Lon manoeuvres his hand to the back of a shelf. 'Only pale ale. Evan likes dark.'

'Times are hard all over,' says Simon.

'I'll survive,' I say.

Simon is tugging away in another corner of the tank. 'This has spread everywhere. Didn't you hear my dad say this would be a slow grower?' The pile of green on Simon's knee has made no perceptible difference to the little landscape. 'Fucking climate change.'

'You'll have to forgive his rages,' Lon tells me.

The urgency that hit me on Viv's sofa, which I hopefully mistook for horniness, has been slightly dampened by the smallness of home life. Still, if they push it I can muster enthusiasm. Whatever it takes. I'm not going back to Viv's tonight.

'Tell me a story about today,' Lon says.

This situation: when Lon first invited me over to meet Simon and close the circle, they fed me lamb vindaloo and asked about my work. Since Nettie prefers that we only discuss our program with those who need to know, and since I didn't anticipate a long courtship here, I described my work vaguely, as a small part of a large project on suicidality for the psych department. Even that shocked Simon, who couldn't imagine regularly talking to the suicidal (and he designs open-plan offices).

I tried to normalise it, nudging Lon for details of the suicide rate at Willow Wood. He quashed me, told me it happened but that he could usually identify a depressed resident before they got close to making a plan. 'All they need is engagement,' he said.

I let it go. For that night, my story was close enough to the truth for my conscience to make it from the dinner table to their bed, which was what I was there for. But they kept inviting me back. Lon pities the single cook and I like dinner, so I kept accepting.

My thing about sleeping with couples is that when it's good, it's very very good and when it's bad, you can leave. They'll still have each other. Nobody gets hurt.

Saturday nights eventually became Sunday afternoons. A few farmers' markets later, it was starting to look like a romance. Over carbonara one night, Simon gave me a key to their apartment so I could tend the greenery while they went to visit his sick grandfather. When they came back I tried to return it, but Lon said, 'Simon thinks it will simplify things if you keep it.'

'Simplify what?'

He batted his eyes and told me to ask Simon.

Looking back, that night was my last chance to tell them about my job. Simon mentioned how his grandfather had been asking anyone who came into his hospital room to kill him and how much that upset the staff. I brought up 961, how the old man might have qualified for it.

'Well, that wasn't him,' Simon said proudly. 'In the end he turned down all the morphine because he needed to go through the suffering. It was hard to watch, but that's his generation. He ended up in a coma with loved ones at his side, and that felt right for all of us.'

Before I could ask a soft probing question about turning down a dying man's request, Lon piled on. 'I don't know how the Mercy can square itself with the practice. It's obscene.'

'Mmm,' I said.

'Your suicidal people don't have anything to do with that, do they?'

'No. Nothing,' I said.

Simon shook his head as he pondered my job again. 'You live in a dark spot.'

Which is why, whenever Lon asks for a story about my day, I summon up patients from the past. Fortunately I have a reasonable archive.

'One of our frequent flyers swallowed a razor blade and nothing happened. For two days. She came into the emergency room demanding scans for a made-up backache. She insisted she didn't want an X-ray, she wanted an MRI.'

'That would have sliced her apart.'

'That was her plan. A doctor there recognised her right away. She confessed, got sent over to us for observation. Now she's being watched twenty-four seven. She says the urge has passed. Unlike the razor. We're pushing laxatives. Bulking agents. She's resisting. I think she's still hoping for a medical emergency.'

'See?' says Lon. 'You're in the wrong area. My patients love taking their laxatives. No convincing required.'

'Wait a minute.' Our conversation has distracted Simon from his weeding. He brings his handful of terrarium salad to the kitchen and dumps it in the compost. 'Can someone truly shit out a razor blade with no consequences?'

'Apparently,' I say.

'Keep me posted on that one,' he says.

I never asked Simon what is simplified by my having their key, but we've settled into a routine about it. I ring the buzzer, one of them greets me, asks why I don't use the key. I say it's for watering the plants but, still, I always seem to stay the night.

'All right. Bedtime.' Simon strips off his t-shirt and shorts and drops them at his feet in the middle of the living room. He's forty and black, with little bits of grey peeking around hairy corners highlighting those facts. His turtlish head is countered by his busy brain and body. He's the only one of the three of us with an active gym membership and healthy snacking instincts. Lon promises me we'll start behaving more responsibly when we get that old. We're still on our beers.

Simon looks confused. 'Are we doing this? I have a training session in the morning.'

The cosy suggestion is suddenly offset by my thought that somewhere in the city, Geraldine is getting into bed alone. I won't forget her name. I promise.

I am a good house guest, and drop trou as requested, wondering if my dick will comply. Simon wraps an arm around my neck and pulls me to him. Our bodies touch. I'm made of balsa and he's mahogany. Maybe solidity comes with age too.

'Actually,' says Lon, 'I was on the verge of suggesting we sit out on the roof for a while, if only because it's such a hot night. We could go up there naked. I've never seen anyone else up there—'

Simon closes his eyes to silence Lon, which usually works. This is Simon's foreplay, a minute of enforced contemplation.

I close my eyes too. What appears? Teddy on a metal shelf in the morgue, slowly draining.

Reset.

Mum tucked into her single bed, tapping her feet under her sheet in anticipation of whatever tomorrow holds.

I open my eyes.

Simon's are still closed. He's breathing with intention. Gratitude for this day.

Lon smiles at Simon and me, joins into our close embrace.

'You're clothed,' Simon tells him.

'Use your imagination,' Lon says, pulling us together tighter.

This is what I came for: the sound of two other people breathing, slightly out of sync, rhythmic and content.

Oblivious, healthy.

There's closeness, some kissing to choice locations, but it ends in distracting conversation about logistics for the morning. Simon has his meeting, which he's stressed about, and Lon has an early shift. We call it off, which is fine. In bed, I settle between them, grateful that my virility is not going to be tested. This is the first time the three of us have got into bed and nothing has happened.

Lon is asleep in minutes, and Simon, of course, isn't concerned either. He kisses me goodnight.

———

I wake up staring at the slow rotation of the ceiling fan. Simon's even snore is on my left and the fuzzy slab of Lon's back is on my right. Sleep makes them that much more impervious to the world. Simon rotates towards me as one hand reaches up to the top of my pillow. His fingers come to rest in my hair. What if our sexless milestone has meaning? Did they sense and respect my hesitation? Or have I lost my appeal to them? Or, have we turned into an old married throuple?

Somewhere in the bedroom, my phone hums. I slide down past their legs and reach for the glowing pocket of my pants. My movement doesn't wake them.

Viv's face blinks brightly at me from the screen. The picture was taken at an animal sanctuary. She's flirting with a monkey. It's flirting back, fingers reaching for her nose. The time underneath shows 3.17 am.

I walk her to the living room before answering in a whisper. 'Hi?'

'Hi.' She's panting excitedly. 'I require your oath.'

'For what?'

'Give it to me first.'

There's a low whistle in the background. 'What is that?' I ask her.

'I need assurance,' she says.

The whistle turns into a shriek. 'Is that the kettle?'

'I'm making tea.'

'Are you at home?'

'I am.' She is so chuffed.

'What are you doing there?'

'I'm making tea. What are you doing where you are?'

'I'm at Lon's.'

'And Simon's? That sounds friendly. No, none of my business. The point is, I walked here. On my own two feet. And I conquered the stairs. Isn't that wonderful?'

'Stay there. I'll be home in ten.'

'No you won't. It's late, you've got to shine bright at work tomorrow. No need to save me.'

'Does anyone know you've gone?'

She laughs at the absurdity. 'I left a note. They won't find it, because I'm going back soon.'

'It's the middle of the night.'

'I'm aware of that. I'm not looking for assistance or advice. I'm simply sharing my good news.'

'It's the middle of the night!'

'Would you rather I not call you next time?'

'Let's discuss it tomorrow.'

'If that's what you'd like. Just trust me, baby. I'm going to have a cup of tea, take a short nap on my couch, and have a shower. Aren't you happy for me?'

———

I sit on the floor and watch the terrarium until I convince myself I can see the plant from Simon's father anchoring and hoisting itself upwards throughout the globe, mini palms unfurling leaf by leaf against the glass.

The sun, already a summery orange at five-thirty, bounces through the window and formally announces a new day.

I do a few random sets of push-ups and squats.

By six-thirty, I am on the couch, almost back asleep, when a message comes from Nettie. *Quick catch-up at the student lab, 8.30?*

The student lab. This is going to be hardcore. I reply: *I thought you'd never ask.*

I call Viv.

'Hello,' she sings. I don't hear the echo of an airport terminal in the background, which is a positive. Instead, the self-satisfied cadences of public radio fill the air. Viv's breathing is still rapid, at least sixteen resps a minute. It may be a pathological response to the implant. Or she's been moving furniture.

'What are you up to now?' I ask.

'What are *you* up to now? You never came home.'

'You told me not to.'

'I had a stab at reviving my plants. Loosened the soil so they can take on moisture. They're feeling better now, thank you.'

'Good work.'

'Plants need water, light and time. Like every one of us. You haven't managed to put much of a stamp on this place, except for your handsome pile of boxes.'

'I've been meaning to.'

53

'That's the fall of the Western world, right there. *Meaning to.* Where are my birds?'

Her menagerie of painted ceramic toucans and parrots, mementos of journeys to warmer climates, each one lurid in its own impoverished way. They used to sit at eye level, clustered into an unlikely and odd-sized flock on the bookcase, begging to be hidden. That, I managed to attend to.

'Hall closet, third shelf,' I tell her.

'As long as you haven't sold them.'

'They're extremely safe from that.'

She probably stayed up on a sentimental jag, calling other retired good Samaritans in other time zones to reminisce about their and their country's better days. No doubt the suitcase of her clothes that were too good to even take to Willow Wood has already been located. She's probably sitting there in two blouses and a dress.

'It was refreshing to move around with nobody skulking after me.'

'What are your plans for the day?' I ask.

'Sintra will be coming soon to make sure I've made it through another night. I can see her little face, shocked at the sight of my empty bed. "Oh my, where has Vivian gone to?"' Viv gives an uncharacteristic and appalling Indian-inflected imitation of surprise. This confirms what I've long suspected: people aren't in touch with their inner racist when they check into places like Willow Wood. It's the preponderance of foreign nurses with accents that makes ridicule, the only weapon left, too easy.

'Mum.'

She insists that she adores Sintra, that it's all in good fun. She's moved on, anyway. 'I'll make my slow way back. Let's be truthful, I'm in no position to repossess my old life.' A flicker of insight. 'Coming here was a test for myself. And I've passed. That's enough for now. I hope your night was as satisfying, whatever your arrangement is with them. When I saw you yesterday, you looked like you needed it.' With no more warning than the end of that sentence, her image on the screen flares out to a pinpoint.

Lon comes into the hallway, with a morning boner leading him towards the bathroom. 'The reservoirs are down,' he says. 'You should take your shower with me.'

I do need it. The idea of Simon sleeping in the next room adds a frisson of adultery to the act. The prospect of his eventually joining us carries a spark too, though he usually takes weeks to finish. (That, along with his generally even demeanour, makes me suspect an antidepressant, but he hasn't mentioned it and I've resisted doing the forensic work in their drug cabinet.)

Ironically, Lon and I end up wasting water. His hands are on me with true Catholic-school urgency. He graduated directly from a military twelfth grade to a stint as a callboy, a low episode about which he experiences zero shame and about which I can't hear enough. It put him through nursing school. The end result is that no one would call his technique anything less than professional.

Then there's this uninvited image: across the city, in the bathroom that Teddy built, Geraldine is standing in the shower, avoiding the girls, avoiding today, staying under the spray as long as she can.

I look down to see that my attention has waned. This is not a good side effect of my new job.

I lift Lon's mouth off me, levering his body up to standing while I kneel in front of him. The switch has the drone of reciprocity to it, but no one complains. I concentrate on the task in front of me. It helps that Lon is an easy mark this morning. When his legs tense, I fake it for the first time in my life, pretending to finish myself off directly over the drain.

When we're drying ourselves, he rests his chin on my shoulder, close with still-damp, post-coital softness. 'Guess what's on my mind?'

'What?'

'The toasted-cheese-sandwich truck comes today.'

———

Nettie is in position in the lab at 8.25 am, standing between the hospital bed and the window, rocking back and forth on her heels while she flips through her phone. She's arranged Sven, the bandaid-coloured dummy, in bed and tucked him in snugly. He has a moulded blond pompadour a few shades yellower than his skin and a weary smile. Every orifice of his has been worn soft by practising nurses and doctors. Getting him to take a drink should be easy.

She knows I'm in the room but it's only when the door clicks shut behind me that she puts down her phone. Two strips of fluorescent ceiling lights shine down on her glasses, obscuring her expression. Whatever she sees when she looks in my direction causes her to walk around the bed and hold her arms open wide.

'And how *are* you?' she mocks, meaning it.

'*Fine.*' I go for the hug. She catches me by the shoulders, preventing a full embrace. This keeps professional boundaries where they belong but still bestows a warm glow onto whatever is about to commence.

She lets me go. 'I'm to blame too. I assumed you were doing more than note-taking all along, that you were understudying, getting comfortable.'

'I was. I was roadworthy, but—'

'—but now we move forward. Go: help Sven with his wish to die. Adult children by his side. No second thoughts.' She takes two plastic cups from the supply closet and puts them in my hands. 'Fill them two-thirds of the way.'

If you're demonstrating what you know about priming an IV line or debriding a wound, you can move quickly, describing to your assessor your actions and the precautions you will take as you go. For a procedure that is essentially a dialogue, though, it's in the acting. There's no room for rushing. I keep close to Sven but not too close, giving the established script space for tears and goodbyes with his imaginary children. I've cast them as two adult sons, and I improvise complex family dynamics, giving one of them poorly controlled bipolar disorder. Possibly too much, I know, but I'm trying to impress. The non-favourite, who was far more useful and devoted, has signed his acceptance but requires his own careful handling as he is full-strength Greek Orthodox. I convey calm and gentle like nobody's business. By the end of the preliminaries with the imaginary children and the moulded patient, there is unanimity in the room.

The second cup remains safely on the end table through it all. Once I have asked Sven again if today is truly the day, I hand it over and step back.

After he has swallowed, I tell him, 'You and your family have a few more minutes together. They're yours. I'll be over here.' I step back, warm, spacious and appropriate.

When I risk a glance in Nettie's direction, she's still got her eyes on Sven. She taps her fingers against her upper lip and turns to me. 'What do you believe has improved with Sven over Teddy?'

'The placement of the cups, for one.'

'That is correct. Plus, you normalised this intervention better than yesterday's. At any rate, I saw less panic in you. But why?'

'Teddy's kids showing up rattled me. And Geraldine's doubts. Which I know can happen. Anything can happen.'

'What else?'

I came prepared for interrogation. 'Remember Norma?'

Nettie thinks. 'The viola player. Breast with bone?'

'Yes. The room was so tense when you walked in. Remember the daughter's face when you reminded her it would be recorded? She acted like it would be used against her. You didn't flinch. You didn't ignore them, but you didn't try to coax them either. In the space of a minute, your level of comfort prevailed. It was where they wanted to be and you led them right there. I've watched that session a few times. The assistant should set the temperature for the scene, no matter the outcome. That's what you do.'

'Thank you. The pedestal is nice.'

'I tried to do the same thing with Sven just now, to assert my position in the room, to ignore the world outside and move us forward with a sense of specific purpose. Keeping that honesty—and that focus—would have prevented the spill. That, I think, has to become my habit.'

Nettie tilts her head sideways till her neck gives a click. 'All right. I appreciate that and appreciate that that's what you were aiming for, but my discomfort with yesterday was about more than the spill. It was a symptom of a larger issue.' She squeezes her neck with her hands. 'Try not to take this as a global criticism—'

'Please. Let it rip.'

'That comment you made earlier, to Sven's sons, about the last minutes being for the family. It made me want to ask you, *Who were those other minutes for?*

Ah. It wasn't the spill, it was my essence.

'It's for the patient and me to make or not make our transaction and provide the drugs,' I say.

'That is correct on every other ward. Not with us. The reality for Teddy and his family is that our role is smaller than that. Non-existent. You are, in the most demeaning sense, an assistant, nothing more. That's why I thought you would be comfortable walking into the room yesterday. Whether you're full of disgust or feeling weepy that day is irrelevant. Whether they're ready or not is irrelevant too. Whatever you picked up watching me with Norma was simply the way I am. Scale back on the empathy or you become a player. You are a step behind, supporting. The words do the work for you. Aside from handing over the cups, your presence is barely required.'

'I'm there to support,' I parrot, resting my hands on Sven's thigh.

'Do you know what I remember about Norma's death? The way she weaved her fingers into her daughter's as she fell asleep. I saw dirt under the daughter's nails. What was she doing that morning? I asked myself. Gardening? Digging a grave? It was a throwaway thought. I only know of their anxiety at the start because you talked about it afterwards. For me, those minutes with them were unconscious.'

'That makes me feel so completely green.'

'That's acceptable. You are. Just be less interested in connecting, in some expected endpoint. In the end, this is for your own survival. You'll sleep better. Look at Lena and how it impacted her.'

I think about Geraldine. I think about thinking about Geraldine. Faking it into the drain.

'I get it,' I say.

Nettie leans back. 'I'll tell you a story that's helped me. My aunt was a nurse in a small town. One of these picture-perfect cow towns, complete with the permanent stink of manure and slaughter hanging over the place.'

'Your mother's sister?' I ask.

'Not my father's. There isn't much farmland in Shanghai. This aunt lived past ninety, independent until the last three weeks. She had a lady friend we never knew about until the woman swooped in there at the end to take care of her, but that's not the story. My aunt's job, from her teens onwards, was to ride her bicycle all over the town and visit whoever couldn't make it to the doctor on their own. She knew everyone's details. They trusted her. They eventually gave her a car, which they let her keep when she retired. That was a different era. Seventy-seven when she finally stopped. When I started studying, I asked her once if she got a lot out of the job. She said my question was peculiar. If she was bandaging a wound, she said, she'd become the bandage. If she was giving someone their pills, she was the medicine cup. The job needed doing, she did it. What more could she do?'

'Sounds Buddhist,' I say.

'Who knows what else went on in her house? *The job needed doing.* That's been a useful anchor. The work is it. Keeps me out of my own head. Otherwise I take up too much space.'

I pick up the cup. 'So: I am the Nembutal.'

'There you go.' She takes the cup and crumples it. 'I'm going to scram. I want to deliver Teddy's report to certain parties in Oncology.'

'It's not complete.'

Nettie wriggles her hands, typing in midair.

'You didn't have to. I was going to finish it this morning. I was waiting for the debrief.'

'Why? Were you waiting to find out from me how the intervention went yesterday?'

I make a guilty face.

'It's over. It was your first. The end. Reflect and move on.'

And she's off to the seventh floor, taking her indefatigable glutes to the staircase.

———

I go back to our office to look at Teddy's report. Nettie filled in each screen, clipped it to the video file with the death certificate, and published it last night at 10.36. The chief variance noted in the summary was the unplanned presence of his daughters. The spill was minimised. My apparently glaring presence was minimised. I have been spared.

She has, however, exercised her right to record comments on the assistant's performance. This is normally my domain, but this time it's hers. Her cosmos has no such beast as blame in it, and yet:

Due to an unexpected staffing shortfall and the wish to respect the patient's preferred timing for death, this intervention was conducted as scheduled with a new clinician in the role. I assigned a staff member familiar with the patient and his family. He has not been as rigorously mentored as our previous assistant. On review, an unnecessary dynamic was noted between the facilitator, the patient and the patient's partner. This appeared to involve heightened empathy for the family, resulting in an observable need for control of the situation and even approval in his role. The dynamic did not conflict with the patient's wishes and this was, in the end, a successful intervention. As noted, it was the assistant's first intervention.

Our objective remains the development of a teachable, scalable model that may be replicated elsewhere. If there are conclusions to be derived, we will include them in the final filing. Because our aim is to reduce inconsistency across different centres and staff members, we will continue to evaluate the impact of personality traits on the intervention, remaining mindful of the wellbeing of every participant, including that of the assistant.

Not global, my arse.

The phone on Nettie's desk beeps. I swivel and reach across to answer. It's from inside the hospital, a patient's room. The number is familiar.

Uma. The dentist. My two-thirty. The clock flashing green on the wall says nine-fifteen.

'Hello, this is Evan' is met with silence. 'Is this Uma?'

'It is,' she finally says.

'Are you looking for Nettie? She isn't at her desk.'

Another pause. Our scheduled meeting will be her third, to confirm the plan for her death. The visit is to quadruple-check she's okay. If she's grown attached to Nettie, I can defer.

I say, 'We're scheduled to—'

'I'm supposed to talk to you, I know. You don't lose track of an appointment like this. I'm cancelling.' She didn't want to talk to Nettie. She wanted voicemail.

'Did you want to change the time of our meeting?'

'No, I—'

The researcher in me is ready. The tip of my pen is touching a blank page on Nettie's notepad, awaiting dictation.

'I'm—' In the background, someone mumbles in her room. 'Yes. I'm not going to do this.'

'If you want, Nettie could come by and see you later.'

'No! I don't want to be drawn back into any more talk.' Her words are for the other person in the room, who is no doubt gesturing to Uma to hang up. 'I don't mean to sound rude. It must be easy for you, but I can't talk about my death, sun-up to sunset.' She takes a sip of something, then chokes, falling into a coughing fit that borders on gagging. Still hacking, she says, 'I've said what I have to. Bye now.'

And out.

I guess Uma wasn't a good fit after all.

The referral process needs work. As outlined in Measure 961, a patient has to voice their wish to hasten their own death on two separate occasions to get the ball rolling. These requests must be unprompted and documented. If an astute clinical reader of said patient's notes catches this, they must then send a referral to the patient's treating doctor, advising them to review the history, confirm prognosis, and make sure other possible treatments have been discussed, from the hot chemotherapy bath in the abdomen to easy-listening piano tunes with the music therapist. If there isn't a reasonable expectation that one of these might ease suffering, and if the doctor considers that the patient's profound hopelessness and likely ongoing expected misery sit within our parameters, he or she is required to initiate a discussion with the patient about their legal option of an assisted death. This almost never happens.

In the early days, when we were setting up shop with few customers, Nettie decided to run a surveillance trace on people using a few keywords—*suicide, Nembutal, euthanasia*—in the Oncology ward. One junior doctor was heard being directly asked by a patient—in front of his family members, no less—for all of the above. The doctor assured him, 'We don't do that here.' Since Nettie followed that up, pointing out that withholding available and requested treatment was malpractice, the 'team' has been more forthcoming with referrals.

She went further, developing an application to scan patient notes, searching for broader terms (*dejected, despairing, distressed, downcast, downhearted*; and that's just a few of the Ds). She screens out conflicts that may complicate our work—uncertain disease progression, difficult family dynamics, unstable psych history, financial hardship. Then, once we've found a potential candidate, we discuss referral with their treating doctor. When that happens, they know Nettie's watching.

I'm trying to recall how Uma reached us, when I see Nettie in the doorway.

'Uma pulled out.'

She nods. 'Her partner was only seventy percent on board. I guessed that was coming.' I start to roll away from her desk, but she presses me back in place with one firm hand. 'What reason did she give?'

'Nothing we can use. And she doesn't want to talk about it or see either of us again.'

'Did you record the call?'

'No.'

'Good.' She glances at my few notes. 'The walls have eyes.'

Ethics has determined that patients who have left the program do not, for our purposes, exist. They may not be discussed or contacted again without a new referral. I fold my notes in half for the shredder.

'Thank you,' Nettie says. 'Next: guess which psychologist is restricting the involvement of his trainees with our program.'

'Any of them?'

'Death is apparently not a normal part of the hospital experience.'

'It isn't in any of the ads,' I say.

She doesn't even smile. 'I want to show him a few clips. I'll start with Mimi and move on to Salvatore.'

'That's just cruel.'

'Not as cruel as I'm feeling. We're meeting again in an hour. I need to run first or I'll take it out on him.' She reaches past my knees for her jogging gear under her desk.

I was in the park near Viv's place one night when Nettie ran past in head-to-toe blue spandex, hair up in a matching scrunchie. At least fifteen kilometres from her home, but there she was. And there I was, sitting on a bench eating a burger and dribbling grilled onions onto the grass. Either she didn't see me or she had the good taste not to acknowledge.

She takes off downstairs as I escort the sensitive documents to the shredder, turning them slowly into ticker tape.

What's left for the day is a rather sluggish client list.

There's Sanford. Sixty-eight. Former CEO of a company that leases farming machinery on an industrial scale. Motor neurone disease is taking a leisurely trip up from his legs. Sanford enjoyed cruises when he could still manage the little steps; once he started to rely on a wheelchair and an attendant, not so much. Thrice-divorced, no children. Big real-estate holdings too, from some smart early moves. He's philosophical about it all, even about our cautious progress, which is moving only incrementally faster than his illness. 'As long as you get around to me while I can still choke the stuff down.' He's expressed a preference for a male assistant, if possible. Up until yesterday, it wasn't. He says, 'This decision is different for a man.'

Indeed it is. For instance, picture Dad, driving along a leafy country road and considering his options. He would have been Sanford's age this year. Aside from the business prowess and the smart early moves, they could have been dead ringers. Dad's zooming along the road, the radio going in and out of static from the mountain reception. The wife and kid versus the guardrail. A tough one. Only a man could make that call. Speeding up, just like Sanford: right here will do.

I scroll through the rest of Sanford's record. The disease is working him over. One week it takes out a hip flexor, the next it sends a demonic itch to the centre of his back. Primary issues: he's frustrated and constipated. He doesn't truly need to be occupying a hospital room for this, but he's got the money, so he's on the executive floor. Judging by the glowing notes, he seems to be charming the nurses up there: *warm and talkative*; *very helpful during interventions*; and, suggesting a breach of ethics, *extremely generous with staff*.

There is a Marianna listed as a possible witness. An ex-wife? Sanford's next meeting with us won't be until after his medical review. Given the new opening in the schedule, I make some notes and shoot a message to Nettie to see if he might be interested in fast-tracking it.

———

When the bus drops us at the entrance to the park, Viv awkwardly kicks off her sandals, affecting ease with no success. Picture Frankenstein's monster having just watched a video on how to kick off sandals. She tilts forward far enough to pick them up and miraculously not fall forward, then hands them to me.

'Protect them,' she says, walking with purpose towards the soft ground around the lake.

These are not any old sandals. When she first brought them home, she took them for a catwalk around the living room. Doing fractions at the coffee table, I became enamoured of the sponginess of the cork heels. Her splurge was justified because they would be worn at her first tournament. She didn't like exploiting her sex there, but she was proud of her toes. They're not dainty, and nowhere near catalogue-ready, but they are a pleasing shape and—she would punch me for saying so—ladylike. When the money flowed, pedicures held a regular spot in her schedule; when it stopped, she filled a purple plastic lunchbox with foot lotion, clippers, pumice and various grades of files required to keep her toes appealing and suggestive of sex. When her symptoms confined her poker to her laptop at the kitchen table, she kept her toenails painted and these sandals on just the same. 'You get more done if you put yourself together like you care, if you don't look like you're sitting next to the toaster.' Even now, though the leather straps are cracked at the buckles and the cork is ossified, they are too cherished to wear through the park.

'This,' she pronounces, wiggling her toes in the shady plenitude of wetlands. She's pushing them into the mud as joyfully as she can, which, with the sun backing off slightly from its recent burn and with her muscles remembering their purpose more each day, is pretty damned joyful.

'This.' She stomps again, reaching out for my arm, not for stability, but to shake me, to make sure I get her point. 'This!'

I agree. 'This!'

She veers to the left in order to investigate a log that's fallen across the marshy back corner of the lake. The place is more conducive for dusktime hookups than for leisurely ambles.

'Nature's provided us with a bench!' Her shoulders rise and fall to maximise each delicious inhalation. She beckons me after her, right past nature's bench. 'This is all I've wanted for so long!'

A mother duck and two fuzzy yellow ducklings scatter into the shallow water to get out of Viv's way. She points them out to me. 'Looks like a duck, quacks like a duck, poops like a duck. Must be a—'

'Very convincing duck decoy.'

She points me out to them. 'My funny son.'

They regroup and move to the shore, where they keep watch, attempting camouflage in the parched grass. They loop their necks forward, jostling their yellow heads to see what Viv is going to do next.

With agility, she side-steps a condom and an abandoned pair of women's underwear. 'See this? Responsible people come here.'

There have been two steady weeks of gains. The manic edge has softened while her movement has continued to improve. The makeup has been toned down. She's taking a walk in the park. The sun is shining on us all.

Her head turns towards a low whistle. 'Is that a magpie? It most certainly is.' She takes two muddy steps towards the bird when it flies off. 'Everly, take off your shoes and come stand here with me.'

'Mother,' I say. She flinches as intended. 'The name is Evan.'

'Still? A mashed potato of a name. Your father's fault. Everly was such an improvement. I'm sure you keep him tucked away in there.' She points to my chest.

The duck family make a run for the water. 'Come closer!' she says to me.

'I can see from here. Let me just be your shoe sherpa. One of us needs to keep their feet dry.'

'You're only punishing yourself.' She pads her feet up and down, squishing for maximum audible effect, waving her arms in circles on either side of herself like slow propellors. 'My soles have always been tough.' Double meaning intended. 'Come on. Why won't you take off your shoes?'

'Don't wanna.' I will freely admit that I'm staying on dry land in case she falls. She could still misjudge her capacity, and I'll have to get her out of the lake to coax her, step by leaden step, back to the bus stop.

'It's because I drank when I was pregnant with you.'

There's no stopping this train. 'Probably.'

'It was your father and his Cuba Libres. It started earlier, when we were drinking with the locals, trying to blend in. If I didn't drink, Claude wouldn't drink, and we couldn't have that. I'd have one and he could have three. He'd cheer up a little and, if I was lucky, he would make chicken *mole*, his one dish. That put him in a festive mood for an hour or so. It seemed worth it. We both preferred him with a shot or two of rum. But now, with you such a stranger sometimes, I'm not so sure.'

'I've grown to accept my low-grade brain injury,' I say.

'It may have been more than a few times a week during that first trimester.'

I cast her an intensely forgiving gaze.

'Joke as you like. Those drinks must have played a role in your development and who you've turned out to be.'

'And why I'm not standing in the mud.'

'Yes.'

'If you had only drunk a few more, maybe I'd be right there by your side,' I say.

'Is the dirt your whole issue? Look around. There's grass. There's sunlight. We have the afternoon to get your precious toes clean. For better or worse, even Claude would be next to me right now.'

Dad? For real? According to years of her mocking stories, he only liked the outdoors when it was tidy. No mud allowed. Even in the past two weeks, as up as she's been, Viv has never attempted to memorialise his love for the universe's mess.

'He'd have his feet all the way in,' she adds. '*He* could accept the world as it is. Not get bogged down.' She slurps her toes around for emphasis.

No. This I remember well: the night after the funeral, she was standing in front of the open fridge, picking with her fingers at a chicken she had roasted when Dad was still alive, talking to a friend standing at her side. I remember that chicken. I held onto that wishbone through the first three relocations. I remember Viv saying, 'Limited, limited, limited. Claude kept his special grey goggles firmly on, always. I see it now, that this was inevitable. If there was a dandelion in front of him, it was a weed. Any actual problem—a flat tyre—it was the apocalypse.' Viv's sudden awareness that her son, her personal recording device, was standing there in his baby-blue suit, still funeral fresh, made her close the fridge, lick her fingers clean, and lean over to wrap me safely in her arms, protecting me from such fathers. 'It's a metaphor,' she told me, which didn't clarify the goggles any better, so she went on. 'And that's why he didn't see the many paths that the world has for us, bright paths like you.' There: the scold was turned into an inoculation against my father's limitless limitations. That tree and he, they had it coming.

This afternoon, though, he's become the kind of man to dive head-first into life itself, with both feet in the mud.

'That's a new take on Claude,' I say.

'Who's talking about Claude? I only said that he—unlike you, *Evan*—would have at least been brave enough to enjoy it out here. Maybe he's an extreme example and maybe a touchy one. If so, I'm sorry. My concern is always for you.'

I throw her some shade. 'Who brought you here? Whose idea was it?'

'Then go all the way. Let me enjoy it. I'm your mother. Come stand next to me.'

'Won't you want me to help you out when a syringe bubbles up?'

'That sarcasm, it's a tic. You think it justifies your sense of remove. It's not even a character trait. It's a symptom. Its only function is to keep you out of the game.'

Her students loved this kind of abuse. She ventures into deeper mud at the edge of the water. Her right foot is braced against the rotting bark of a decaying log. She pushes back and forth against it, forgetting her lecture and instead giving her open-armed attention to the afternoon sun.

The golden light penetrates the overgrown shrubs around the pond, tracing a halo around Viv as she rotates her hips, her shoulders and articulates each of her fingers like Shiva herself. She stops to scowl at me. A thought has interrupted her ecstasy. 'Do you think you're suicidal?'

'No. Thanks for asking. Why?'

'Your job. It isn't exactly cheery.'

'You thought it was a good idea when I started.'

'Don't be scared to walk away while you're ahead. There's too much of your father's shadowy side in you.' She makes her way to drier ground while keeping a mistrusting eye on me, as if I might drive off a cliff if she turns away. 'Speaking of your work. There's a stunning Jordanian woman at my place—wears her headscarf, has the prayer mats. The woman is extremely sick. Not-getting-better sick. She might benefit from your services.'

'Is that your prescription?' I ask.

'She has liver failure or cancer. Something. Whatever it is, she spends more time at the Mercy than with us. First it was the surgery, then one infection after another. She comes back from each appointment more beat up than before, always holding her side. It's like in those movies of a prisoner being brought back in from a torture session all black and blue. Once a week she endures this. Now her doctor has finally owned up. She has a few months left—short ones was how he put it, as if the number of days in a month is negotiable. They may want to try out one more drug on her. While they still have use of her body for experimentation. She said yes to them. I asked her if she had a choice about it. I don't think she fully gets what's ahead. She used to be in the front of the pack at tai chi. Now she stays in her room falling apart, praying and crying and working on her brave face for mealtimes, where she can hardly touch a bite.'

'What I'm hearing is that you think her time has come and she might be interested in learning more on the subject of assisted dying.'

'Deep down she's entertaining thought of it. She has to be.'

'And only needs a push,' I say.

'Aqila has been so unlucky in this life. Only has the one niece, who comes by every few days, drags her to appointments, fluffs her pillows and brings her fruit. To make matters worse, Aqila thinks her situation is some godly whim that she must endure. She's too old to qualify for a liver, or too sick. I don't know details. The next time they send her over, I could let you know she's there, get her room number, and you could pop your head in. Just as my son, visiting. Friendly. If the conversation goes that way, maybe she'll ask about what you do for a living. That's your opening. No harm there.'

'You can't refer a friend,' I tell her.

She gives me a sympathetic smile. 'This woman may not know death is a possibility.'

'She said yes to more treatment.'

'You know how they corner you. And this niece who comes probably bullied her into going through with it.' Viv looks disgusted. 'I don't know what that one's angle is. Forcing more treatment on a dying woman.'

'It might not be force. It might be she's after the two percent chance of a good result. You don't know. And some people like the caretaker role. Some people don't mind being cared for. *Mum.*'

'Stop calling me that,' she says. 'It's manipulative.'

'Only in certain quarters. Anyway, Muslims don't tend to come to us. It's not the done thing.'

'Then tell me who comes through your hallowed doors.'

'White agnostics. Middle class and above.'

'Sick rich white people to the front of the line, naturally. Nicely educated, too, I'll bet, the narcissistic pricks.'

'Generally, yes.'

'And everyone else? Are they culturally inappropriate? You think this poor woman should die in pain because she hasn't said the magic words? Bullshit.'

After months of her slow-moving domestic reporting from Willow Wood, it is a thrill to see her this righteous. I hope it lasts. Hope. Probably what Aqila is going to die from.

'You signed up to help more people than just people who look like us, didn't you?' she asks.

'It's where we are right now. Baby steps.'

'Don't tell me I raised an apologist. Who's stopping you from doing the right thing?' She points to my forehead. 'If you want a better planet, you have to be willing to leave your own neighbourhood.' She raises her palms towards her face like spotlights, shining them on herself, a prime example of a trailblazer.

'The law is still new,' I say.

'Then what a perfect time to make it fair. If you're not going to, I'll go ahead and talk to Aqila on my own.'

'About killing herself?'

'I am capable of letting the conversation roam in that direction,' she says with a sly spark.

'Go right ahead,' I say. 'But don't mention your son the dying assistant or our specific service.'

'I already promised you. I can be subtle.' She accentuates this last point with a one-legged curtsey, and tips forward. My arms shoot out towards her to catch her, but she manages to right herself with one palm on the ground, her hand splayed near a used blue condom. She looks back at me. 'Any problems?'

'None,' I say.

She pushes herself to standing, wiping the dirt from her hand on her thigh. 'Don't hover. I'm not your job.'

'You're right.' Since the initial phone call from the hospital bed, she has skilfully maintained her tale of utter independence by never once explicitly asking for anything. The prevailing narrative is that I moved back to mix up my social possibilities, moved in to save money, researched her medications to expand my knowledge base, took her to specialists to make professional connections, and, on a monthly basis, contribute to the bill from Willow Wood out of the goodness of my heart. The woman is a grifter.

Up on her toes, digging her feet down into a new patch of mud she's found: 'All I'm looking for is a tiny bit of belief.'

'The truth? I don't feel like it. Your mind is where it used to be, which is wonderful, but your body isn't there yet, so part of me doubts your judgment.'

Her rapturous pride comes to a halt. 'You're doubting me?'

Poor word choice. To her, doubt is the opposite of life. Not long after my father's incident with the tree, I experienced what any psychologist—*had I been taken to one*—would have called terrors. To deal with the grunting, heaving dead bodies that were stationed around every street corner and behind every parked car, my mother hatched this effective home remedy: *Tell them you doubt their existence. Say it to them. Say it to yourself. It will make you strong.* So, yeah, doubt.

She stiffens her shoulders for battle. 'If I go skydiving tomorrow, you still know who you're dealing with.' Actual chest-thumping. 'This is me.'

Just then her foot catches on a root branch that's sticking out of the mud.

The good son, standing a few feet away, channels Nettie's aunt to give the patient what she needs: I hold still, maintain the requested respectful distance. My mother will fall or she won't. I am not here to expect or doubt or do anything.

And, with no other power than her own strength to aid her, she stays vertical. She looks back at me with a *hmph*.

The desire to kiss her implant right on its electrodes is one I'm pretty sure a good nurse would resist. Even coming from her son, it could be read as condescension.

'I'm gaining ground,' Viv says. 'I know it. So if you start managing me, even a teensy bit, you will live to regret it. When I come back, I'll haunt you. I'll move your furniture. I'll tip over your soup while you're eating.'

I smile.

'And your cereal. You won't get through a meal in peace.'

Charmed, I take two steps closer and sink down into mud.

With both hands she grabs me by the arms and shouts to the treetops, 'Gotcha!'

—

Sanford's bed is in zero gravity support mode, a reclining setting reserved for the lucky few up here. He would have been a beefy guy once. Now the air's been let out of him and the muscle tone is gone. His eyes angle over to me in the doorway. 'Look, they sent me a man after all. Good for me.' The words set off a coughing fit. His hand makes it halfway to covering his mouth. 'Don't nobody move, I've got this.' The other hand fingers the bed's controller. Despite his wrist being tied to it with a white ribbon, his forefinger can't reach the stick.

'Can I help?'

After a few more ineffective swipes with his finger, he gives my offer a nod. 'Mornings,' he says, as I wrap his fingers around the controller. He squeezes it to life, and brings himself upright enough to clear his cough. The bed has a dozen comfort positions and no guardrails, adding to the illusion that we are in a boutique hotel. His legs extend straight out, separated by a pillow, the way they were put there, his bare feet flat against the upholstered foot of the bed.

'Prop me,' he says. I stabilise his position with pillows at his sides.

With repositioning accomplished, he introduces himself and I dip my head in a gesture of respect to his obvious wealth. Of course, the Mercy prides itself on the equality of its care throughout the campus, but these pillows are goose down, not fibrefill. There's more: dedicated chefs, pastel-coloured uniforms and, riskiest of all, carpeting. Every patient has two cameras on them, one directed from behind the bed and one from the doorway, a fact which research shows *magically* minimises drug errors and yields clearer communication with patients.

This attention to recorded detail is what led Sanford's neurologist to make his first pitch to us a month ago. Nettie was sceptical. Sanford is disabled, not imminently terminal. 'Let his lawyers straighten out his landholdings. Then we talk to him.' She wanted to get through a few more ninety-nine-percenters before assisting anyone from the executive floor. Other programs have had issues with moneyed patients. One well-married widow promised the administrators of her hospital a garden atrium on her way out. As soon as she was dispatched, the funds flowed in. The hospital hired a landscaper and the family hired a lawyer. Out of nowhere, the anti-dignity people, or whatever they're calling themselves, called a press conference, saying the hospital had gained from her death, which was somehow worse than it getting a garden after she simply died in the hospice with a bowel obstruction. But Sanford's doctor advocated for him, exactly the way Nettie likes.

'Are you wearing perfume?' he asks me.

I tell him it's aftershave, which sounds more butch. 'Is it strong?'

'Nah. It smells like a barber shop. I'm just glad the nose is operational. Get started. What's your story?'

'In what regard?'

'I want to know who I'm talking to. Homey details. Are you new at this? Married, divorced, what?'

'No, and neither. I came up here to introduce myself and talk about the plan.'

'So introduce yourself. Straight? Gay?'

I blame the cologne. 'Gay.'

'Male nurse. Seemed like there was a chance. And not married. Single?'

I squint, trying to emanate a polite confusion as to why this information might be relevant to his death.

'It's not discrimination if you're going to help me kill myself either way,' he says. 'You can give up a few basics. Are you with someone or what? Yes, I need to know.'

'No. I'm not with anyone.' Lon and Simon, actually. The three of us sleep under one sheet.

'I see. Looking.' His eyes widen with visions of who knows what. 'I'm divorced again, which will keep this simple. She wasn't a real helper around the house, then I got sick.' With his free hand he hitches up his sheet to show me his puny calves, glistening from executive-level moisturising. His brief questioning was just a lead-in. 'This disease forces you to cut losses. I didn't want her being the one feeding me mush. Whatever or whoever you may be into, don't hang around with selfish women—or men. Please, do not under any circumstances marry them. Judy was all right for garden tours and wineries, but she'd need to have the right gear on in order to take a piss. You should have seen the toilet she found for her bathroom.' He slows down enough to notice he's still talking. 'Do you see? My throat's already back in business. But Judy. Everything was a contest or a slight. On top of that, she'd be paying somebody else to feed me the mush anyway. Might get some on her sleeve. And I hadn't even dreamed about the suppositories back then. Paid her what she deserved and, after a few operatics, that was it. I cut out the middleman. Here, I've got my room and my view and a lot less talking. What else does a body need? If I'm in the mood, there's company. There's you, for instance.' He looks at the hardwood end table next to his bed, adjusted to the height of his elbow. There's a glass of orange juice on top, as if for a photo shoot, complete with frosty condensation and a strawberry perched on the rim.

'Help yourself,' he says. 'It's fresh. They brought it ten minutes ago. Doesn't agree with me.'

'No, thanks.'

'If I need help here, I press a button and they run to my side. Better than home. Well trained. They listen to me yammering on my steroids. They listen for as long as they can stand it, do what needs doing, friendly enough for the job description, and then they go. For the time I have left, it's what I need.'

'Which is what I'm here to discuss.'

'Aha! Yes, my death. Your department is another business entirely. Very interesting people, for medical. The only ones in this place willing to go all the way. I'm listening to *The Tibetan Book of the Dead*, a chapter a day. It's provocative, but I can't exactly talk to the others in the lounge about the *Chikhai Bardo* and my dissolution. Which is a shame. Upsets the women. That's why I asked for a man. Our brains work differently. Even gay brains. A joke, don't sue. I told the psychologist. We love life as much as women do, but the second we're presented with a fact like this, we don't want to go around crying on shoulders or joining a group. We're not wired to be patient. We don't revel in the process as much. We want results. Am I right?'

'I might say that everybody handles death differently.'

'Stay neutral, sure. Knock yourself out. I know what I know. Men want to get to the end of things. Climb to the top, take it apart, find out how it finishes. Women revere the journey, the process. Which absolutely is their prerogative. Am I right? Don't bother being diplomatic, I know I'm right. Since you're here, the fact that I asked for a male was obviously passed on, so I'm assuming there are no objections from on high. So my feelings have been affirmed, in social-work speak. And I'm grateful, because my own HR department would have given me hell for even acknowledging there are two sexes.'

'No objection. For what we're doing, it's a reasonable request.'

He can't raise his head but he can raise his eyebrows. '"What we're doing"?'

'Assisted dying.'

'Thank you. Really, you should have the juice. Someone took the time to squeeze it.'

I remove the strawberry and drink.

He watches my throat as I swallow. 'Who knows what hothouse they're getting the oranges from. That's not our nightmare. Not mine.'

'It's good,' I say. He watches my hand as I replace the glass on the table, effortlessly. A hundred little actions I'm not even aware of are needed to keep me from dropping it. I'm oblivious.

'Now let me ask you,' he says. 'Why did you turn down the juice the first time?'

'I don't know.'

'Is it against some rule book?'

'No. I just didn't say yes.'

'Forgive me if I'm still curious. So it's against a rule book of your own making? I need more than that. Somewhere you knew you wanted it, but you *thought*. You thought something. You were concerned it would look a certain way. Is that it?'

This feels like a job interview going wrong. 'I suppose.'

'But then you said yes. Is that a personality issue for you, this hesitation?'

'I held back at first out of some, I don't know, archaic form of politeness, then I drank it,' I say. 'End of story.'

'When I told you to. Not when I offered. Like you were waiting for the order.'

'Hold on. Aren't you revelling in the process here?'

His mouth flattens, almost turning up into a smile. 'Sorry for picking on you. If you're giving me my last drink, I don't want you hesitating. Life is too short to pussyfoot around.'

'I won't pussyfoot.' I make a point of eating the strawberry with pleasure. 'Unless you want to discuss my juice-drinking habits further, can we move on to discussing your death?'

He manages a nod. I've got the job. 'Continue.'

'I'm here to discuss the date. Before we get into it, there's a woman named Marianna you've mentioned as a possible witness. We don't have much information on her.'

For the first time since I came into his room, he deflates. 'She's not coming. You can take her out of the picture completely. Look.' He points to the sheets bunching up again near the bottom of the bed. 'Help me slide up here. Brace my legs.'

I grip his calves while he lowers the bed to flat. His controller hand raises the bottom of the bed to lift his knees up. I push against his body. It's like moving a futon. He's up and straight for a few seconds before he slumps back to more or less the same position he was in. 'My butt is closer to the centre, at least. Much obliged.'

'Did you ask Marianna to be present?'

'Yes. She's a guru I've met at a few retreats. Wife number two introduced us, right when we were splitting up. She's helped me over the years, but she's not on board with this.'

I'm conscious of the cameras in the corners of the room. 'Does she have any objections she wants to discuss?'

'She has no right to objections. She's not friends or family. And she gets it, my wanting out of this skin prison. She respects it. She just doesn't want to be here. I knew it was a huge ask.'

'How was that for you?'

'Disappointing is how it was for me.'

I let the word fester. His fingers, working well now, tap the side of the controller, as if he could eject me from the room. Although giving him the time to fully express his inner process is therapeutic, this gap I'm leaving feels sadistic.

His expression hollows out. 'I wanted her here. I was very disappointed about it—sad, okay?'

There. He felt his feelings, verbalised pain and explained away the witness.

'Does that impact your feelings about taking the Nembutal?'

'Are you asking if I want to die more naturally? No. Thanks for asking.'

'What I'm getting at is, will you be comfortable going through this without her present?'

His eyes are glistening. 'I'll be me, comfortable or not. Time is up on this line of questioning. I appreciate your concern. I do. I just can't wait for her to come around and hold my hand while I take the poison and die, as you all so neatly put it. For our purposes—yours and mine—Marianna will not be here on the day.'

'I just want to be sure that any available emotional supports are—'

'Blah, blah, blah. There aren't any. It's you. Are you in?'

'Yes,' I say.

'At least fake it that you're enthusiastic. Let's settle the date and get this over with.'

'That's what I came here to do.'

'Could have fooled me. How's the end of the month looking? Is your schedule chock-a-block?'

Don't give in and don't bristle. At one of her last assists, Lena let herself be flustered by a patient's hostility. A young mother, bowel cancer with mets spreading through her pelvis. Fat with ascites. Her kids were in the next room with the social worker. Her husband was in the bed with her while she was drinking her drink. She handed the empty cup to Lena and asked, 'How come you get to live but I don't? Tell me that.' Lena, the empty cup shaking in her hand—must have had a big night out the night before—had no answer. 'There's nothing special or beautiful or better about you or what you're doing. I wish this was the other way around and you were about to die. Why don't you go stand in the corner.' Lena did as ordered, waiting by the window with her arms folded. The woman didn't let up, shouting after her, 'This isn't the morphine talking! It's a genuine question. Why do you get to live and I don't? It's a total fucking mystery to me.' You can't see Lena's face in the recording, but the woman went on. The husband did nothing to quiet her down. No *I love you*s there. Her last words were harsh ones, directed at Lena.

Afterwards, the husband didn't even acknowledge the diatribe. He just went to get the kids, while Lena washed the body and went through the documentation. Nettie, who watched the recording with me, said, 'Lena shouldn't sulk. She's only a symbol to them.'

So, for Sanford I flash professional engagement and personal disengagement. He doesn't want to know me. 'Is there a day you're thinking about?'

'How about I'll die next Tuesday?'

'Yes, fine. Did Nettie discuss the consulting suite with you? I can arrange for you to come down there to have a look.'

'I prefer the view from my room, thank you.'

'I don't see why not.' But someone will. No way they'll let us creep up to the penthouse of clinical excellence. And before any member of the board gets a vote, there's Carmel, the nurse in charge of this country club. She will have to be appeased. Still, the customer is king, so I say, 'I may have to make some inquiries to—'

'I've already arranged it.'

'You did?'

'What do you know? There's emotion in you after all. It's approved. No inquiries to be made.' Sanford raises his more functional arm up to the bar that dangles from a discreet steel pole over the bed.

'Do you need a hand?'

'I would ask you if I did. I don't have problems with asking for what I want. Sometimes I just like to hang. Also, I'd like to die in the evening.'

'What time?'

'Eleven. My best hour.'

My healthy detachment leads me to consider the financial details: if the ward is hosting, they'll have to kick in for my overtime. If I start the paperwork and the drugs around nine, it could be one in the morning before he's in the morgue and signed for, entirely at time and a half. It will be like an entire extra day's pay. They can put that on his bill. 'I'll confirm it with Carmel,' I tell him as I leave.

'Be my guest.' He rattles the chain of the bar back and forth against the pole.

———

Nettie is at her desk, knocking her keyboard upside down to get crumbs out. She looks up. 'Is all in readiness for him?'

'Marianna won't attend.'

'Family?'

'Guru.'

Nettie wipes the crumbs into her wastepaper basket. 'Well, that's a setback we can endure. When?'

'Next Tuesday. I'll put it in the schedule.'

'I worry about him. The avoidant type. It's like we're participating in his lifelong dodge.'

'Avoidant? He's a master of industry.'

'Three wives? Avoidant. If he has a guru, maybe I'm misreading him. He wanted a male, so that works. Next: would you be interested in assisting with Iris?'

'Isn't she today?'

'Correct. Now, actually.' Nettie points to a blue kidney dish on her desk. It's holding a cup of Nembutal. 'Short notice, I'm aware. Two daughters and her partner are there—partner is named Lenore. They're completely aligned with each other, how this is going to go, what it means. They won't be looking to you for much. You go in, do what's needed, then leave. They'll want time with the body afterwards. Let them do the washing. They've brought their own soap. What do you think?' Nettie checks the time in the corner of her monitor. 'She had her metoclopramide nearly an hour ago.'

'Are they expecting me?'

'They're set for you or me. They're reading her favourite poems to her. Very in-the-now about it. We don't matter. You've seen her before, haven't you?'

'I have.' Tall, angular woman with small round tumours, like bits of fried bread, all over her torso, spreading outwards to her limbs and up her neck. She can barely move without one bursting with bloody pus.

'They wanted to bring their own incense for the smell, but fire laws et cetera. They brought smoke alarm–proof candles instead.'

'I'll do it.'

'Yes, you will.' Nettie hands me the kidney dish and puts the paperwork in my other hand. 'They're in C22. Bring your recorder.'

'It's in my pocket,' I say. 'Also, on Sanford. He wants to do it in the executive ward. In his room. At night.' I let her imagine the obstacles for a moment, before adding, 'The venue and timing are already arranged and approved, through Carmel.'

'I'm stunned that hasn't blown back in our direction. Score: us. Anything else?'

I feel an urge to stall, to put some time between Sanford and Iris, but Nettie is nodding at the kidney dish, which is, in the end, where I really need to be.

She says, 'Then go.'

⎯

No mistaking the daughter when she greets me at the door. The same long dark frizzy hair as Iris had in the healthy pictures she showed us and a green metal eyeglass chain dangling down that makes her look even taller than her mother.

'Sorry, are you Denise or Toula?' I ask.

'Toula. And you're Evan, not Nettie. Come!' She waves me into the consulting room. The candles have filled the place with ylang-ylang and lemongrass, to cover the earthy smell of human putrescence. The chairs, the couch and the metal bed rails have been draped with orange sheets, transforming the room into one big pustule that camouflages the patient on the bed.

Iris is tucked in on her side with one arm on top of the sheet, and a few pinkish growths visible. A faded patchwork quilt is folded next to her head. This would have to be a memento, but the placement is clever: the busyness of the red and green diamonds make them the only visual in the room that jars.

Iris's mouth is spread wide and she's shaking with silent laughter, her eyes nearly closed and her chest heaving. Her face is puffed from steroids. Lenore, with a tight perm of silver-blond hair, is snuggled under the covers and sharing the laugh. A book of sepia-toned nature photography from another century is open flat at her side.

Toula presents me. 'Evan is here.'

The women don't even look up. As is right.

The other daughter, Denise, composed of similar familial dimensions, is draped over the arms of a chair, looking more removed then Toula, as if she's here in body only.

Recently framed photos are spread across the bottom of the bed. Iris and Lenore in a rowboat; Iris leans towards the camera with the oars held close to her chest, her chin tilted up, and her mouth open in a predatory grin at the camera.

She was a leg model, who hung around after shoots, became a creative and then a principal at an ad agency, eventually buying the place and building it up. Divorced. Then Lenore came into the picture. They got disgusted with advertising and sold the business. Iris was training to become a psychotherapist when, bam, three years ago, a rare cancer started popping up.

There are a dozen well-shot pictures of Toula and Denise at different ages, growing from girls in identical blue velvet dresses into women in separate frames, doing their own thing with their own friends. No pictures of the father. They were six and eight when Iris took them and left.

A breach of conduct: everyone, including Iris, is holding a half-filled wine glass. The bottle, with a visibly French label, is on the tray table. The issue of alcohol has been raised by previous patients, all of whom were told that no intoxicants are allowed in the room. Iris didn't like the answer, apparently. I've seen Nettie ignore this sort of variance. I'm happy to do the same. Unless she drinks the entire bottle, she should keep the Nembutal down.

This morning I reread Iris's exit interview: *I can handle death. It's no surprise. What I can't cope with is becoming this repulsive to myself.*

The tumours that are visible are determinedly random. They don't follow circulation or nerves. In places, they are as evenly spaced as polka dots on a dress, and in other places they form tight clusters. The psychologists agreed that severe disfigurement falls under existential suffering. It wouldn't have been easy for a model, leg or otherwise, watching the cysts bloom and then bleed and then stake out more territory.

A thicket of these buds circles her wrist and cover the back of her hand, but they mercifully stop when they get to her palm, which will allow her to bring a cup to her lips.

Her bed has been turned towards the window, where a small painting is propped on the sill, partially blocking the hazy sunshine. The picture is in bright children's book colours. A round grassy hill with a square log cabin perched jauntily near the top, curly smoke coming from its chimney. The day is fading in make-believe land, from pale sky above down to dark stripes of night blue and a few twinkling stars along the horizon. The subject of the painting seems to be the twisted tree next to the cabin. One leafless branch droops to the ground and doesn't even attempt to turn back up. With the surrounding lawn trimmed and vivid, and the smell of pie no doubt wafting from the house, the singularly dead branch suggests that the whole scene might be real. The picture is the central view from the bed, as though it's her target.

I stifle my curiosity about the picture's meaning. Iris and Lenore talk to each other and the sisters talk to each other, not denying my presence, but not incorporating it either.

'Should I come back in a little while?' I ask.

Iris raises her head and then her eyebrows at her daughters. The gesture, left over from glamorous days, causes one small tumour below her ear to leak. 'No. I'm ready when you are. We're not doing goodbyes.' She nods the assembled into position.

I begin, 'As you know, we need to formalise—'

'Yes, whatever you have to do, do.'

I clamp the camera to the tray table. I ask my questions. Iris says *yes* in the right places.

When I come to the end, she gives another nod and her daughters gather around the bed. 'Climb aboard. Lightly, lightly.'

Lenore adds, 'Bring your wine.'

For the benefit of the director's cut, I turn my head as if I didn't hear. My focus is the liquid in the cup I hold, not even rippling in my steady grip.

The challenge for Iris's beloved is to hold her without aggravating the cysts. Lenore's free hand rests on some intact skin on Iris's shoulder. Toula and Denise each find clear spots to touch—her right calf, her left palm.

Iris looks around at the way they've placed themselves and says, 'There, you've already divvied me up. In no time I'll be ashes and it will be easier.' Lenore's adoring eyes stay steady and dry.

Amid the careful ballet, a bloody and golden smear appears on the sheet near Iris's elbow. She gingerly sits herself up, expanding the red spot. Toula notices and restrains the urge to dab or cover it.

Iris extends her free hand to take the cup and brings it close to her. There's no philosophical peering into the abyss of it, no tentative sip to see how the future tastes. Once it's in her hand, she holds it up, and the others, on cue, raise their glasses to drink. Iris knocks it back faster than they do, as though it's been a long night of drinking games and her turn has finally come to lose. As she swallows, Lenore's fingertips trace Iris's shoulder.

Toula laughs and cries, 'There you go!'

'There I go,' Iris says, gripping Toula's wrist.

Keeping her gaze on her mother, Denise takes the cup from her and holds it out for me to take away.

'Well, it tastes worse than they said.'

Lenore offers her the glass of wine. Iris gives me a guilty smile and turns it down. 'I'll be all right,' she says, wiping her mouth with a corner of the sheet.

Six *I love you*s fly, a relatively small tally.

'Just hold me,' Iris says. 'That's all.' Wrapped up in their touch, she keeps her focus on the painting.

The three other women maintain their contact, letting her rock slowly between them. The drug couldn't have hit her system yet, but she's starry-eyed, swaying, never leaning too far in any direction, but seeming to sense how each is positioned to catch her when she falls.

Iris reaches forward, hands towards her knees, to let out a moan that grows. The further she leans, the deeper the note. She breaks off to inhale and then resumes, louder, primal. Another breath and it goes up a decibel. Toula's mouth opens, as if she's ready to add her voice.

I step back, willing myself invisible.

Viv and I won't make a scene like this. We don't do feelings this naked. Her parting message won't be a roar. No, she'll be saying, *Isn't that interesting?* as she steps off the cliff, as the lion's teeth close around her neck. Any other response would require an acknowledgement of the facts. Viv likes to stay upbeat.

Wendell, one of Viv's middle-period boyfriends, threw me a hint that there might be an alternative interpretation of life. He was a grizzled Burmese academic who was just like dear old Dad in that he hadn't lived up to his early expectations for himself. He never published. He said it was funding, Viv said it was motivation. Regardless: as a healthy, practical adjustment to reduced status in his field, he resolved to make his mark on more impressionable students, by teaching year seven to nine history. Even more practical, he made my mother laugh. At the end—because inevitably he didn't live up to her early expectations of him either—he came back for his few things. As he carried his overstuffed duffel bag out through the garden door, I saw that he had tears in his eyes. He wished me lots of luck and said, 'She isn't always right. Let yourself fall in a hole sometimes. Let out a yell if you want. It's not against the law.' I nodded and agreed, hoping my manners would make him stick around longer. They didn't.

So we're not the keening kind. Rainy days may happen too, just not to Viv. After all, if we'd jumped into Dad's grave after him, beating our chests and lamenting our lot, we'd still be there. Viv likes to say she does what she can with the cards she's been dealt.

Toula kisses her mother on the lips. There are unapologetic full-throated groans happening all over.

Iris looks around, silently excusing herself from the psychosocial responsibilities of everyone else's grief. At this point, her focus is closer: Lenore. The painting on the sill is just shapes to her now, like art to a dog. Even the urge to stay upright seems like a relic. In response to nothing, a grin flickers across her face: a past mystery solved, an acrid burp? The drug is on its way to bringing her whatever enlightenment she might be due before her brain stops.

She catches my eye and whispers something to Lenore, who passes the message to me. 'Thank you for being here for us, but would you mind waiting outside? We'll come when we need you.'

'Of course. I—'

'Leave the camera running. We won't touch it.'

'Goodbye,' I say without any added freight, turning the handle and pulling the door slowly after me, to keep it from clicking when it shuts.

As soon as I'm gone, the women, minus Iris, get louder and begin to chant. There's a simple rhyme to their lines, even through the door—some grim children's song from a time when such things were allowed. That's why she wanted me out, so she could nod off to this lullaby without a stranger watching.

At the far end of the hallway a teenager with a buzz cut and a pinned leg is practising 360s in his wheelchair. Rehab must have sent him down here.

The muffled dirge in C22 gets louder.

Not that I'm bitter, but who will be here for me, toasting my departure? Even Nettie's aunt had a *special* friend. But there are no guarantees. I could stay lean and mean on boiled spinach every day until I'm ninety-seven, spend each night next to a completely harmless partner, resisting hourly urges to escape, warping my wanderlust through six days a week of something that pays the bills, raises ten children, each one kind and wise, and even then, death could come to me in a corridor like this one, on a stretcher, listening to the overhead vents rattling and a junior doctor promising to figure out what's causing my sudden sharp headaches. Before the doctor, my own beloved, or any of those children—painters and professors and airline pilots—could start to chant me across the river of forgetfulness or even come and massage my feet, the hallway will go dark and I'll be alone, essentially unattended, my body already losing heat. The thing is that it's all musical chairs.

Why do we play?

My death will look nothing like the pageant of tenderness behind this door. First, there's the slim chance of assembling, much less siring, such faithful handmaids for my last instant. Giulia might be willing to officiate, if anyone knows enough to call her, and if she can get the days off. Lon and Simon? They'd be too horrified. An ex or two could turn up to gloat. No, none of them will be there. They are all, like me, only passing through. There will just be another bit player with me at the end. Assuming my final breath isn't a blessed surprise—a late-night vice grip across my chest (my father's father, age sixty-four), a wrong step into crossfire during a mall rampage, or the ever-present threat of a sudden tree in my path—the people by my side whenever my last bit of air blows out, whoever it is whose eyes I'll be looking into pleadingly as they mop my brow or escort me to the gallows, it's more likely than not that that person is still, today, a stranger.

Makes me wish I had the patience to at least accumulate a few pallbearers. But that was never on the cards. Viv and I turned relocation from one city to another into a sport. *Holding still will always be hard for you*, a therapist once promised me. She had a heavy jet-black fringe more appropriate for a lead guitarist than a social worker. *Who would you say your role models are?* The question returns to me now, and the only person coming to mind is Iris. If the game is all about the very last move, Iris has it nailed. That's how I want to die, and it's on the other side of a steel door.

The chanting drops off to low voices, an outburst of tears. One morbid laugh. I check the time for the notes. They don't need me in there to tell them what's happened.

The teenager turns and speeds in my direction. Sports injury. No doubt the metal frame around his leg is a badge of honour, damage from a fierce tackle on the grass under a brilliant sun. Sure, the thing's a hassle because it ruins the season, but soon it will be good as newish. When he's older, gone to fat, and the mornings turn damp in the winter, he'll look back on that afternoon game with a bittersweet twinge.

He glances up from the work of spinning the wheels to notice my ear against the consulting room door. He grins. 'I won't ask.'

I grin back, our matched smiles making me regret the middle-aged ache I gave him. When Lenore opens the door, he rolls away.

A waft of lemongrass and the view I've been imagining—the daughters, their faces wrung open, and Iris in the middle of the bed, mouth half-open, with no expression at all.

Lenore is still breathless. She throws her arms around me and digs her chin into my chest, puts her wet cheek against my neck. 'Thank you thank you thank you thank you thank you thank you.'

'You're welcome,' I say, hoping the kid in the wheelchair is watching.

Without any warning, I cry. Not with silent professional restraint, but with gulps and tears. Lenore, weeping herself, is still louder.

If the football hero sees, he'll think I'm family. No problem. At least there are no security cameras in this hallway.

I choke, catch on my sobs, and with an uncontrolled snotty shudder, regain my breath. Lenore gives me an extra squeeze for comfort. I take it, wondering if there'll be a moment for me to ask what the picture of the tree was about.

I question the appropriateness of this assistant for this role.

Lon is stretched out on the thin slab of sun-baked grass that runs between the ramp and Willow Wood's front door, taking a half-nap. He doesn't smoke but insists on taking smoking breaks as often as if he did, since most of his peers do. Viv says it's an awfully convenient form of workplace protest. His arms are flung out, pulling his navy-blue work shirt up high enough to reveal a band of skin and a longitude of hair.

I block the sun from his face until he opens his eyes. He squints up at me. 'Make a complaint. I'm not wearing my badge.'

'Still. Hygiene.'

'I'll disinfect when I go back in. Doesn't matter anyway. No living organism survives this temperature for long. Look.' He points up the slope to a barely shaded spot near the concrete porch, where a scabby black and white cat lies belly up, paws out, in an identical position to Lon, as if they had both fallen from a plane. 'The kitchen takes pity on her, but not enough. Easy to get parched in this heat. A UTI takes hold, and you know the rest.' He makes a hissing sound at the cat. She doesn't move. He hisses louder, again with no response.

'Is she dead?' I ask.

'No flies yet.'

'That's got to be bad for business, though.'

Lon returns to his resting state and tries to shoo me away. 'Move. *You're* bad for business. I have three more minutes.' He closes his eyes.

I stand back and let the sun fall on his face.

'Tell me a story,' he says. 'A happy one. No suicide today. From the cruise boat.'

'Six Hundred People with Diarrhoea?'

'Save that for Simon. I want one from the Sex with Passengers category.'

'You know all of them by now.'

'I don't.'

He does. There were rules on the boat and they weren't often worth breaking.

'Then tell me about your boss,' he says. 'What did she do today?'

'Kathy?' It was a bland enough choice, once my lie needed expanding. Nettie's name, which is too distinct in the first place, has been attached to Measure 961 since the beginning. An army of Kathys must work at the Mercy.

'Surely she's given up something interesting by now,' Lon says.

She has. Nettie's parents were sick or sickly from their fifties onwards. Chronic, gradual decline. While her brother went off and had a life, she stayed home to do their shopping, second-guess their doctors, and so on. She blames no one, says we're too far into a new century to excuse it as Dutiful Daughter Syndrome. She just loved them more. Father died finally, but mother took way too long. Dementia. The woman started forgetting things one day, stopped recognising people six years later, and didn't lose the feed-me reflex for another eight. Afterwards, Nettie made up for lost time, working and studying, while keeping her own eyes on a better death. As soon as 961 passed, she wrote her job description. Since then, she's had her name on papers and more proposals. Her free time is devoted to extending the measure to allow patients with cognitive decline to give consent before they're incapable, so they can avoid her mother's slow death. *Dementia's my issue*, she says as if she's the First Lady.

'Nah. Kathy doesn't give me much,' I tell Lon.

'Professional. Do you give her any details?'

'No.'

'How about me? Do you give me anything?' Lon swings out a foot to trip me. I jump out of the way.

'Need-to-know only.'

'But I need to know,' he says, stroking my ankle with his foot. He stretches into the sun again.

The cat hasn't moved. This is the question that taunts a hundred night nurses in a hundred doorways: dead or just asleep? The chest isn't rising or falling. The paws are open heavenwards. The nose is as pink as a kitten's, and the fur, which doesn't even shift in the slight breeze, hides the rest of her. I tighten my vision and flex my internal muscles of death assessment to determine if the cat has achieved mortal stillness.

No; I convince myself that her body still carries a charge.

Lon looks up, shielding his eyes with his hand. 'Great news about your mother, by the way.'

'Thanks. It's great about yours too.'

'I mean it,' he says, letting his hand fall back.

'Oh, I mean it too.'

Lon tries to kick me. I catch him by one ankle and he lets me.

'You're not resisting,' I say.

'I'm waiting for a massage.'

'Here?' I rub his slender talus.

'Later.' He kicks himself free. 'I'm at work. Please.'

I drop his leg.

'Honestly,' he says, 'Viv is a wonder.'

'Did she get a straight flush?'

'Come on. She's checking out. She's doing the thing that people don't do.'

'What?'

'Checking out. She asked enough people until she got a yes. You didn't know?'

Of course. This was the long game since before the implant.

Suddenly, I'm seventeen and we're at the lobby counter of a casino resort. She maintains subtexty eye contact with the bronzed young man on the other side of the marble, discussing the hotel's occupancy rate, finding out whether he has access to the swimming pool during off hours, how strong he is at poker. She's not making headway and they both know it. She continues to flirt with him out of habit until her bill is printed out and presented. The room rate appears exactly as it was stated at check-in. Even the charges from the minibar are there. As we walk out, her summation of that particular learning moment is: *If you don't ask, you'll never know.*

I picture her working over the staff of Willow Wood, getting them to deem her fit for independent living.

Even backlit, my surprise is evident.

Lon sits up. 'Wow. You're just finding out.'

I nod.

'Trish is handling the discharge. It was embargoed information until yesterday. I thought Viv would have bragged to you by now.'

I shake my head. He brings his knees up to his chest, then rolls forward, launching himself up into a standing position, landing on his feet right in front of me. If we were any closer we would kiss. He brushes dry twigs of lawn off his shirt and pants.

His jump triggered the cat's alert system. In an instant, she flips over onto her paws, briefly taking the pose of a vigilant sphinx, then falls back, takes a lick of a forepaw, and shuts us from her eyes.

My mind is flicking through recent visits, cataloguing the various people who chose not to inform me about Viv's discharge. 'Did she make all of you promise not to tell me?'

'Let's turn this into a positive. Walking out of here on your own two feet is a rare enough event. Organising it without informing your immediate carer has to be in a special category. You must be impressed. She's earned it. She's been shuttling to and from appointments over in the rehab wing. I don't know if she's been stealing stuff or what, but she comes back with half of their equipment room. The weights and bolsters. The dexterity balls. You would have seen those when you've come.'

'Nope.'

Lon recalibrates. 'Let's stick to the boundaries of this. I'm your friend, I'm fond of your mum—excessively—and,' he pulls his badge out of his pocket and pins it to his shirt, 'I'm an employee of this facility. Let's go with the idea that what I've told you is hearsay. They mainly keep me around because English is my first language. Rumours get garbled. I can't be sure it's true that she's leaving. There: I'm out of facts.'

I cover his badge with my hand. 'When is this happening?'

'Next Tuesday. At least that's the hearsay I heard said this morning. Trish was on the phone. Happy?'

'That's one word for it. Just wondering how she'll manage. What about the stairs to her apartment?'

'Who have you been visiting? The woman's a gazelle. You should see her on the StairMaster.'

'Can she make practical decisions on her own? Has anyone tested that? Do they think she can manage her finances?' Naturally, they do. Even though I sift through her bills, even though I fill out the disability forms and keep her creditors back, and even though I managed to refinance the mortgage out to twenty years when Marais gave her less than ten. I colluded, and insisted to everyone that she was the origin of wise decisions. Now that she's high on whatever's switched over in her brain, she believes she can manage on her own.

'I'm guessing you haven't heard about the poker?' Lon says.

'I thought gambling was banned.'

'Online is a grey area. Front office probably doesn't know, but your mother told one of the cleaners she's on a two-week heat. Up sixteen thousand dollars.'

'They're giving her that kind of access?'

'No one uses the business centre. Let her be: she's a success story. Even if management did find out, they would only butt in over a downward trend, but until then—'

'Where is the duty of care?'

Lon puts his hands on my shoulders. 'Evan, where is the love? She's better than when she came in. The surgery worked.'

'Marais still hasn't seen her. He won't let this happen.'

'Sorry. They brought him in to do a review and he couldn't have been happier. The only one worried is you. Trish took him and the occ health person over to your place, where your mother gave her greatest performance.'

I shake his hands off my shoulders. 'They came to my house?'

'Her house. And Marais was proud. Even took movies of her in action. I'm guessing you didn't know about that either. I only heard about it this morning. I promise.'

'How much of Trish's phone call did you miss?'

'I'm going to close my pretty mouth now.'

'And this has been brewing for weeks, while I've been visiting her and seeing you guys?'

He laughs. 'Turns out I *can* keep a secret.'

———

Trish is in the hall near the kitchen, a file in one hand and a half-wrapped brownie in the other.

'I hear there's news about my mother.'

Her pupils dilate. I actually see this happen. She crumples the plastic wrapper. 'Yes, Evan. There is.'

'When was I going to be told?'

'It's obvious we need to speak about the plan in detail. Why don't you come into my office?'

And not have a scene in the hall? I'll pass. 'Here is fine.'

While I over-emote about the irregularity of the secret-keeping, Trish leans forward and keeps her hands clapped together around the brownie, displaying utmost respect, if not for my benefit, then for that of anyone who happens to be passing by. 'Your mother wants this chance to try. She deserves this. We'll schedule supplementary services for home to make sure she's—'

'So should I be looking for an apartment for myself and stop thinking I need to cover her mortgage or the price of a nursing home? Or am I her part-time caretaker now? Where do I fit into these plans?'

'I absolutely hear what you're saying. You want to keep her expectations, and yours, realistic. You want to know that she's safe. And you have to be mindful of your family's resources. Let me start by assuring you: so do we. Very much.' Trish is treating me like the irate son of a resident. It feels good to know where I stand. 'We are one hundred percent aware of how lucky she is to have you looking out for her future.'

I can't decide whether to take that last dig as a dig. 'Thank you.'

This change in Viv's plans—a constant I should be used to by now—seems to have transformed me from caring carer to self-involved son, worrying about petty details like time and money. Could it be PTSD from all the other surprise moves she's sprung on me? Or simple selfishness, that she's moved on from this whole business of deterioration to whatever's next, and I'm—?

Trish ducks her head and gives me a coy smile, a move that I'm sure has calmed many an annoyed family member. 'The important thing is that she's better now, right?'

'Right.'

'We're in this together for your mother,' she says. 'Dr Marais was good enough to come over here for a review. That day was probably the most awkward, because your mother brought us to her—and your—apartment, to show how she would do in her home environment. She was adamant we not tell you, and—patient's privilege . . .'

I ought to act violated, but I can picture Viv's resolve in that scene. Trish didn't stand a chance. 'Go on.'

'We were there for a short while, long enough to observe her in the kitchen and the bathroom and on the steps to the apartment. She went up and down beautifully—six times. Rejuvenated. I've seen many residents come through, but none have cut a path like her. Staff here are positive she can and should be caring for herself at home. We'll do whatever's needed to make the transition smooth. I understand that it might seem like a fantasy to you. Hearing about it when it's practically a done deal must be even stranger.' She straightens her back. 'Again, I'm sorry for not telling you earlier. I was doing my best to advocate for your mother.'

'It's not your fault. I know how she operates.'

Trish leans close to me again, with relief. 'I guessed you would get it. You're her son, after all.'

Viv's not in her room. Her bathroom is empty too.

I picture her in the activities centre training for her next event, trim in her teal leotard, standing with her legs spread and gripping an exercise ball with both hands. At her feet, an array of pilfered foam rehab pillows.

A scrawny man in grey sweatpants and a greying white t-shirt is the only one there. Flat on a mat with a baby barbell in each fist, he's staring hard at the ceiling, tightening his lips in order to swing his arms up over his body.

I find her in the business centre, hunched over an ancient computer. From the side, I can see her mouth, half open in a crooked smile at the monitor, which is tilted away from the door.

'Busted,' I say.

She turns on her most charming eye contact, as her hand floats up to rest on the screen. 'Oh, here you are. Lovely.'

'You know, if you just toggle to another window, it would be more effective than trying to cover the crime with your hand.'

'I'm sure there are ways and I'm sure you know them. I'm not here to deceive. If they want me to stop, I'll stop.'

'What happened to your games with Evie and Jesus?'

'That was practice. I'm after real money.' She catches me scanning the screen behind her. 'Don't look. The bankroll is down for the day. I had a more than adequate two pair just now, but so did redbuck63. You're an excuse to get out. Give me sixty seconds?'

'Whatever you wish.'

'Don't start,' she says. 'One minute.' With a careful swing of the mouse, she swipes her cards across the screen, clicks shut a series of windows, and signs off. A month ago, turning herself back to the desk would have taken the whole sixty seconds.

With her gaze still tracking the site's slow signout, she says, 'Tell me what you think about the plan for me to move back home. Truth.'

'What?'

'I gave the green light to tell you yesterday. According to my sources, you've been on the premises for at least half an hour. You and Lon always seem to find each other, so spare me your surprise.'

'Wait, I'm the con artist here?'

'No scene, please.'

'I did hear it from Lon. As your flatmate and carer and son even, I would have liked to have been told. And earlier.'

'Stop this. Timing is not the real issue, is it?' She swivels the chair to face me. 'You've been told. What do you think?'

'Do you care? If I tell you I've got concerns, you'll call me names.'

'Well, I'm going to do very well at home. There'll be a few overnights first, to satisfy the authorities. A community nurse will check in. An occupational therapist will keep watch. Then I'm free. No more of this rabble.'

'There'll be logistics for me to figure out, but clearly that's my problem.'

'The couch is yours as long as you want, so that's only an issue if you make it one.' Viv pushes herself up, taller than she's stood in a while, and walks out of the room with a fluid swerve to her hips. 'Frankly, I'm surprised you didn't find out earlier. This dumb little village. Assisted living? Everyone helping and watching and stopping by to catch your next dribble. My nightmare. Assisted dying is what I call it.' She stops to whisper, 'No offence to your occupation.'

Lon approaches from the other end of the hall at relatively high speed, carrying somebody's clexane injection in a kidney dish. He slows down at the sight of us.

'Thank you for your discretion,' Viv says to him.

'No probs.' They manage an awkward fist bump.

'Whiteness.' Lon puts his hand on my shoulder. 'I hated lying to you. I did.' He means it.

'I made him do it,' Viv says.

'She technically does pay my salary,' he says.

I don't add that I do too.

'If it gets too tight at home, you know you can always crash with us,' he adds.

Viv can't hold back her curiosity. 'Is Simon comfortable with that?'

'He certainly is,' Lon says.

She catches a frisson passing between her son and her nurse. 'Everyone has an angle,' she says.

Lon raises his eyebrows high, says, 'You're both welcome,' and turns the corner towards the residents' rooms.

Viv stretches, rotating her arms, just as I pictured. 'Were you going to tell me you knew about the plan or were you going to have me shock you with my news?'

'I didn't have a strategy.'

She gives me a pat on the shoulder. 'That's the way. Take it as it comes.'

———

Next patient for dispatch is Leo, ninety, with his girlfriend, Myrna, eighty-six, attending. Their interviews are full of a sense of wonder—that they lived so long, that they found each other, that we're going to let him die before things get too bad. He was a chef, famous for his dumplings, with three Chinese restaurants across the west side by the time he retired. Myrna was a photographer who got rich on a book of portraits of children from around the world. Even she ultimately decided that photographs of children were twee. 'If I had the strength today, I'd go back and take pictures of all their grandparents. That would be a different book.'

They met in one of the retirement communities that Viv looked at early on, when she was curious to see what she couldn't afford. A printed menu at the dinner table each night and an activities coordinator in a red polo shirt. Leo and Myrna were married to other people when they met, but as happens in such places, their spouses died, which meant that even before they'd hooked up, each had already made one big trip to the cemetery. In the few years since, old age has effectively blended this little Chinese man with this little white woman. The only distinguishing details are his thick white crew cut and the thin veil of chestnut-dyed hair on her head. They may have met late in life but they have nearly identical glasses, dark eyes and fleshy noses. Time puts a Groucho Marx mask on us all.

'I loved my May, but she was gone,' said Leo, taking a shallow breath after every third word. 'A few weeks later, I took Myrna to one of the dances. We caused a fuss.'

'We only wanted to dance,' said Myrna. 'We're both short. It made sense.'

Leo had his first symptom three months ago. Pancreatic, advanced. Given his age, treatment options are scarce. Only some palliative radiation and the usual drugs to keep him digesting food, but it isn't working. Barely eating. To control the pain and get him through our questions he's been wavering between sedative fog and agonising breathlessness. He said, 'It's time to stop while I can still think.'

Myrna has no qualms. 'You don't get to this age by being dewy eyed.' Then she asks, 'Can the light be turned off?'

I comply.

'Much better,' she says.

I make my way through the bulk of my script, until Leo asks if we have time for a priest.

Last rites, especially on short notice, are a big ask. The brotherhood is not fond of our work. I tell him, 'I might not be able to find a priest for you this morning,' letting the last words hang there to see which he wants more, the priest or the Nembutal. 'Do you have a priest who knows you?'

Leo shakes his head, then wipes his nose on his wrist.

I ask, 'How about a person with spiritual training? Would that do?'

'Can they come now?'

'I think so,' I say. *I think.*

'Then yes,' he says. 'Send them.'

Myrna asks, 'What do you possibly have to get off your chest now? Tell me.'

'It's nothing to do with you.'

Myrna takes this without any sign of hurt and gives me the nod.

Pastoral Care don't want much to do with us either, but I make the call. A woman answers, lets me explain the situation as best I can. The silence on the other end is not that of a servant of a panoply of gods, but of someone trying to fit in one more damn thing. 'Do you know what he expects from this meeting?' she asks.

Leo and Myrna are watching me. 'He asked for a priest. He's asking for support.'

'Suicide is considered a sin in certain circles,' the woman says.

'Yes,' I say. 'Do you think someone would be able to come by soon?'

'Give me ten.'

She shows up in five. Once again I'm banished to the hallway while my flunky recorder gets to see everything. What if the woman has been summoned to perform a last-minute wedding and I miss it? Or what if Leo killed a man for his dumpling recipe and needs to confess? I strive to remain unengaged, clear my mind by concentrating on how an elongated spine leads to good posture which leads to a balanced hand which means I won't spill the Nembutal. I lean against the corridor wall, aiming for a casual stance that won't attract the attention of passers-by.

The door opens. 'It was a non-denominational version of last rites,' the woman mutters to me as she exits, keeping her distance from me and the cup.

Myrna welcomes me back. Leo's face seems looser than before.

He remains in charge as we go through the final questions, giving deeply considered responses to each while Myrna's chin bobs along silently.

'Yes, I would like to drink the poison and die.'

But first, Leo asks if he can interrupt the script again. He has to tell us that during the war he helped a wounded soldier die. This story has come up during two earlier interviews. Who is he trying to reassure? He won't tell us how he helped, because 'it was not as easy as how it goes here'. The point seems to be directed towards me, as if to suggest that what he and I are doing is a good deed done between men on the battlefield.

Picturing Nettie's watchful gaze from elsewhere in the building, or maybe later, I nod in selfless acknowledgement.

He leans up to Myrna for a peck. They say their tender words—two concise *I love you*s—and embrace as tightly as they can manage, holding on until the muscles give up.

'I'll have it,' he says to me.

He drinks.

The shock of the act gives them pause and they hug even more desperately than before, and settle down to staring at empty space. Two people watching the tide go out. I offer to leave, but Leo says, 'Stay here. For after. For Myrna.'

Pointing with a knobby finger, she kindly asks me to go to the window. It's not banishment. She's shy about her tears. I pretend to look outside while keeping watch on their reflection.

After a minute, I hear him say, 'Myrn, you know I'm not so sure about this all of a sudden.'

In the ghosted reflection she leans over the side of the bed. 'What are you saying?'

Yes, Leo, what are you saying? We don't have a big window of time for regrets here. Speak now, or the protocols won't save you.

Leo clarifies: 'It's that I worry for you.'

Excellent news. No need to code him for a gastric lavage. One woman, having drunk and swallowed, sat quietly for about ten minutes before asking Nettie offhandedly what would be involved in saving her. Striving for calm, Nettie had to explain that the moment had passed. A minute later, the patient's barely consoling last words were, 'Never mind, I was going to die anyway.'

'What are you going to do for company?' he asks Myrna.

'I love that that only comes to you now. Hon, I've been lonely before. I'll get by. And we'll be together soon enough.'

'Promise me you won't fritter away a single afternoon,' says Leo.

'I promise not to fritter.'

He nods and raises his voice in my direction. 'As long as it is, this is still a short little life.'

Noted.

Making the most of this extra time to dispense wisdom, he tells Myrna, 'Pay the bills on the same day they come in. Don't muck around waiting for the due date. You get confused and then there are late charges.'

'I promise,' she says. I catch her checking the clock on the wall.

'And don't stay in your room. Get fresh air. Change your point of view. A lot.'

'I will.'

Finally, he pats her arm. No more words.

Leo goes quiet but the slow breathing takes so long that I actually do end up looking out the window. I can make out a trio of psych patients sharing a forbidden cigarette in the yard. When they finish, one of them lovingly stubs it out on his calf, then picks at the burn.

I check back on Leo. Myrna's peering closely at his frozen face and pressing her fingers against her cheeks. She turns her ear to his mouth to listen for breath. I let her run through her emotions, composing herself for a full minute before she calls for me. 'Excuse me, um—what's your name again?'

Invisible enough for you, Nettie? 'It's Evan.'

'Evan. Would you please check on . . . ?' She nods in the direction of what is no longer him and is now his body.

I go through the steps, taking his non-existent pulse, holding the bell of the stethoscope to his silent chest.

'One minute he was comfortable and then he was gone,' says Myrna. 'What happens now? Do I call the funeral director? What do I tell people?'

'There's no rush. Would you like to have some time alone with Leo?'

'I've said what I had to say.'

'Then I'll call the doctor.'

She jolts, as if I'd suggested the crash cart.

'To certify Leo's death,' I add.

'Yes. Please.'

While I alert the appropriate people, Myrna circles the bed. 'So small now,' she says. I don't know if she's referring to him or to herself or to what's left of her life.

'Can I get you anything?'

'No. I'm still absorbing it. This is the way death ought to be. Not the torture my husband went through. He had a heart attack. Next thing we're in the hospital. They couldn't save him, but they worked on him for half an hour. Beating on his chest, trying to drag him back to this world. Revived him twice. I knew he was dying, that he wanted them to stop. They finally listened to me. He should have been allowed to go peacefully, but the reflex of the world is greed, always trying to get some more. This, what you did today, convinces me. Leo got to say, *Enough*. And that means everything.' The people who make Nembutal would be thrilled by such an endorsement of their product.

I wash the body while she watches, extolling the peacefulness of his death the entire time. 'So simple and so beautiful. So simple.' Myrna could do an ad even, tell Leo's story to the camera. By the end everyone would want a bottle.

Nah, she's too old. They'd want someone younger. And cuter. In an MRI machine, looking weary. *Have you had another disappointing scan? If you're facing a short prognosis, or if you've been struggling with intractable pain or paralysis, or if you've just run out of medical trials, then maybe it's time to think about Nembutal. For decades, Nembutal has proven to be an easy-to-use and fast-acting drug for people with terminal conditions. You take control. You decide.* We finish on the patient in a deck chair, in the middle of a bountiful, flowery meadow, surrounded by his photogenic family. We lie a little and show him eating a piece of celebratory cake. *A bit of drowsiness and soon you're resting in absolute peace. Forever. Your family can be confident that you're no longer suffering.* With a smile, the patient gives his family The Look. They look back, and we know it's time. Then cut, leaving something tantalising to think about. *Use only as directed. Now in cherry and chocolate.*

Then it hits me: Nembutal is off patent. No one would make enough of a profit on it to bother shooting a commercial.

———

Once Leo is washed and dried, Myrna lets me cover his face with the sheet.

'My niece offered to come today, to stay outside, in case I needed her,' she says. 'I said thank you, no. We're not so close. I was smart to keep her away, because it wouldn't have been right if I'd had on my mind that she was waiting in the hall. It would have been distracting. Death is death. You can't call it a great tragedy at this age.' Her fingers brush Leo's hand, which is sticking out from the sheet. She's more intrigued than heartbroken. 'He's still warm.' She pulls her hand away. 'Well. Give me a few weeks, I'll put my affairs in order and I'm going to want the exact same thing.' She rests her hand on Leo's sunken chest and stage whispers to him, 'I'll be joining you soon.'

Before I can even think of a tactful response, Myrna makes her meaning clearer. 'Where can I get that stuff for myself? I can do it at home. You don't have to have me here.' She takes my hand tightly in hers and yanks me down to her level. 'I'm ready today, if you want to know the truth.'

The camera would have caught that for sure. On replay it would only be conceivable that I didn't hear her if I was in the cafeteria.

Please stop. Why is she asking me about this? Doesn't the activities centre at her place have wi-fi? Don't they have a noticeboard for dealers? I come up with the most anodyne response: 'I can't advise you on this.'

Just then, the doctor knocks and enters.

Myrna accepts his condolences. 'It was beautiful,' she tells him. 'So simple.'

'I'm glad to hear that,' he says, as if she has reported that her headache has cleared up. He goes to work on the death certificate.

Myrna nudges me towards the doctor, as if now would be the time to get her the prescription she wants. I put out my hand to quell her enthusiasm. She's already said too much.

He finishes and leaves. She nods at me. 'I understand. It has to go through official channels.'

'This is a big day for you, for the two of you, but Leo was sick and going to get sicker. You're a healthy person. What you're talking about is a very different thing.'

'It's not that different.'

I take her hand as I revert to script. 'I can't imagine what a difficult moment this must be for you.'

She puts her face close to mine. 'Are you going to help me or not?'

Loud and clear, I say, 'I hear what you're asking for, which can't be easy. I want you to hold this idea softly today.'

She looks puzzled for a moment. 'Oh, I understand. You think the notion just hatched this morning. It's not so. It's been with me for years. This isn't anything shocking for an old person. I'm only asking for a name.'

Leo farts low and long. It's practically a full sentence of farts.

Myrna straightens and smirks. 'A gentleman till the end.'

The orderlies arrive to exchange paperwork for a body. Soon Leo is rolling off to the morgue. Myrna doesn't even watch him depart, she's so focused on me. 'Are you going to help?'

I'm wishing the niece were here. 'If it's all right with you, I'd like to make another call, to someone who can meet us here, someone you can talk with a bit more.'

'Anybody who can help will be welcome.'

I let her misinterpret my meaning. She thinks I'm hooking her up, when I'm actually turning her over to the authorities, by which I mean a social worker.

'I'm as ready as Leo was. There's no doubt in my mind.'

Alejo will talk her out of it. He has a way with geriatric depressives. Hopefully she won't take too long to comprehend that he's not the man for the job either. If she doesn't stop discussing suicide with hospital staff she's going to be getting electroshock, not Nembutal.

The moment he enters, she sees the tortoise-shell glasses and the plaid vest and she knows she's been had. As she stands there in the empty centre of the room where Leo used to be, her little bird chest goes up and down and her hands squeeze into fists in front of her. She sends an accusatory glare my way, but recovers enough to tell him, 'Thank you for coming on such short notice.'

'Thank you for asking for me,' Alejo says. 'Shall we go back to my office?'

'Yes,' she says.

She is still thanking me when Alejo takes her arm and leads her out to the hallway. Her fists have gone slack.

I write my reflection before I even leave the consulting room, expressing my pleasure with my dispatch of Leo, satisfaction with Myrna's satisfaction at Leo's death, and a gratitude to protocol for knowing what to do when Myrna asked for Nembutal. I don't mention the guilt.

COMFORT MEASURES

THE OCCUPATIONAL THERAPIST, Joan, has my mother on the living room floor, gliding back and forth on a foam roller. As of one week ago, this is normal. Viv is in her yellow fleece tracksuit, a purchase from her recent winnings. Her calves and feet are up on the couch while she shimmies effortlessly. A folder from Willow Wood marked *After Care* is open at Joan's side. Joan checks off boxes as my mother hits her targets.

Viv sees me in the hallway and pivots around on the blue tube. 'Loose and controlled,' she brags. To emphasise her progress, she pushes the roller away and starts in on random Pilates poses.

To make up for the staff's collective sin of not communicating about Viv's discharge, Joan has clearly been directed to liaise excessively with the son. She gives me a detailed account of the past three hours—showering, dressing, house cleaning (more than has been seen around here in recent months) and meal prep (ditto). For an early lunch, they made crumbed flounder with potatoes and a salad. After washing up, Viv marched up to the fourth floor of the building and down to the lobby, pacing herself and never wobbling.

'Happy?' Joan asks me.

'Happy?' I ask Viv, who gives a fake smile. 'I'm happy,' I tell Joan, who pulls a phone from her pocket and holds it out to my mother for her thumbprint of approval.

'Then I've earned my keep.'

My mother gets up on her knees to press her thumb against the screen. 'There.'

'Till Thursday?' Joan says.

Viv winks. 'No promises.'

The woman is entranced.

As soon as she's gone, Viv turns to me. 'Well, that's the last parole visit for a few days. Time to make a run for it. Are you staying with the boys tonight?'

'Undecided.'

'Whatever works for you works for me. I only need you for the next hour. I'll figure out the rest. We're going to the bank, for some business that still requires my keeper's signature. Any objections?'

None. Now that she's left Willow Wood, there's more money to go around. She has reasserted control of her own, relieving me not only of the duty of making sure the bills are paid but forbidding me from contributing any further. The whole thing assumes the pension and her winnings will be enough, that she won't be dependent again, that she will always be a good judge of what she needs. The only anchor she has is Willow Wood, which is holding onto her original $145K deposit for three months as a placeholder. That was Trish's idea, just in case.

Viv grabs bright white sneakers from the hall closet and, raising one knee at a time like a flamingo, pulls on and laces up each sneaker—without sitting down or falling over. It is impressive.

She slips her backpack onto her shoulders. 'I have a proposal for you: when we're outside, would you walk behind me a little bit, about half a block behind? You can observe. What do you think of that?'

'All right.'

'On top of what I did this morning, the walk from here to the bank and then the library should give me nearly a mile of further exercise, and in the blazing sun.'

'If you're up to it.'

'If *you're* up to it. If I continue to pass muster, what do you think you'll do?'

'Go to Lon and Simon's for dinner.'

'I mean with your life. You can only couch surf, or whatever it is you're doing with them, for so long.'

'Your concern has been recorded. Let's get to the bank.' I steer her to the door.

'Don't handle me. And don't hang onto me. I'm better on my own. It's time for you to go forth and—' She flicks both hands up and spreads her fingers wide to indicate exactly where she'd like me to go.

———

Following Viv's fall, the building taped the stairs with no-skid yellow strips. She takes each one with care and ease.

'Will you be able to manage these when you're in a hurry?'

She looks back up at me. 'Why on earth will I be hurrying?'

To avoid a possibly deserved lecture on mindfulness, I wave her on, staying at the top of the stairs to give her the lead.

Out on the street, I see a small slight stranger in a yellow tracksuit already half a block away. Each foot lands on the pavement with purpose. Her elbows smoothly power each step forward. She dodges through schoolchildren and turns the corner without even looking back to see if I'm behind her.

First a camping store window and then an accordion player catch her attention. The musician has sleeve tattoos on both arms. He's serious, playing 'Habanera' fast, as if for a carousel. He's too young and too ratty for the spangled instrument, which is why everyone else looks the other way as they pass him—which is what undoubtedly draws her in. She reaches into her pack for her purse.

I let myself get close enough to note her offering. Ten dollars. The old Viv would have given between one and five. Her online winnings have been steady though—or so she says. At least she didn't take out her chequebook.

But she is cautious in other domains. Where she used to sprint across Barkley Avenue if the light was turning red, she dutifully canters in place while the light cycles back to green. A younger woman on the opposite side, holding a yoga mat under her arm, makes the dash across, racing an oncoming bus and stumbling just as she reaches the kerb in front of Viv. My mother puts out a hand to keep her from falling into the street. The woman accepts the assistance, flashes earnest thanks, steps onto the kerb and keeps moving. The light turns green and Viv sets off, her chin high as she crosses to the other corner and pushes open the bank's giant brass doors.

I find her in the waiting area, standing with her hands on the back of an empty chair. She's holding her ticket number and watching the screen.

'Am I allowed to wait with you?' I ask.

'If you wish.'

'I've wanted to tell you about a patient of mine. Your "better on my own" reminded me.'

'Go ahead.'

'A wealthy man, about your age, he's onto his third wife. He gets diagnosed, something degenerative. Things get rough and he needs real nursing, intimate nursing. Guess what he does?'

'Starts going to hookers?'

'I didn't think of that.'

'Never rule it out,' she says. 'A man with money. He might not tell you everything. Or are hookers on one of your forms somewhere?'

'No and no. What he did tell me is that he divorced her. At the time when you think you'd want the most backup.'

She leans against the empty chair. 'He let her go. How unmanly.'

'Remember when you were diagnosed, thanking your stars you didn't have a husband to console or pretend to be healthy for?'

She looks momentarily surprised to be reminded of what she'd said, as if wondering if it's true. 'Interesting.'

'What's your read on my patient?'

'Well. He's come to you, hasn't he?'

'Yes.'

'My read doesn't matter. That's as eloquent as it gets. Didn't need the wife. Didn't need to go on being sick. I get it. Whether you're sick or not, he doesn't want to count on people anymore. Wives and nurses only get you so far. There's your moral.' Her fingers tap the rim of the chair for a minute. It's a good moral. 'I wonder what stories you tell about me.'

'None.'

'Lies. Stand over there.' She points to a row of tellers' windows that's been repurposed into a self-serve coffee station. 'I'll let you know when you're needed.' She holds up her ticket. 'Six more before me.'

I retreat to watch her monitor the progress of each teller with the intensity of a meerkat, so that she is walking towards the available teller before her number is even called. A moment later, I am beckoned.

The teller, a man in his twenties wearing cufflinks seriously, explains the situation. Viv wants our joint account to be closed. With sufficient ID and both of our signatures, this man will transfer the remaining funds, and her recent winnings, into a new account that will be entirely under her control. 'Are you in agreement with that?' he asks me.

Viv's eyes stay focused on the three forms awaiting my signature.

I say to Viv, 'If this is what you want, I am. But it's not my idea of best practice.'

'What does that mean?'

'It means safety first.'

'Explain the risk please.'

'For most of the past year, I've been scrambling to manage your finances. It was necessary and I've done it.' I wait for a thank you, but it doesn't come. 'Getting rid of the joint account means that, *should my assistance be required again*, there will be the same paperwork and hassle in getting this set up. Given what we've been through, best practice would be to keep this account open. That would look sensible to the average person. It would be tidier.'

'Would it?' she says. 'Oh well.' She nods at the pen chained to the counter.

As soon as I sign she directs me back to the coffee station while she withdraws a wad of cash. She counts it twice before squirrelling it into the innermost pocket of her backpack. She gives me brief side-eye as soon as she's zipped up to let me know that I can resume tailing her.

A block further, when she reaches a bakery window, she tilts her head for me to catch up.

A field of tarts spreads before her on the other side of the glass, even rows of chocolate, lemon and raspberry. She points out a lattice-top tart on an upper shelf. 'Look at that Linzer.'

'It's nice. Are you going to buy it?'

'No. I want you to stay with the Linzer a minute. With the crust all geometric and evenly browned to perfection, do you think, from looking at it, that it tastes good? Truth.'

'No idea. It looks like it should. Photogenic. Could have been in the window for years.'

'Best practice, as you might say.'

'Might I?'

'*Tidy*. How it looks and how it tastes are different matters, aren't they?'

'I get it. I trust you.'

'You don't. You watch my hand when I reach for a cup of water. The very nerve that you would trail me like this, after everyone else has given me the freedom to fly—what is that?'

'You suggested it.'

'It was a test and you failed. Just stop. I was sick and you got caught up in the drama of things. You scampered back, upended your life for me. I never asked for it. I apologise now for even letting you come.'

'*Letting* me?'

'Don't be a martyr. I want you to be free too. I'll call the mortgage people and get you your money back.' She goes on, 'You don't need to hang around. It's your nature to get stuck on the sadness. Your father was like this, loved the theatre of things. You can do better.'

'Have I been in your way? These are things that a son might do and a mother might be grateful for. You don't get to pathologise it.'

A blond girl of about four, with pigtails and a glittery tiara, comes running up to the bakery and pushes in front of us. We both shut up. A woman who could only be her mother is close behind. The child points at the glass, squeaking about a meringue with mouse ears and nose and whiskers drawn on in chocolate. The mother stands at the door to the bakery. 'You want it? You got it,' she tells the girl, and they go inside.

Viv turns to me. 'You want it? You got it. Here it is with no psychology. I appreciated those things you did for me, but you are not a captive here. I'd like to see you move on. Are we done?'

She turns and walks away, brisker than before.

———

I walk back. Towards home? That concept isn't feeling stable at the moment. (Viv on that first relocation after Dad died, assuring me that we would be okay: *Home is the shell on your back.*)

I wish I had a transcript of her initial call from the Mercy, the one that brought me scampering to her side. Why didn't I record that? It might help to diagnose me.

Firstly, is it the theatre of dying that draws me to work each day? No. I am there because of my conviction. And a need for approval, Nettie might add. But it's a job and these are people in distress. I don't want to cure or coax them. Still, it's human to want to know if I'm being helpful.

Am I closer to developing my inner Nettie's aunt? No. But I kept my deeper feelings out of the room when Iris was dying. I betrayed Myrna, as per guidelines. Even with Viv—I did sign the bank forms for her. I must be getting closer to that Zen state of nursing. It's practice that I'm after, not attainment.

Is that what Viv was talking about, my need to hover? Maybe if I found a more spiritual role (death doula!), leading Sanford through the bardo, plucking my lyre while he lays there wheezing and Cheyne-Stoking for days. Would that satisfy my errant desire to help?

Wrong. It would be too slow, too soft. Viv wouldn't respect me in the morning.

She can have her couch and the payments on it. And her space.

Admittedly, after The Fall I did go full caretaker on her. For the drama? Some would say I acted out of filial duty. That's too old school for her, not what I was bred for. I came back to Viv because I wanted to. Happy to do it, happy to resist planning my life, like Mama taught. It's not my problem if she treats me like a stranger.

Find your sustenance anywhere, everywhere. Don't get complacent. She learned this the hard way, she enjoys telling me, reciting all the bargains she made with herself in the early days of their marriage: *I was going to leave as soon as I met someone with more zest for life*; but after I came along, her deal was that she'd take off when I turned eighteen, or when I was twelve, or just as soon as she could get a job that paid. *By the time I was formulating life in parcels like that, I already knew the next step.* (Ditch, so to speak, Dad.)

Once she's restated the litany of rum deals she never had the strength to follow through on, her voice drops to a whisper to polish the next pearl, as if it has just come to her for the first time and if she reveals it too loudly a dozen goons in black Kevlar will break down the front door to arrest her for saying the unsayable. *Darling, they want us to get attached to places, to other people, to things, because they want us to stay exactly where we are. We're more useful to the state when we're holding still.* The solution? She stitched it onto a sampler that she hung above desk after desk after desk at each of her jobs as if to underline its Dr Seussian point: *Go where you go, do what you do. No one is waiting to live your life but you.*

What did I make of this? Nursing. For the practical, it represents a steady income. For congenital short-termers, it represents an endless source of possibility. One gig after another, each one a new promise. No matter the initial lure of a new job, once any probationary period ends, management can be relied on—much like other staff and the occasional patient—to show their true ugliness. If disgust doesn't move you along, boredom will, or, at minimum, a friend of a friend will give you a lead on the next situation to try somewhere else.

No complaints from me. Each move has allowed me to witness the full shit-covered mess, from maternity to palliative, each job preparing me for my current one. The takeaway—from watching not just a thousand patients, but flatmates, and employers and shags and, of course, Viv—is that we are not here to linger.

I find myself up the street from Viv's apartment. The crowds are gone, but there's free parking here, so the cars are packed in tight. In front of me: a row of low grey buildings from another time, with planters full of flowers on their window ledges and balconies. I don't want to go home. There, the first sign of an impending move. But what if we *are* here to linger, to plant marigolds? I keep walking towards the apartment.

Might it have been more useful to all parties if Viv had lingered longer with the person she'd promised to love and protect?

Not how she framed it.

And after Claude, the long flow of broken bonds, mystified acquaintances, the abandoned apartments and irritated employers and the many Wendells were all reduced to justifiable points of inflection, necessary contractions in the long bloody labour that is life. A grudge would burst into bloom one afternoon: th a removal van would be at the door. Or, I'd come hom to find a cab packed and ready to take us to the static

A constant adventure.

When we landed at the commune, I was given the option of deciding on a new name for myself. I chose Ever, because it sounded neat. Giulia, sensitive to appearances outside of the commune, was the one who advised me to opt for the adverbial form. And I knew that Viv (who was keeping her name as it was) liked the Everly Brothers, so it was designed to please on all fronts. It wasn't until years later that the rock star therapist noted that *ever* means *constantly*, not a concept that was large in my life then. Big deal. I made it to five sessions with her before ending it. Besides, the name was only in full use for the nine months till we left. There was an issue with kitchen duties.

At least it gave me Giulia. Even at age fifteen, she read Viv quickly. The first week at the commune, Viv and I shared a bed, a king-sized futon off the pantry. Our room had been painted a glossy red for some reason. Bed and pillows and our bags took up the whole floor, which was painted black. It was our cramped territory. At night I wrapped myself in my sleeping bag on the far side of the futon, but I'd wake up snuggled close, my head next to hers, as though we were sharing brainwaves. When she opened her eyes and found me there, she'd squirm to a distant corner. At one of the nightly meetings, she said she hoped to give her son healthy boundaries; perhaps there was another spot for me? It was a nice line and it worked. That night, I moved upstairs to share that bunk bed with Giulia. She welcomed me with, 'You can have the top bunk for now. I don't think you two will be here for long.'

I've reached Viv's building, but I don't want to go inside.

I look at my phone for an alternative.

Giulia is happy to explain it all. 'You don't love the drama, you love her. That's always been your problem. You'd let all other dramas drown in the sea before giving up on her, even if she was swimming away from you.'

'Harsh.'

'Isn't that why you called me?'

'I was looking for consoling.'

'Strange choice then. Sorry. Your other problem is that you don't call me enough.'

'That doesn't mean I don't care about you. What happened with the Baby Lover?'

'We're not calling him the Baby Lover anymore.'

'Did he stop wanting three kids?'

'No. Dave's next to me. Driving. We're about to buy an old dresser for your room.'

'Then he just heard you say Baby Lover.'

'He's heard me say a lot of things by now.'

'Wow.'

'Don't panic. He hasn't moved in. He's got a really good deal on his place. Your room's still free if you're freaking out there.'

'Thanks.'

'The point is, if you called more, you'd know about Dave. He's super deluxe.'

'It's a two-way phone,' I say. 'You can call me.'

'If I did that, it would get too easy for you. You'd leave it to me. If you want to maintain access to my services, you have to work.'

'That's ridiculous.'

'You're ridiculous.' This stalemate makes me homesick for her. She adds, 'Re: consoling you about your mother. She's independent again. That must be hard for you. Whatever will you do? Move away?'

'Harsh II, the sequel.'

'Okay, Everly, we're at the house, and a dresser—that does not look a bit like its internet pictures—is being dragged out to the street by a muscle giant who neither the Baby Lover nor I will want to get into an argument with. I've got to go. Call me again soon. This was fun.'

I head back to Barkley Avenue, with plans.

I vow to call Giulia more.

I vow to call Lon and Simon more.

I vow to accept Viv's offer of the money and get a place of my own. Grow basil and parsley. Get a couch.

I vow all sorts of things and then go into Celco's and spend too much on a shirt for Sanford's death. It's a narcotic shade of navy blue, the kind of thing I would never buy, with a collar that's so minor it wouldn't support a tie. This could be the uniform for all my assists. Though I wouldn't want it to become so distinctive that other staff see me wearing it in the cafeteria and know what I've been up to. I could try wearing it to every other gig. Whatever. Sanford's worth it. No need to log an entire reflection about it.

———

Lon and Simon are flattered when I call them while the sun is still shining. Apparently this is a first.

The evening is expectedly domestic. We eat some tomato-surprise thing with breadcrumbs and anchovies that Simon found in a magazine. After dinner, Lon sits on their bed, working through a continence training module on his laptop. Simon is constructing a model of a bank's private entryway for prestige clients. I sit on the couch with a beer, reading an article from the same magazine that provided dinner about a baby boom among refugees, until Simon asks for my help with the model.

As he fiddles with the most propitious foyer design, I stabilise a little sheet of wood between my forefinger and thumb, thinking, *Funny you've come up with these two steps to this sunken reception area, because this guy I'm helping to die would so appreciate a ramp.*

'You all right?' Simon asks.

'Fine. This isn't too heavy.'

'Why did you call today? To come over and read?'

'No, I'm happy to help with this,' I say.

'Not what I'm talking about. It feels good, having you here with no purpose. That's all. You can read, or hold up my retaining walls, whatever makes you comfortable. Plus, you're someone else for Lon to yap at.'

Lon says from the bedroom, 'I can hear you.'

Simon goes on, 'We're glad you called. That's all.' He bends forward and gallantly kisses my knuckles. Then he calls to Lon, 'What was it you thought Evan was having?'

Lon calls back, 'Panic?'

'You gave it a name.'

'A trilemma,' Lon says.

Simon smiles at me, holding eye contact until I blush.

Lon calls in, 'Has he run out of the room yet?'

'Still here,' I say.

Simon asks, 'Would you want to come away with us this weekend? We were thinking of a mystery drive, two hours. We'll stay wherever we get to. You can choose the direction and we'll go.'

This may be the kindest offer I've had in years. I don't even know what direction I would choose. 'Sure.'

'I'm not camping,' calls Lon. 'A motel, at minimum.'

'Wherever we want to go, we'll go,' Simon tells me. 'Friday?'

'Friday.'

Without any more long looks or further discussion of plans, the evening winds down. I participate in their mid-week sex (thirty minutes or less; no anal). My performance is appropriate for the occasion, not extraordinary and not disappointing, and thus a relief. Leo and Myrna flicker through my mind only briefly. After we've mopped up, my hosts easily drop off to sleep.

Not me. I feel the need to go home, but Viv is there, sleeping soundly. Untouchable again, without a single need—Giulia's right—because she's well.

I could go to a hotel.

I could get the money and look for an apartment in the morning.

Better yet, leave town. Go back to Giulia and the psych ward and the chicken-scented apartment. My room is waiting.

No. My companions snoring innocently beside me will expect to see me in the morning. And Sanford will be counting on me tomorrow night. On Friday, a road trip.

Wrong. False thinking. Lon and Simon are merely providing a surface closeness. What do they know of me? I could spend my days working as a circus clown for all they know. And what do I know about them? Where are we headed, with such little data? Towards a directionless weekend, that's where.

And the day after tomorrow, Sanford—whatever he thinks of the shirt—won't be counting on me for anything.

I could go anywhere.

I'm already gone.

This much I do know: Lon hoards temazepam in the bathroom. I slide out of bed and take two.

In the morning they have to wake me. I am forgiven for raiding the stash, but they enjoy prodding me out of bed, pushing me into the shower, making me shave, getting me dressed, giving me cereal. I fight it all the way, but they prevail.

The nagging even feels good.

———

Our office received a request for a call to the penthouse.

In case there are any interdepartmental surprises, I open Sanford's file on the screen. Nettie slows her fingers over the keyboard as I make the call.

There's nothing to fear. Carmel, normally an old-school matron in complete control, is simply nervous about tonight. 'He's made his farewells to his associates. They don't stay long. They keep coming in and out. The friends, I'd say he's keeping them in the dark, telling them he's fading fast—but, going by his signs, he really has months left. Is that a problem?'

'If the lawyers are content, we're content. The friends will think he had a premonition. Or they may understand.'

'I suppose,' Carmel says. 'I brought him coffee just now. He said he didn't have anyone left to say goodbye to. Not depressed, but not—I don't know, not complete. Is that usual? Is that just my concern?'

'I couldn't say.'

'You may want to show your face up here this afternoon, ahead of tonight. For extra support.'

'Will do.'

Before I go up, Nettie beckons me to her desk so she can straighten my collar. 'Sexy shirt.'

———

Sanford has been wheeled over to the window. His head is angled down towards an old book in his lap, green and worn, the yellowed pages propped open by a small pink polka-dotted beanbag. His hands have fallen to rest palm up on his knees. Sunlight is reflecting through a droplet perched on the end of his nose, unsure if it's ready to let go.

'Excuse me, Sanford?'

His upper body pivots in my direction, his head tilts down further, and the droplet makes the leap to his top lip.

'Evan. Is there a problem?'

'No problem.' I venture into the room. 'Here to say hello.'

'Hello?' His head relaxes back down towards his lap.

'Yes. How are you feeling?'

'Come sit.' He swallows a few times. 'This was in the lounge.' He extends his fist towards the book in his lap, *Leaves of Grass*. 'Poetry. Never before. And never again. Only took it because I can stare at it and stare at it without needing to turn the page.' He drags his hand to the middle of the page. 'I found this though. This is what I want. The third and fourth lines there. I'm reading them over and over to make it stick. My new mantra. Have a listen: "Clear and sweet is my soul, clear and sweet is all that is not my soul."' His eyes turn towards the window and he repeats the lines. He looks at me. 'How about that?'

'How about it?'

'Absolution. Absolution's the wrong word. A clear sweet world that's everywhere at once. When I was growing up they used to call it God, but no more. I'm not sure if absolution is even right. The second year into my second company, we scored this giant Chinese contract. It meant that from then on I could tell everyone else to fuck off. A powerful moment in a man's life. You haven't had it yet, I can tell, but you will. Magnificent feeling. The world then was as clear and sweet as anything. Not God, just *Fuck off*.' He laughs at himself as his eyes go misty. Another bit of nose dew is gathering.

'Is that how you're feeling?'

'Yes,' he says with a bit more brightness in his eyes.

He stares at his fingers as he clenches and unclenches them on the edge of the book. 'Did Carmel talk to you about the deck? There's a gazebo on the roof with a good view of the city. That's where we'll do this thing tonight.'

'Will I need to check—'

'I'm always ahead of you but don't worry, you'll pick up speed one day. After nine, the place is shut up, lights off. Nobody cares if we use it. Carmel said there may be issues, afterwards, with bringing me down from there. My body, it seems. There's no full-size patient elevator if you need to bring me down on a cart. Something like that.' He looks around at the armrests of his chair. 'I can stay in this.'

'That shouldn't be a problem.'

'If it is, it's not mine.'

'Definitely not,' I say. It wins me one lopsided smile. 'Is there any special reason you want to be outside tonight?'

'It's not inside.' He leans back to look at me, still sizing me up for the job. He drops his head back down towards the book.

'Is there anything else?' I ask.

'There is nothing else. But thanks.'

I leave like a dutiful employee without waiting for a goodbye, which I feel, even though he hasn't said anything about my shirt, gets me another smile.

———

Due to the late date with Sanford, today stretches out across a split shift, with four unpaid hours ahead until I'm back at the hospital. The choice is between Viv's place, where she will likely be playing

Texas hold'em on her computer, or the boys', where I know Lon will be enjoying an afternoon off.

I consider a documentary at the arthouse theatre near the hospital for about a minute. Then I line up a quickie with a young couple (okay, I have a predilection for the comfort of strangers, two at a time). They're history grad students who have been doing something tantric all week and want a witness present for their big finish. More importantly, they're within walking distance. We send the requisite photos and stats back and forth until they give over their address.

Half an hour later I'm there. Doorman building. The apartment is air-conditioned, and apparently funded by someone who's more solvent than a pair of minimally employed, bearded students who have been edging towards orgasm since last Thursday. I keep my clothes on, show enthusiasm at the right moments, and wonder to myself if there'll be time for a quick bite before going back to work—baked Ziti at the Italian place?—all while they're fervently rubbing their way on any soft surface to a hands-free finish. They get closer and closer and closer, declaring their undying passionate love for each other and, as an awkwardly convivial afterthought, to me. The whole show is over quickly. I leave feeling unsurprisingly unsatisfied. It just wasn't intimate somehow.

There's still time to kill, so to speak. I go to my soon-to-be former home and respectfully ring Viv's bell. Even allowing time for her old shuffle, there's no response. I let myself in.

A balled-up sandwich wrapper rests on the kitchen counter. Further investigation leads to a plate in the sink with a mayonnaise smear of chicken salad on it that has already formed a skin.

The light in the bathroom is on. The only other evidence of her recent presence is a damp waft of rose soap coming from the shower.

Outside the bathroom is a closet, one side of which I've been permitted to colonise. I slide the mirrored door to examine her side. The upper shelves, usually packed in tight, are in loose disarray, evidence of a hectic search. Her canvas weekender bag is gone. More noticeable is the new position of her little treasure chest, an old jewellery box, complete with gold-painted detail and a fake-ruby clasp. It is neither fireproof nor flood-proof but Viv has stored her valuables in here for as long as I can remember. During the move to and then from Willow Wood, it occupied the left corner of the top shelf, beside shoeboxes. Now it's been brought down to the middle shelf and left in a basket of panties. I wiggle the lid. It's still locked.

Back in the kitchen, an inspection of the garbage shows she still doesn't like pickles.

No note. Maybe she's only gone out for a little while. I check the bathroom. No toothbrush or toothpaste. Another circuit around the apartment confirms it. She's gone.

The assembled facts: she had a shower and a chicken sandwich and packed up, I presume, whatever worldlies she needed from the chest.

And really, no note. This is a sensitive one. We always leave notes. When I was fourteen, Viv was trying our luck in the back end of a more affluent suburb. Better school, for her and for me. At least that was the idea. The bad kids planned an end-of-term bender. A watermelon filled with vodka and a keg were at the top of the schedule. Caught up in their own celebratory spirit, they invited a wispy nerd like me. I wasn't even fake friendly with any of them, and the feeling was mutual, but I accepted. High school.

The event was to take place deep in the park, behind the main gate to the reservoir. The festivities wouldn't kick off until 11 pm, after security had cleared the place. This was well past any plausible time for an outing, but Viv had given me the front room of the house we were in that year, so sneaking out was easy. With the exuberance of flight, I biked as fast as I could from our street along the road to the park. An assortment of teenagers who were destined never to leave town came into view.

Tonight, I had resolved, I would change my fortunes. Before I'd finished my first beer, I was drunk on my own lies. Anyone who would listen heard about my father's tragically spectacular death while climbing a glacier, the houseboat he had left us, how Viv and I had sailed the world for years, docking where we liked, lifting anchor when we were bored. I was too old for lies this majestic, but no one stopped me. No one even bothered to ask how our houseboat had come to port in this landlocked town. They weren't listening. Still, Nadia, the girl most likely to let me touch her breasts—I was still confused enough to think this was what I wanted—handed me a second beer.

As I popped the top, I heard Viv from a distance. 'Everly. Thank goodness.'

There is no way to pretend you don't know your own mother, especially as she stomps through a crowd of locals you don't particularly like, especially when you are kind of glad she's there. With her recently hennaed ponytail scrunchied high on her head, hers was the only kind face I could see.

'Hey, Vivian,' said a guy with a moustache, who was currently serving his sixth year of high school.

'Hello, Gunther,' she said. 'Makes sense you'd be here.'

The audience half hid beers and whatever they were smoking.

'Just celebrating with friends,' I said, even as these friends stepped aside to clear her path.

'I wouldn't count on that.'

I started to introduce her. 'Viv, this is—'

'Not tonight.'

'It's cool,' I said. 'I'll be home in a while.'

No one bought it, least of all her. 'Don't make this a big deal. Come, now. And not with that.' She pointed my beer in the direction of the garbage. I threw it out, mouthing 'sorry' at Nadia, who looked amused.

I wedged my bike across the back seat of the humiliatingly old brown Volkswagen and we bounced away. The crowd closed up behind us as we left, as if I was never there. Still, from then on every one of them remembered to call me Everly.

On the ride home, Viv told me that, in the time it took me to drink one beer, she frantically checked the cinema, the schoolyard, and the railway line behind the house, before following two cars down towards the reservoir.

'I was only hanging out.'

'Hanging out.' She patted my shoulder. 'Aspiring to the greatness of those friends of yours.'

I argued their case. 'You only see them in one light, because of their grades.'

'Yes. I don't have access to their finer points. Such as?'

'They invited me.'

'That was friendly. Next time, if there has to be a next time, we leave notes in this family, okay?'

'Dad didn't.' Even I was surprised at how readily that came out.

This hurt enough for her to ease up on the gas. 'You're right. But you and I do. Okay? It's the house rule from this day forward. Promise?'

'Promise.'

I retrace my steps through her apartment one last time. No note on the fridge, no note on the coffee table, no note on the back of the front door.

Viv's rules often expire without warning, though. Given the lecture I received in front of the bakery yesterday, time might be up on the note mandate. A note would only coddle me.

Still, I walk through the apartment once more, in search of an explanation for her absence, now potentially in its twenty-fourth hour.

Nothing.

———

Night has fallen on the executive ward. Mood lighting only. A Filipino night nurse is bent over a coffee table by the ward station, fanning out interior design magazines. When the elevator door opens, she straightens up to greet me. As soon as she sees the badge clipped to my belt and the wire basket the pharmacy prepared, she returns to puttering, moving the leather chairs into a conversational grouping closer to the picture window that overlooks the park.

All the patients are in their rooms. Carmel is at the nurses' station, looking as institutional in shape and demeanour as the beige desk and counter in front of her. She notes my punctuality—three minutes early—and waves me over.

'He had his last meal at five, as per instructions,' Carmel tells me, and looks at the basket in my hand. 'All good?'

'All good.'

'You're taking him upstairs and bringing him back. I can't ask my staff to assist. They know him so well.' The night nurse by the conversation pit is within earshot and looks vindicated.

'Understood.'

She says, 'I've packed a bedsheet into the back of his chair. Keep him in there, after. So strange to be planning this. Throw the sheet over him before you come down. Call, and I'll be by the elevator. We'll make it work.'

———

Sanford is in a maroon checked bathrobe, wedged into his wheelchair with pillows all around him. 'You've got the goods?' His lips shine with a film of broadly smeared Vaseline.

'I do.' I show him the basket.

He hurls himself sideways for a closer look, almost losing a pillow in the process. I stuff it back into place. He keeps the cups in focus as he slouches down in the chair. 'Let me have the one that keeps me from throwing up, get that going.'

As I officially explain the medication that he just explained, I pull the plastic top off the cup. He nods and *yes*es me until I put it into his right hand. Using the crook of his left arm for support, he brings the cup to his lips. With concentration, he holds it in place while his throat slowly passes the syrup down.

'There.' He lets the cup fall into his lap. 'To the rooftop.'

'Do you have anything you want to take with you?'

'Like what?'

'I don't know. Something to hold onto. Any items of significance.'

'Are you for real? If there was one item of actual significance left, I wouldn't be killing myself, would I? Here's a free tip: don't ask anyone that question again. Let's go.'

He tries to direct the chair out of the room, but only manages to rotate himself into the wall behind the door, then jam himself into the corner even further from the doorway. In one last attempt, he rams the chair against the mini fridge.

'It's these rooms,' he barks at the controller. 'Today is not the—' The chair hits the fridge again, hard. Finally, he lets his hand fall away from the knob and shuts his eyes. 'Can you?'

'No problem.' I drive him out of the room, trying not to master the steering too well.

The separate elevator that goes to the roof deck is at the end of a long corridor that's tastefully downlit and carpeted blue. No conversation is made. The elevator doors open and, with a bit too much speed, I swivel the chair into the car and turn him to face the front.

He fingers the edge of his bathrobe as we make the slow ride up. 'It's not a family heirloom, but it's homey. Your item of significance, I suppose.'

His admission brings me a flash of satisfaction, which I quickly get in check. I am not here for his love or for his anger or even absolution.

The doors open onto the dark wooden deck and the night sky. The garden is a curated array of planters, currently loaded up with azaleas and surrounding an inoffensive arrangement of chairs. Sanford's head wobbles as he drives forward into the humidity. He inhales without coughing. 'This air is more real than what they pipe in downstairs. I know about the garbage that lives in those filters.'

At the end of the deck is a ramp with handrails that leads up to our destination, the gazebo. It's full Victorian kitsch, including dangles of fretwork lacing over the edge of the roof, all wrapped in a red and gold finish. Given the hospital's air-conditioning exhaust grimly droning on the far side of the tar-paper roof, the bright vibe is a big stretch.

Sanford steers his chair up to the landing, wordlessly allowing me to correct his course with my index finger whenever he veers too close to either guardrail.

'Great night for it,' he says when he gets to the top. A small vase of daisies sits in the centre of a cafe table.

He nods at the basket. We are all business. I place the drugs and paperwork squarely on the table and clip the camera to the railing. He lets me proceed, showing more respect for the legalisms than I expected. Once the last necessary *yes* is recorded, I put the cup into his hand.

Again he engages his left arm to raise the cup to his lips. Halfway there, the physical apparatus suddenly gives and the cup lowers towards his lap, tipping inward, stopping itself mid-chest, just short of a spill.

As I anticipate the potential horror—having to keep him here while I requisition more Nembutal, and his aggravation about the delay—I reach my right hand out to steady the cup.

'It's going to be all right,' he says, twisting away from my hand with another tremor that splashes enough Nembutal to darken a small patch of his bathrobe. We both look in the cup. Still enough to kill him.

My hand overrides his. It takes a merging of forces to bring the cup level. 'Do you want to put it down for a moment?' I ask.

'I do not.' He rotates his left shoulder, as if the hinge is merely rusty and winding it back will ready it for the task.

I keep my hand an inch from the cup—hovering, as Viv might say—while he makes several attempts to raise his arm. He can bring it no higher than his chest.

'Let's give you a moment,' I say, trying to extract the cup from his weak grip. As I do, he pushes his left hand under his right.

'There we are,' he says, latching onto my wrist for extra support. 'We can do this. Now: lift. Together.'

I keep my hand firmly on his wrist, which is beginning to shake from the position. 'You drank downstairs on your own. If you want to do this, you need to do it on your own. You know that.'

'It comes and goes, you know that,' he says. 'Let me, please, or I'll—' There are tears forming. He has no threats to give me, which makes his weak rage even sadder.

'I'm sorry.' I relax my fingers and try to untangle my hand from him and let go entirely. He can have the cup. He can spill it.

With a desperate surge, he digs his fingertips into my wrist and yanks me closer. Our pretzel pose stalls below his chin. He leans forward, forcing my hand and the cup up to his face. 'You're only bolstering me. Don't overthink it. What else are we going to do?' He drags the cup and my hand closer, his mouth opening towards the rim of the cup.

I do three things at once. One, I lift my elbow slightly, as if I'm pulling my hand away and say, in a clear, recordable voice, 'No, Sanford. You have to understand. Legally, I can't take part in this.' Two, I turn, blocking the camera's view of three, which is me making my hand look limp enough to convince anyone watching, even myself, that I am not doing what I am doing. Our three hands glide the remaining distance to his lips, like a pointer across a Ouija board.

Mouth makes contact. He gulps at the cup until I'm afraid he'll choke. After a few seconds, he pulls his head back so he can swallow a few times. He doesn't choke.

I say, 'Good.' So much for neutrality.

He leans in and drinks the rest without faltering. My hand is still right there with him. Near the end, when victory is slackening his grip, my index finger positions itself on the bottom of the cup. The distal knuckle, which even while supporting this enterprise has attempted to remain wilfully ignorant, now decidedly breaks the law: it contracts, tipping the bottom of the cup upwards to make sure Sanford gets the last drop, to compensate for the spill on the bathrobe. As he swallows, moisture drains from my mouth, my body.

He almost nods as he drinks the last of it. When he's finally done, both arms fall to his lap, leaving the cup in my hand.

'There. That was more effort than it had to be.' He licks the inside of his cheeks, his teeth, and his lips. 'Well, I was right about you. Thank you.'

'You're welcome,' I say, taking a less than confident glance at the camera.

'Listen,' he says, 'a change of topic, but I don't know how much time is left and I thought of this. Have you ever been to the restaurant at the Swayburn?'

'Yes, once.'

'So you know it. They've been sending me my dinner here. I've been a good customer of theirs for a long time. Made me a lobster tail for my last meal. They do the best T-bone in the city. The chef knows what she's doing. I have an account, to be paid through the end of the month. Take yourself in before then, bring a friend, mention my name. I want you to have a meal, on me.'

'That's a kind offer, but I'm not supposed to—'

'Not supposed to what?' he mocks. 'You already provided your service. This is your tip. Don't refuse me.'

A fire engine passes below us, siren on. Somewhere in the city, someone is waiting to be pulled to safety. And yet here's Sanford, looking philosophically out over the city, sending me out for a T-bone. It comes to me: I saved him.

'What's the time?' he asks. My phone shows 11.17, but as soon as I open my mouth to tell him that he turns back to the view. 'Scratch that. I just want to take it all in. I'm not spending my last moments watching the clock tick.'

It was what he wanted. I did more than assist and I am proud.

A few stars come in and out of the clouds, a few bright constellations that only make sense to humans. They're carrying on their own business up there—frightening cavemen, providing homes to future colonies. They make me see that Sanford's approval doesn't matter anymore. He'll be dead in minutes and no one will know the degree of my assistance.

And they free me from Lon and Simon, who are getting ready for bed right now.

Free me from my mother, who has probably checked into some casino and is smiling at her cards even as I smile at the yellowish sliver of moon.

The cup is still in my hand. I feel as free as if I'd drunk from it myself. When I first told Giulia about this job, she said, 'Be careful.' She's not always right. This is where I belong.

The drone of that siren disappears into the city. I turn to follow it and glance up into the wooden rafters of the gazebo. A shiny ball is blinking its round red eye at me, recording everything happening below it.

I stare at the eye in the sky for a second too long, long enough for my expression to say, *Caught caught caught caught caught caught.*

I wish I had taken the anti-emetic.

From memory, this is the medical board's stated policy on situational ethics and personal judgment in assisted deaths: *Owing to the moral complexity and legal ramifications of these interventions, we are forced to regulate the behaviour of those present in clear and absolute terms. We anticipate that no governing body will be willing to consider 'grey areas' or extenuating circumstances that may bring the role of the assistant into conflict with the law.*

Sanford has a few minutes left. My only job—for him and for the camera—is to continue as if all has occurred according to protocol.

'You don't think about death when you're a boy,' he says to the city below. 'I made it through school, college, all the way to my twenties without even one death to mark me. Then the grandparents dropped off—finally, yes, but an inheritance helps. Then I noticed people starting to fall off. Distant people. A tropical disease, a drug allergy, avoidable accidents. Never a situation I'd have found myself in. Hang-gliding? These individuals were never that close to me. It was news but had no lasting effect. They were unlucky and I was immortal. My fifth-grade teacher told me I was destined for greatness. That was my only flight path. The plan was, I would remain untouched by any of the bad genes or bad choices stopping everyone else in their tracks. Didn't even hear about one suicide till I was in my thirties. That was other people.'

An unsmirched youth sounds idyllic. I'm trying to stay with it, imagine him young and swinging, with bluster and money and wives, but all I can see is six-year-old me in a corduroy suit at my father's funeral. Then it was the grandparents, all four gone before I was twelve. Then Viv's last serious boyfriend, who I thought was going to save us—bicycle + truck + blind spot, which only made Viv run faster. By then, I had the picture. We were a collection of bad genes and choices, the ones Sanford deftly avoided.

'Time catches up, though,' he says. 'Wait. Not even. It's there all along. My boss walked around with cancer a whole year, not telling anyone, not even his wife. Before he died, he handed over his job to me. So that worked out. I even dated the wife for a short time, but her grief was too much. My best sales rep, AIDS. Didn't even know he was sick. Then more, faster. I get a call about a balloon accident half a world away and the happy honeymooners, these good-looking kids I'd sent a case of a very good meursault to, they were coming home in wooden boxes of their own. The kind of thing that happens to others, not you. And then you hit forty and it picks up speed. There's no pretending anymore. My father, then my mother. Bang. Bang. It was expected, but not appreciated. Then my ex-wife. BANG. That's when you know it's only a question of when. These phone calls at strange hours keep coming. Still, I knew I was invincible, that because Dee got clipped early, I would somehow bank an extra ten years. Here's the truth: it's a shooting gallery, and you're lucky every day until you're not.'

He puts his hands on his knees, pushing his legs apart an inch or so. 'Oof. This,' he looks at his body, 'was keeping pace with me since the day I was born, always there. I believe that. Who ca

It's this.' He looks at me as if he's just realised he's got company. 'And it's you.'

A helicopter hovers nearby, no doubt called by whichever security guard has the task of monitoring the gazebo camera. I act natural.

'I'm glad it's you,' says Sanford. 'I am.'

I let myself enjoy one last unincarcerated flush of gratification.

'My brother!' Sanford dribbles. 'That's the bastard I am. I forgot my brother! Petey. My baby brother.'

He didn't come up in any of the interviews. I recover enough to ask, 'Does your brother know what's happening here?'

Sanford shakes his head. 'He's dead. Heart. One Thursday afternoon, I was at work. He was at the local pool.' He closes his eyes. 'I sat at that desk for decades, never using my legs when I had them. I deserved his heart attack.'

I feel sorry for Sanford, not having anyone here but me. 'No one deserves anything,' I tell him.

'That so?' He closes his eyes and his tongue makes one slow trip across his lips. He reaches weakly for my hand and I give it to him. His head weaves, falling fast. Abruptly it pivots in strong disagreement with something, then juts forward, as though he's willing himself towards the edge of the balcony, to jump. With my free hand, I guide his head back into the neck cradle. The touch springs his eyes open, glazed but definite. 'Don't . . . Don't—' he says, but can't complete the thought. He's fighting sleep. 'Don't . . . feel . . . a thing.' His voice is so even and the words are so far apart that they barely sound like a sentence.

Don't feel a thing. I don't know if it's a command or a report. At present, I'll take it as advice.

He sags down into a familiar sack that tells me there will be no more voluntary sounds. I loosen the chrome toggle of the neck rest to straighten his head, if only for the purpose of presentation. With a gurgle, he passes swiftly through sleep into unconsciousness and beyond.

In a few minutes, the papery skin on his forehead goes from smooth to empty. I check my watch. Let's give him ten minutes to be sure.

The helicopter lingers. There must be an accident somewhere.

Through self-preserving willpower, I keep watch on my patient and avoid looking back into the camera overhead. I'm looping the recording through my mind, to see if I can reach a verdict on me before somebody else does.

I get out my stethoscope. No heartbeat.

Pulse is absent at wrists and carotids.

The folded sheet Carmel put in the back basket is made from a far higher thread count than you'd get downstairs. I cover him with it and call her.

'He did well,' I tell her, officially launching my cover-up.

'And you?'

'I'm okay.'

'For the life of me, I don't know how that's even possible.'

I stare back at the helicopter until it curtseys and flies off.

———

Carmel hurries us out of the elevator. 'The hallway's clear at the minute. Though you never know.'

The rest is painless. I pilot him back to his room. Carmel conducts the orderlies as they transfer him onto a gurney. She helps me with as much of the documentation as she can, pressing Sanford's stickers into all the right places, until the doctor swings by and, after examining the cooling corpse, certifies that he is dead.

By 12.45, Sanford has been delivered to the morgue.

The night nurse packs Sanford's belongings into a black leather overnight bag. A thousand dollars' worth of pyjamas, wire-rimmed reading glasses, a squishy ball to keep his hands strong, miscellaneous electronics.

'How well did you know him?' she asks me.

'Not very well.'

Her eyebrows go up with polite scepticism for our enterprise. 'He was a very nice man,' she says. 'Nicer than many.'

Tomorrow the bag will be messengered to some lucky recipient. Moderately startled by the news of his death, she or he will review the contents, separate the sad from the functional, and feel the essence of the windfall—good fortune and another chip away at their fantasy of immortality. Will they sail past the news untouched or will it send them off in a new direction?

I leave the ward, vibrating from the night nurse's disdain. My guilt is tempered by the fact that Sanford needed me. Plus I didn't spill the Nembutal and didn't hesitate. I was nice too. All I did was lift my finger. I fulfilled my purpose.

———

The few hours left of the night for sleeping are not productive. Viv's still-empty apartment is one reason. I find a small faded blood stain on her pillowcase. It briefly takes on the importance of a critical clue, but the fact is that a two-night AWOL is certainly within her repertoire. Once I was twelve and had been deemed responsible enough to manage (feed myself and keep up appearances), she confidently took weekends away with few details provided, before or after. Unless of course, the trip bore some kind of fruit, such as a turquoise leather jacket or a few days' winnings. Her return would be low key, in any case, with zero apology for her parenting style and all emphasis on my big boyness for having entertained myself. The dismissal she gave me in front of the bakery, compounded by the lack of a note to explain, convinces me, even in the middle of the night, that the blood on her pillow is evidence of nothing more than gingivitis.

My other reason for sleeplessness is the work to be done on my alibi. If my movements in the recording bring about any questions, my recorded statement of disavowal should protect me, but I need to cue up my actions with my statements to develop a clear narrative for any angle of surveillance. I rehearse my surprise at being questioned, practising calm expressions of innocence and, if pushed, confusion leading ever so slightly towards indignation. Not too far, and not too fast, I decide.

Downstairs, in the hazy light of morning, a garbage truck notches its way through the middle of the street. The men run to collect the bins on opposite sides, empty them into the munching maw at the back, and swoop out to collect the next two, stitching their way to the corner.

There may be easier jobs in this world.

An hour later, I slip into position at my desk. Nettie keeps her eyes on the screen but asks, 'How was Sanford?'

'A lot of talking.' On the bus this morning I scripted one sentence to sync with the video: 'He did struggle with his arm in the last minute, getting the cup to his mouth . . .'

Her head cocks. 'Did he make it?'

'He did. Disease-related weakness at an inopportune moment. Almost spilled it. Not avoidance. His intention was clear. In the end, the arm made the journey. No problems to report.'

'Document whatever's relevant.' Her inbox pings and she's distracted back to her screen. 'I'll watch later.'

'I haven't seen it yet, so any feedback is welcome.'

Next patient, assuming I'm allowed: female, fifty-two, with seriously disseminated breast cancer. Not particularly symptomatic yet, but the deterioration hasn't started in earnest. It will come. A nurse, she's lived all over like a missionary, specialising in refugee camps. No children or spouse. Cheryl has outlived her prognosis by eight months. The only carer is a sister who has attended exactly one consultation. She wholeheartedly supports her sister's right to die. She is also paying for her room.

Nettie leans back in her chair, headphones on, watching a pharmacology lecture. In the corner of her screen, Sanford's death—my recording of it—third in her queue—is hours away.

After reviewing Cheryl's files, I recommend psych consults for the patient and the sister, separately, to bluntly ask about the role of money in the decision. I then publish my clinical write-up of Sanford's death. I also compose a tender, guiltless reflection to be attached to the file. No mention of the degree of assistance ultimately required.

Later, when I pack up, Sanford is fourth in her queue. She's watching a home assist, a recording from somebody's concrete back-yard somewhere with a barbecue going. The patient is in the centre, an old man with his middle-aged children watching the camera. Nettie lowers her headphones to wish me a good night.

I go to the apartment. No Viv.

There's one quick rotation through the TV channels to confirm nothing is on, and then scrambled eggs, eaten standing up in the kitchen. I am asleep by nine.

———

At 6.30 am, the phone hums. It feels as if I woke up at the moment the signal was received. It's Nettie. Calling, not texting.

'I need to have a conversation with you, in person. Outside of the hospital precinct would be best. Do you know the new playground at the back of the park?'

My forehead goes damp. It's not only outside the precinct, it's a city block away. She doesn't want to be seen with me. 'Sure.'

'Eight-thirty?'

'Can I ask, what's this about?'

'When I see you.'

———

Nettie is waiting by the slide, shifting her weight back and forth between her feet like a fighter getting ready. I lift the latch on the low green gate as she scans the perimeter to see who might be around.

There's a jaundiced Indian man being pushed past the fence in a wheelchair. Despite the steamy morning, he's tucked into his seat with white hospital blankets up to his chin. The woman in hospital whites steering him looks over at us once before leaning in to listen to something he's saying, then laughs a genuine laugh and keeps moving him along. The rest of the commuters speed-walk by without even a turn of the head.

'It's just us,' I say.

'Evan, I hate having to ask you: are you recording our conversation?'

'No.'

The pause that follows is so long that I feel compelled to insist, 'I'm not.'

Still she hesitates. 'I'm sorry. Can you show me your phone?'

I hold it up.

'Please, switch it entirely off.'

I do.

She pulls out her own, pressing the wake-up button to show me that the screen stays black. 'Mine is off too. What I'm about to say is between us.'

'Can we at least sit down?'

She doesn't respond and doesn't make a move towards the bench. 'Tell me what happened with Sanford.' I summon my composed sentences and she adds, 'Please give me the truth the first time. I don't enjoy this.'

'He needed extra help getting the cup to his mouth,' I say. 'I gave it to him.'

'How did you give it to him?'

'His hand wouldn't reach. If I hadn't supported him, he wouldn't have been able to—'

She holds out her index finger to stop me.

I bargain. 'He wanted to drink. He said so in a clear voice. You heard his words.'

'You poured Nembutal into a patient's mouth. I watched you do it. The degree of assistance doesn't matter. You did it.'

Here we are.

If she has some other recording device going, I don't care. 'He was almost there.'

143

She is no longer trying to be kind or coax out my confession. Now that she has what she came for, her face goes steely. 'You're going to defend it?'

There's nothing to say.

She scrunches her eyes closed. 'I saw this when I met you. I mistook it for belief in our project. You think you're just there, doing nothing, but you have a dangerous—I would say pathological—need to be part of the proceedings.'

'That's not true.'

'Pouring it into his mouth? Is that the same as handing someone a cup?'

'No. I joined his effort. He couldn't do it alone.'

'Our entire project, the questions, the safeguards, they are there to protect you, to keep you from crossing this line. The training, every minute of every interview, is there—and recorded—to protect the patient and to protect you from the conversation we are now having.'

A pair of joggers trot by. Our heads turn in unison to watch them. They briefly check out two tense-looking adults standing in a playground without a child.

Nettie leans closer. 'Now that you've done this, how do you feel? Deep down?'

'Deep down I see 961 less like the bible and more like a regulation. If I'd stopped him up there and sent him back to his room, I would be having more regrets right now than I'm having. That's how I feel. I can't change that. I helped.'

She turns her head away from me.

'I'm sorry,' I say.

She stares at the blue rubber mats under the swing set. 'Well don't panic—you're safe. I've gone back through the notes. The recordings have been dealt with. There's no evidence of wrongdoing and there won't be. I won't report what happened, but your time with us is done.'

'Yes. I'm sure. Thank you.'

She studies me. Is she looking for remorse? 'I hope I'm not making a mistake. Personally, I would like to fire you. Covering for what you did is the only way I can protect my program. Here's what you'll tell HR when you resign: You weren't a good fit. Because of their bias against me, the problem won't be you. They'll put my next hire through much more screening. You'll work again. The Mercy is always short staffed. They'll hire you anywhere else in the hospital, if that's what you want. I don't particularly care.'

I look down and see that my hands are shaking.

'The only good words I have for you are that yes, you helped,' she says. 'I get that. I do. In the world outside the law, there's nothing wrong with what you did. But you won't catch me putting that on paper. The fact is that you have to live inside the law or you have to live with the consequences. This time, you only have to live with yourself.'

I feel fundamentally warned. 'Yes,' I say.

'Goodbye.' She lets herself out without looking in my direction, leaving me in the playground.

I walk over to the swings and select a moulded black plastic seat at the end. My feet connect me loosely to the mat beneath me as the chains let me dangle in little circles. I turn my phone back on, log into the hospital site and officially text in my resignation to HR. Reason given? *I wasn't a good fit.* The reply comes immediately, possibly automated, assuring me that my remaining pay will be transferred to my account at the end of the week, that pending a discussion with Nettie there may be other opportunities for me at the hospital, and, though they recognise this may be a busy time for me, would I like to attend an exit interview or fill out a survey about my experience with the Mercy Hospital in the next seven days? I opt for the survey, but not now.

There's no word from Viv. She always loved the prospect of sudden joblessness. At the moment I'm not seeing the charm. I straighten my legs against the ground and let go, shooting forward.

Your feet go back, the swing goes back; your feet go up, the swing goes up, further. Next thing you know you're flying and it keeps going as long as you do. If it weren't chained to the pole above me I'd launch out over the fence. The air rushing past helps. I pump higher and higher. I didn't break the universe. Just the law. And Nettie protected me.

My eyes are on my work shoes, pointing out in front of me, still polished for Sanford, swinging up and swinging down. Everything behind them is moving—the empty playground, the treetops and sky, down to the matting, then up again.

The treetops, the sky. This, I am sure, is where Viv would jump off.

The hum of the phone in my pocket slows my ride. It's an unfamiliar number.

A woman's voice says, 'Am I speaking with Evan?'

I stake my feet, dragging the swing to a stop. 'Yes.'

'Good morning. This is Joan. We met on Monday. Your mother's occupational therapist.'

'Ah.'

'It's fantastic that I was able to catch you. You see, I'm at her building, downstairs. We had an appointment. I've been ringing with no luck at all. Her mobile goes direct to voicemail and her landline rings out. At first I thought she could be having a shower. So I gave it a while, but—no luck. The office patched me through to you. So sorry to bother you at work.'

'Right.'

She's waiting for me to get tense about this situation. I tell her, 'She hasn't been home for a few days.'

'Where did she go?'

'I don't know.'

'We're supposed to make Thai salad with sprouts and beef.'

'She would have liked that.'

If I didn't have the right answers for Nettie, I really won't have them for Joan. She doesn't wait for them. 'I'm concerned that she would skip our appointment. Would it be possible for you to come meet me here, just so we can go upstairs to make sure she's not home right now and in some sort of trouble?'

'I don't think she's in trouble. She took a little trip, I think, and she didn't leave a note saying where she went.'

'Still, for my peace of mind, I'd like to go upstairs at some point. I can wait for you now—my morning is blocked out for her, so I can hang around till lunch—or come back and meet you later, after your shift, if you like.'

'I'll come now.'

'Really? Fantastic. Can you just get away like that?'

'Today is light.'

———

Joan is in front of the building, bent over and doing windmills, one hand touching her toes and one hand reaching up. A green-netted bag of groceries sits on the ground beside her, with bouquets of coriander and lemongrass sticking out of the top.

'That was fast,' she says.

'Better off checking.'

Inside the apartment, there have been no changes in the past two hours. Joan does the emergency search for a body while I do a calmer sweep of the place for clues I might have missed.

'See?' I say, pointing to the spot in the wardrobe that was occupied by the missing bag. 'She's taken a mini vacation.'

Joan marvels at my resilience in the face of a missing mother. My goal is for her not to read it as irritation. 'Must be a unique bond you two have,' she says. 'She told me you were an accomplished nurse. That you're going to save everyone in the world. Spoken like a mother, don't you think?'

I can imagine Viv on her foam mat, doing windmills of her own and spinning stories for Joan, to keep them both entertained. 'Yes.'

I look past Joan into the kitchen, and that's when I notice the volcano postcard, Viv's prized bookmark, resting on the far side of the kitchen counter. I must have stared right at it when I was eating scrambled eggs last night, but this time I see that it's anchored in position with the clip of a pink Willow Wood pen that she must have swiped.

'Wait,' I say, going to pick up the postcard.

Here's her note. The handwriting is small, with a quiver of instability in it.

Everly, I'm off for a few days to the beach. I'm looking forward to the silence. Call if there's trouble, but I'll be turning off my phone till it's time to come back. I won't be gone long and you can get yourself settled elsewhere without having to think about me. Love.

Call if there's trouble, but I'll be turning off my phone. Classic. Well, there's the note.

I show Joan.

'Okay. I'll need to let the office know about this.' Taking out her tablet. 'Do you have an idea which beach she's talking about? Did she go north or south?'

'No idea.'

'Well, she ought to call in, if only to reassure us.'

'I wouldn't count on it.'

'Amazing that you stay so relaxed. Nurses, though. You've seen it all. What department do you work in?'

I reach for the nearest thing. What comes out, thanks to Lena, is, 'Renal.'

Joan pauses, no doubt perplexed by trying to understand how dialysis is going to save the world. She laughs. 'There you go. I can't picture working in that area myself, but if the job is right, then it's barely a job. It's love, isn't it?'

'It's love,' I tell her.

'Are you going back to work now?'

'I'll grab something to eat first.' There's nothing in the fridge and I'm suddenly afraid Joan will see and decide that I need training in food prep. I gently direct her and her net bag towards the door. 'I'll have her call as soon as she makes contact, and you can schedule your next visit.'

She lingers in the doorway, rearranging the lemongrass. 'I guess this will be my dinner tonight. Willow Wood already paid for it.'

I assure her, 'No one will know.'

———

The doorwoman swings a mammoth bronze door open into a puff of air-conditioning and gives me a wink. 'Good day, sir. Welcome to the Swayburn.'

It's brushed chrome and granite from here to the cornucopia of pink gladioli sprawled across the concierge's desk, which, like everything else here, twinkles. I pass three suited staff members, each splitting their attention between the few people in the lobby and whatever's being piped into their earbuds, before an elevator operator ushers me aboard. 'Good day, sir. Welcome to the Swayburn.'

It's a quick ride to level 47. The doors slide open onto a pathway of carpet with yellow brocade on dark blue. At the end of it stands a similarly programmed greeter—this one wearing maroon—who advises me to watch my step while crossing over the tracks into the rotating restaurant.

An expanse of curving window currently overlooks the older part of downtown, lumpy and grey. Looking past it, through the summery haze, I can see hilly suburbs, and beyond that, just hills.

The crossing guard hands me over to an extremely young woman wearing a trainee badge that says *Kerri*. 'And good day to you, sir.' She's practically singing. 'Welcome to Nimbus.'

'Good day. One for breakfast, please.'

'Certainly. Do you have a reservation?'

I drop Sanford's name, which gets me a clubby nod and immediate escort to a table by the window. 'And how is he doing? I haven't seen him for quite a while.'

Let her hear it from someone else. 'I think he's feeling more comfortable.'

'That's excellent news. Will you be enjoying the buffet?'

I want to say I'll tell her after, but I just say, 'Yes.'

'We have a new pastry chef. Please tell us what you think.'

Kerri whispers a few words about me to the sentinel at the egg station, then disappears behind an enormous curtain that wraps the kitchen. It sits stationary in the building's core, while the seating area around keeps up a subtle spin around it.

Viv brought me here when I was visiting once. We had wine and a plate of stuffed mushrooms, the minimum expenditure to get the view. It was night-time. Her movement was dragging even then, but it was, as she said, a lark.

That's probably also what she said when she left on her adventure. I can't blame her. I'd rather be at the beach as well. She thought Sanford made sense. He would have thought she did too.

I look around the room nostalgically for our table, but the place is laid out in a repeating pattern and turning. The restaurant would have orbited the kitchen thousands of times since we were here. The back of the menu tells me that one minute equals three degrees. It's easier for me to believe the city is doing the spinning and we're up here holding still. If I were Kerri, I'd be spending my breaks in the bathroom with the rest of the stationary plumbing, trying to picture the world holding still.

My first trip to the buffet yields porridge with sautéed bananas, which Kerri pairs with a glass of champagne. I'm not going to argue.

The second course is savoury, congee with chives, tofu and soy sauce. I take half a bowl, leaving room for eggs Benedict. The champagne is refilled at least twice more. In fact, I'm not sure, because it's never allowed to empty.

Kerri approaches me at the fish station as I'm piling salmon onto my plate. 'Today's smoothie is dragon fruit with fresh cherries. Would you care for one?'

I'm completely buzzed by now, from drinking, from food, from getting fired. 'Only if it cares for me.' It's my mother's gag.

'Pardon?'

'I would care for it.'

'I'll have them make one right away.'

'And I need to tell you something,' I say. 'Sanford died two days ago.'

'Oh.' She takes a step back, her adolescent mind blown, as if up until now she thought everyone with degenerative diseases lived forever. 'This is terrible news.'

'I'm sorry. I didn't know how to tell you before. He was very sick.'

'I had no idea.'

I nod sagely. 'He did. He was ready.'

'Thanks for letting me know.'

I already regret dragging a young person into the terrifying truth of mortality, especially in the middle of her shift.

'Were you part of his staff?' she asks.

'You could say that. To the same extent this restaurant was. He said you do the best T-bone.'

She blushes, as if the meat were her own.

'I better sit down,' I say. 'That dragon fruit thing is a good idea.' I've had enough champagne for this particular Thursday.

Kerri watches me make my way between the slowly turning maze of tables and soft leather chairs back to my own. Once I have stacked too much lox on a mini bagel, I notice she is conferring at the egg station, no doubt discussing the news about Sanford.

The room circles me around to a flawless vista of the Mercy's rooftop terrace. There's an exercise class going on, consisting of three healthy-looking geriatric patients marching in place. A gardener loops a length of hose around the perimeter of the deck, avoiding the patients while working on a low flowerbed.

I miss Sanford.

'Your smoothie.' The red speckled drink is delivered in a highball glass. 'Did you want to try the T-bone?' Kerri asks.

'Thank you, that wasn't a hint. There's enough here.'

'Let us know if you change your mind. Sanford was a real friend.'

'Sure.'

The hospital sits there, content with its protocol. No one appears to be in the gazebo. And I'm thankful the area isn't cordoned off with police tape. As Nettie mentioned, I didn't do anything wrong.

A white office tower slides in front of it, hiding one row of windows, then another. Nettie is tucked away safely in the hospital, organising next month's cases, composing the job ad for a new assistant. What she really wanted to do, as she pointed out, was fire me. What I really wanted to do was provide a humane service to people in need.

The hospital disappears completely behind the office tower and soon the entire downtown rotates away. I consider my next course.

A slim couple in their late thirties blocks my access to the dessert table, disdainfully surveying the carbs. Ringless—one divorce each, I'm guessing. After a minute of deliberating, they each select a single pastel-coloured macaron, put it on a plate and head back to their table in silence. I know terminal suffering when I see it.

I settle on a fruit cup, just a palate cleanser. In a few hours Nettie will have approved my resignation. If I call HR this afternoon, I can be hanging saline bags or pushing antibiotics on a general ward by tomorrow. Maybe clipping stitches in orthopaedics. That would be some wicked, subversive shit.

This calls for a double-shot latte and another champagne. I inform the staff and hit the dessert table hard, leaving with a main course plate loaded with a frosting-heavy corner piece of chocolate cake, a blueberry tart and a ramekin of crème brûlée.

Meanwhile, Les Misérables, sitting nearby with their macarons, are having trouble. The man slams his reader down. With headphones drooping out of one hand, he has apparently had enough of her. 'This is my sole vacation.'

The woman, arms folded, doesn't budge. 'Just tell me when it would suit you to leave.'

Seems reasonable, but he only stares at her.

She falls back against the banquette. 'Or, you watch your money tick around for a few more hours, let your coffee go as cold as this fucking room, while I sit here and admire you. Is that what you're hoping for?'

My advice: don't wait for his answer.

He puts his hands on the table, enforcing his own calm. 'How about we just try five minutes of no one being a dick?'

'I'd love it.'

He pushes the buds back into his ears and she turns to look at the dessert table, as if she could use the excuse of the argument to have another macaron. She changes her mind quickly, refolds her arms and catches my glance. I swivel back to my latte, pleased that they found a solution.

These two will not go quietly when their time comes. The last possible procedures will be performed before their doctors start getting real with them about benefit versus harm in continuing on *like this*. Any of their children who show up at the ward, God help everybody, will be delicately urging Mum and Dad to clarify the goals of their care. Even then, these two won't take the hint. With a black fountain pen, their lawyer, acting on their incapable behalf, will confidently tick the boxes *Full Resuscitation* and *All Measures*, yes for both. If it's my shift at the Mercy, I'll be there at the bedside, managing her PEG feed, unblocking his catheter, and proudly remembering my night on the roof with Sanford. Glory days.

The restaurant glides towards a view of the waterfront. The five-year-old revamp, with the museum and the Ferris wheel, already looks twenty.

I picture Sanford at this table or another, trying to convince his guru that he needs her for his last transition. If she had been there with us up on the roof, her spirit might have helped him raise his arm by himself.

Never mind her. It was me. Sanford was glad it was me. Protocol would have been no use to him. I was there for him. No one stopped me, not even me.

Why do we play? For moments like that.

I know what I'm going to do.

Turning my seat to face the window, I get a choice view of the rooftop jungle on the science museum. There's a ban on phone use here, but Sanford would ignore it too. I take mine out and start searching. The number isn't hard to find. After an unusual series of clicks, the connection goes through to a recording that directs me, for security's sake, to leave a brief message. Doing so drains my enthusiasm slightly, because leaving a few words and the data print of my phone number is risk enough, but just five minutes later, when I'm going for a bonus round at the crepe station, my call is returned. A woman's voice, breathless and concerned, asks if I'm the person who called Jasper's Path.

As my crepe is being spread with Nutella, I say yes.

'Then good afternoon. This is Jasper speaking.' They're all named Jasper.

'Thanks for calling back,' I tell her, as the chef gives me a conspiratorial wink about the phone and waves me away, assuring me that as soon as it's done he'll send the crepe to my table.

'And thank you for reaching out to us,' Jasper says. In the background there's the distinct clunk of a pot being put on a stove.

'I wasn't even sure if anyone would be there. After 961, are you still active?'

'I'm not sure what you're after: 961 doesn't cover everyone's needs.' She stirs whatever's in that pot with a metal spoon for several turns, listening, no doubt, to the moneyed clinking of a restaurant at my end. She says, 'Do you have a situation you'd like to discuss?'

'I have relevant experience. As an assistant. Recent experience.' I face the window again, businesslike.

A pause.

This isn't a person to be shy with. I continue. 'As a medical professional, I've participated in several direct assists.'

'Legal assists?' She stops stirring.

'Yes, but that doesn't matter to me anymore.'

This merits a long *hmmm*. 'What are you looking for?'

'I found it satisfying, if I can use that word.'

'You may.'

'And I want to stay involved. If there are any opportunities to help, I would like that.'

'This may be serendipitous,' she says. 'Are you in the city?'

I look out on the grid below. 'Yes.'

'I won't be a moment.' Jasper puts me on hold.

When she comes back on, she's a notch more official. 'We're kind of a mobile response team for our friends, and one of us may be near you. Are you free this afternoon, perhaps?'

'Very.'

'Then it sounds like, at the very least, a conversation should happen. It won't be me. It will be another Jasper. You can find out about us and we can find out about you.'

Kerri delivers my crepe with a deferential bow. They've finished it with two banana slices for eyes and a line of chocolate sauce for a smile.

'I'd like that,' I tell Jasper.

'We're a small group and will always be small. Nothing may come of the meeting. Try not to bring too many expectations.'

'Thanks. I'm thirty-one.'

'What do you mean?'

'I mean I've had to let go of expectations.'

She snorts. 'And please try to limit the personal details.'

———

Our meeting point is a shady and underused pocket park at the foot of a tall apartment building. Weed trees grow from holes in concrete diamonds, and crushed beer cans are generously scattered around.

This Jasper is dressed to forget—white male in a blue Oxford shirt and khaki chinos. When he walks into the park and hoists his eyebrows up to keen attention, I don't know if I'm about to be inducted into an underground organisation or arrested for conspiracy to commit murder.

'Hello, Jasper!' he calls to me from ten paces away.

'Hello,' I reply, more quietly. They should have picked a more common name.

The handshake is warm. His other hand seals the bond. If there is any closed-circuit camera watching, we look like colleagues catching up after too long. He grins hard, attempting to look like he's not reading me as fast as he can.

My read: he's a mouth-breather and he stands too close, a bad combination.

'Now, first: do you represent or are you connected to any body of law enforcement?' he asks.

'No.'

'Good. A reporter? A writer?'

'No.'

'Good, good. Are you recording this meeting?'

The question, coming twice in one day, makes me feel as though I should be recording everything. 'Just in my brain,' I say.

He smiles a non-smile. 'That's permitted. Hoped for, even. Sit down and let's find out what we've got here.'

He sits like he stands—close enough for me to know he had garlic for lunch.

'Have I heard right, that you've been doing good work with 961?'

'Yes, but we're not allowed to say we're doing good.'

Jasper nods. 'I can imagine. At the Mercy, by chance?'

'Yes.'

'As you must know, Nettie joined us for a while. Her efforts were aimed more towards pulling the legislation along, but she sat with several of our friends. In the end, she craved the hospital environment. The structure.'

Ah, so much for anonymity. 'Yes,' I say, containing my sudden fury that no, she never mentioned it to me, not even when she talked about the group by name.

'Are you still working with her?'

'No. The last death I was involved with, in order to respect the patient's wishes, I had to overstep guidelines. Slightly. It was decided that it would be best for me to resign.'

Jasper modulates his suspicion with a tilt of the head. 'Don't tell me details, but—will there be legal action?'

'No.'

'You know that the Mercy isn't the only program out there. Other hospitals are starting up programs too. There's even a regional operator starting a home-visiting service soon. What about any of those for you?'

'No. The structure may be right for Nettie, but not for me.'

A genuine smile breaks through. 'That's interesting. What do you mean?'

'I want to *help*, not just stand there, pretending to be neutral, while I wait for a patient to jump through all of our hoops.'

'Mmm.'

I lay it on thicker. 'How much time are you given to decide if you're going to have chemo scald your insides? One doctor says so and they bump you up to the next appointment. No one stands on the sidelines the whole time giving you an option out. Our patients have to do it alone, and if they're not quite terminal enough, or if they're too sick to give all the consent they gave last week, or if their brother-in-law is feeling a bit too Jesus this afternoon to sign off on it, well, then, we have to abort.'

My dissatisfaction pleases him. 'We agree with you. Everyone must write their own ending their way. And it shouldn't be a doctor's decision. It should be a supported one. Everyone deserves to have companionship and an advocate.'

'That's what I'm after. I don't need to be the nurse. I want—' Nettie's critiques cause me an involuntary twinge, but I say it anyway: 'I want to be a part of things.'

Jasper nods. I'm in.

'Would you mind if I take a look at your phone?' he asks. 'I don't want your name, but I need a quick look at your medical history, and your credit and banking records. Our security measure.'

I offer up the requested data.

I had hoped to meet the original Jasper (or rather the second one; the first, real Jasper offed himself a few years back before bequeathing his estate and his name to the group). Instead, they've sent out their human resources filter. He's scanning through my data.

'Would you like a few vials of blood with that?' I ask.

'Sorry. We have to be on the lookout for anyone approaching us under personal pressures.' He reads through the screens. 'Healthy, single. Things appear as they should. Has anyone in your family taken their own life?' He doesn't even look up when he asks.

'No.'

'Good. Ah—finances?' He hands the phone over to me for guidance. I open up my banking page and hand him the phone again. He rolls his finger across it, hurrying through.

He holds the phone at a distance, scowling at my bank balance. 'Numbers like this are normally a concern if a person comes to us wanting to die. We would refer them on to financial counselling maybe. Are you financially secure?'

'Yes.'

'Let me rephrase,' he says. 'You're very recently unemployed and you've contacted us with—'

'I have money coming back to me that was a loan. I can work as a nurse whenever I want to. I am secure.'

'Very good to hear.' Then he's standing, saying goodbye. The interview is over. 'Sincere thanks to you for getting in touch and meeting. I'll share your thoughts with the team.'

'Thanks,' I say, bewildered at the sudden wrap-up.

He extends his hand to shake mine again. 'We'll call.' And he exits the park the way he entered.

Do I send a thank-you note later or what? Where do I send it?

And Nettie. *She wanted the hospital environment. The structure.* Despite this morning's principled lecture on the primacy of protocol, could she have found a brief, unwatched moment to tell me that she *sat with friends* before 961? Or couldn't I be trusted?

The day has been long enough. I take my champagne headache home, water the plants, and climb into Viv's bed, confident that wherever she has taken herself, she's not coming back this afternoon.

I wake up at 11 am, after the first full night of sleep in a long time, accompanied by an erection—a further positive reading of my departure from the Mercy and a harbinger of better days ahead. This is too distinctly my mother's bed, so I bring the good news to the living room for servicing. The blue parrot in the painting watches, but this feels like a good morning indeed.

No missed calls. Nothing. Now what?

Viv's career-modelling, if not necessarily her advice, has been that after you leave a job you can take a solid week off in order to do nothing. Since I won't be receiving a bill from Willow Wood this month, and since Viv is no doubt parked at a poker table, increasing her good luck, I feel emboldened to think big. A movie maybe?

The phone hums.

'Evan. It's Joan! The OT. The best news!' She's thinking even bigger.

'What?'

'I remembered: the residents at Willow Wood are microchipped. We can find your mother.'

'Not Viv. We had a meeting. They made her sign all sorts of liability waivers to get out of it. She never got one.'

'Well, she must have forgotten to sign one of the forms, because I checked. She has one.'

'She never mentioned it to me,' I say. 'She would have gone down screaming if they tried.'

'If she was at all disoriented during the first check-up, she might have missed it. They can do that job fast. It's in her.'

'Unbelievable.'

'It's good news for us,' Joan assures me. 'Her vital signs are stable and have been stable for the past seventy-two hours. Do you want to know where she is?'

'If my mother wanted contact right now, I guarantee she would be asking for it.'

A judgmental silence follows. 'Trish will want to discuss this with you.'

'Anytime,' I tell her. 'For now, I'm glad my mother's blood pressure is stable. That's enough for me, and it should be enough for you and for Trish.'

Jasper calls in the middle of my nap. It's the woman, the first one I spoke to, sounding less concerned this time. Would I like to come with her to sit with a friend this evening?

'Is this a friend who wants to die?'

'Yes. We've been talking with her for some time and she's ready.'

'Then I'm ready too.'

She's waiting for me at a bus shelter, projecting neither the business-casual look of her colleague nor the earthy calm I would want from a visiting death assistant. It's as if she came home from a long, unlovable day job, splashed water on her face, threw on a crumpled leprechaun-green blouse and rushed back out to meet me. She greets me with a low-key wave.

'We only had to present your story to the others and we knew we'd be able to involve you.' She steers me to the quiet doorway of a closed cafe. 'Now then. I need your phone.'

'I've been through this.'

'Did he patch you?'

'I don't know.'

'You'd know. It masks identity and location for our calls to each other.' She wiggles her fingers hungrily. I hand her my phone, opening up my settings before she takes over. 'I'm putting a limited blanket on here, hiding any calls that travel through our server.'

When she's done, she hits return a few times, sets a password on the protocol, then calls my phone from hers and then the reverse, watching the screens. She hands it back to me. 'There. You're invisible.'

And we're walking again. 'Tonight is a fifty-five-year-old woman. Awful story. Three Christmases back, while she was picking up her cousin at the airport, her brother came home, shot the rest of the family, then himself. Up till that day she'd been happy enough managing a struggling theatre company that I won't name. She and the cousin came home, found the parents and two other siblings, plus her brother, all dead. They didn't cope well, to the extent that they were so incoherent and covered in blood—there's a crazed sound to her story of that night—that when the police arrived, the suspicion fell first on them. Airport security finally settled the order of events and they were cleared. It didn't help. She'd been depressed before, but after this she had to be hospitalised.' Jasper taps her temple, indicating the ward. 'Her friends stepped back. This was too large. She's had PTSD treatments, taken the drugs, tried the therapies. Nothing helps her. Poor woman. *Then*, cancer turns up in her ovaries. The surgeon screws up the surgery, spreads it further. One to five years, they told her. *So* unfair. It was the last straw. In a few years she'd be ready for 961, but she wants to move forward tonight.'

'So are we going to sit there while she commits suicide?'

Her lips tighten. I've used a bad word.

'What do you want to call it?'

'A just-as-natural death.'

'Ah.'

'When you're on the side of the angels, you move with confidence, inward and outward.' Sensing that the invocation of angels hasn't won me over, she speaks more slowly, as if explaining the situation to a hamster. 'Jasper. You will find your own boundaries. There is nothing for you to do tonight but offer her your presence. How does that sound?'

'I support her right to choose her death.'

'There you go,' she says. 'Just go with your gut.'

'Are there protocols?'

She laughs at me pityingly. 'The woman has the motive, the means and a plan. We are there as friends.'

'Friends.'

'Maintain deniability as best you can, for your own protection. Don't look at her name on the front door. Keep your face turned away from any cameras in the building. The police are usually good at respecting a suicide, but you never know. You can put on gloves before entering the apartment if you like. I've got some for you, but I don't wear them. They're medical and impersonal.'

'We're only keeping her company?'

'Precisely.'

'What if something goes wrong? If she gets the dose wrong?'

There's a pause while I lose the goodwill I gained as a hamster. 'She's sourced the meds, tested their purity and confirmed the dosage, all in consultation with us.'

'Do you trust that she's done that correctly?'

'Boy, they trained the faith out of you at the Mercy.'

We're at the destination. It's a grey rectangular tower with staggered balconies. She must have bought off the plan. Jasper waits for me to open the door, so I do.

'What if she wants to back out?' I ask as we walk into the butter-coloured entryway.

No one is around, but she lowers her voice. 'I've never seen it happen. Those with second thoughts, the impulsive, they don't join our group, or if they do, they don't take it this far. They jump

162

off a building, they make their cry for help and end up in the emergency room, or they get on with their lives. Our people get insight from talking to us about the process. By the end, they know what they want.'

We get into an elevator. As it dings each floor up to eight, Jasper and I watch the grey linoleum.

In the hallway, I whisper, 'What happens afterwards?'

'We leave,' she whispers back.

'That's a lot less than we do at the hospital.'

'I hope you'll cope.'

The woman who opens the door looks much older than fifty-five, with a recently moisturised face of smoker's wrinkles and long, frizzy, grey hair that has just been dyed black for her coffin. Her dressing-gown is patterned with roses and thorny vines. The mother's?

'Good to see you,' I say, as if we were in the neighbourhood anyway and thought we'd pop in.

The two Jaspers in her doorway get a once-over and a tired nod. Accepting that we will be the last of life's insults, she forces a flat welcome, ushers us inside and closes the door, trapping us in the front of a long hallway.

'I'm making iced tea. The glasses are in the fridge. We'll drink together. You, yours; me, mine.' Behind her is an unlit wall of movie posters: *Ordinary People*, *The Way We Were*, *The Goodbye Girl*.

'Iced tea will be fine,' I say, trying to gain us further entry, but she stays still, hands on her hips.

'May we come in?' the lead Jasper asks.

'Sure, sure, sure.' And we are led in.

Fatal Attraction, *The Big Chill*. Indeed.

The apartment is alight with green candles, making the place smell like ten minutes of pine spray over twenty years of cigarettes. The living room is cramped, with DVDs in neat towers around a giant television. Four remotes are lined up on the Perspex coffee table. A revolving series of hyper-real nature scenes cycles silently across the screen. A waterfall. A glacier. A tree frog. Opposite is a white leather sofa, gleaming, except for a permanent and slightly person-shaped divot in the cushions, as if the day after the last of the funerals she sat down and has been watching TV ever since. She directs us to sit on the sofa, in between two folk dolls the size of toddlers sitting in the corners. They have button eyes. Each holds miniature maracas that rattle when we sit down. The absence of cameras or unseen witnesses through one-way glass makes the intimacy of the room that much more bizarre.

The woman goes to the kitchen for the tea. Jasper calls after her, 'You don't have to wait on us. We're here for you.'

'You're my guests,' comes the reply from the kitchen. 'And your money's by the television.'

Money? There's a folded wad of bills on a speaker. Jasper checks it out from a distance, looks satisfied.

A moment later, the woman emerges with a red lacquer tea tray and sets it down in front of us. 'Everything that we'll need is right here.'

The tray is crowded with a plastic pitcher, two frosty green glasses, a plate of hazelnut crescents (family recipe), a clear envelope that's fat with Nembutal, and, in the centre, a silver goblet, recently polished, with a dragon grinning as it claws its way around the stem. The cup itself is the dragon's crown.

She pours tea into the two glasses, stirs in sugar syrup with a long silver spoon, artfully drops mint sprigs on top, and wraps each glass in a napkin. She hands one to each of us with lawn-party cheer.

'Now I pour in the medicine,' she says, looking to me for confirmation as she opens the little packet. I nod. It seems merciful that she gets to call it medicine. 'Now the water? One cup?' she says. I nod.

Our host continues to narrate every move she makes, having committed the instructions to memory. 'Plain water from the sink,' she says as she mixes it in with the same long spoon that she used for our tea, then pauses, staring into the goblet. 'This feels very odd.' She shakes the thought away enough to offer us a cookie.

In the spirit of Sanford's orange juice, I take one and thank her. The other Jasper declines, but doesn't seem to judge my engagement.

Our host lifts her goblet high. A furrow of purpose kills any smile she has left. 'To my parents and to my life,' she says, shaky and courageous, as she brings the silver rim to her lips. She drinks it quickly, peeking into the goblet afterwards. With a defiant hand, she replaces the goblet in the centre of the tray, clacking empty on the lacquer. 'My God. I've done it,' she says, turning to hug each of us in her excitement. 'From the moment my eyes opened this morning it's been like getting ready for a trip. Taking care of stupid things. Did I pack my toothbrush? Who's going to water the plants? I had the time so I baked cookies. Now you're next to me and there's nothing left to do. We're here.' She holds up her hand, pulling her fingers together tight and then letting them open into a star, looking at them as if they're new. 'I'd like to die in my bedroom. Come with me.'

The room is a shrine to her parents. They stare out from the walls in half a dozen formal poses shot by mall photographers. Toothy smiles, cloudy blue studio scrims behind them. Mum in a blue floral dress, seated, with Dad in his best suit standing behind; individual ones of the two of them from the same session. There's one of the whole family—maybe even the not-yet-homicidal brother—gathered around a table, each face jutting in towards the centre of the table to smile over a roast. Our host is younger there, grinning, with one hand scratching the ear of a labrador by her side.

We wait in the doorway while she circles the room to review the troops, pausing to give equal time to each photo, before she tips her head in respect and moves on to the next. When she's finished, she sits on the edge of the bed, reaches over to an iPod on the night table and presses play. Greek guitar comes from shelf speakers in all corners.

'This is my father. He never wanted to be recorded. Thought he was no good, his whole life. I tricked him. Stuck a microphone on the table when he was playing. I'm glad I did that.'

There's fumbling on the recording, with false starts and repeated apologies, but he's laughing too. It makes me think of Iris' painting. It makes me wish my father's laugh was recorded somewhere.

'It's beautiful,' I tell her, feeling free enough to say so. 'What was the occasion?'

'My cousin's wedding. He could really play. Thank you. It means a lot to me.'

The queen-sized bed has more folk dolls and stuffed toys, including a seal, a leopard, a blue-eyed doll in a headscarf, all leaning against a wall of pillows. She climbs past the gathering of dolls to a gap in the middle and says to us, 'Here, put yourselves on each side of me. Stay close.' The bed sinks like a pile of feathers under us while she settles herself against a pillow. The fringe of green satin embroidery splaying out from its edges frames her black hair like a brilliant halo. 'I trust you two,' she says.

'We're here for you,' I tell her.

'I have to ask: right now should I be feeling like I could run around the block?' she asks.

Not normally. 'Say more.'

'Maybe it's me, what I'm doing to myself. The fact that I'm right this minute dying, that if you ever told me a feeling could make me want to die before the Lord was ready for me, I wouldn't have believed you in a million years. That a feeling like this could set me against a belief, a belief from decades, from childhood, that tells me why we're here and why we're supposed to endure, no matter what. But I can't endure anymore. There's no point. So,' she folds her hands across her stomach. 'The drug is giving me strange energies.'

After a respectful pause, I ask her, 'Tell me about a beautiful place you've visited.'

'I get this. You're guiding me, slowing me down. How about my grandfather's orchard?' She closes her eyes. 'My mother grew up with an apricot orchard at the bottom of their farm, instead of a fence. No fence, nothing. That was the kind of area it was. In season, you could smell the flowers from the road. And when they fell, they went everywhere, looked like snow. I made the trip back with Mama for a visit five years ago. Dad wasn't up to it, too emotional for him. He'd been away from the old country too long. Refused—'

She searches for a word. It's that Nembutal kick I've come to recognise, followed reliably by, 'Ooh. I'm sleepy.'

Her fingertips trace the line of her sternum. 'There, yes,' she slurs.

Then she stops. Complete. Jasper and I settle in for the quiet wait for an absence of life. We're where she wanted us. Here to give her the confidence, to give her the company, to hear her last few words and now, on her bed, positioned on either side of her, to make sure she dies. The moment is so intimate I forgive Jasper's earlier invocation of angels. I'm closer to this woman whose name and history I don't know than I have been to any of my other cases. It doesn't feel like angels, but it does feel like something. A doorway.

The woman's palms fall to her sides, arms open. There's a tattooed cursive word inside each forearm: *Believe*, on one; *Forever*, on the other.

From the slow regular breaths, there's a steep descent to a series of spaced-out and jagged ones. The skin of her eyelids is perfectly still. Her brain lets go of the thread. Her system loses interest fast.

Jasper calls it. 'She's dying.'

The woman's colour drops like a curtain.

'What happens now?' I ask.

'You sit with her. I'll wash the glasses and clean up so it doesn't look like she was entertaining.'

The death mask is never as pleasant as one would like. Fully at rest, the mouth and cheeks droop downward. She looks grave. I scan the wall of pictures, find a small, gold-framed Kodachrome of a little girl in an orchard full of bright orange apricots.

My phone hums. Lon's grinning face appears. I turn it off.

Lon. It's Friday night and I should be choosing the direction for our mystery drive. It's eight already. They would have been waiting so patiently.

Jasper reappears in the doorway. 'We can go.'

Walking out on a body and closing the door, leaving her flesh alone for hours or days, goes against my nursing instincts. And not knowing who's going to find her and if they've been set up for this jolt. It makes me want to call the police, but they are the reason we can't stay with the body until it's on its way for burying or burning. I suppose none of this matters to the corpse on the bed. I have an urge to add some ceremony to this breach—a warm goodbye, a thank you for the cookies. End of doorway. Nothing. I pull the door closed and that's it.

The candles in the living room have been blown out. The money that was on the speaker is gone.

Jasper leads me back through the hallway of movie posters. As pathetic as they were when we entered, they were at least loved.

At the front door, Jasper tells me that we leave one at a time as a precaution. Me first. She opens the door and sends me into the hall so quickly that it's only in the elevator that I begin to conceive of the frame-up. The slower the elevator travels the faster my mind works. That business about nobody monitoring their activities was a ruse. There's bits of me, digital and otherwise, all over this death. What did she put in my phone? What other evidence did she plant when she went to wash the glasses? My résumé makes me a perfect patsy. She gets the cash, I get the knock on the door from a detective.

The elevator stops on two.

A very old man in a tracksuit gets in, pulling an even older-looking beagle by a blue studded leash. At least the ride is short. I should have worn a hat. I suck in my mouth and tense my brow until I look like I've just come out of hibernation.

'It's so damn hot,' the man says.

I agree with a nod, refusing to leave a voice print.

'Ridiculous,' he adds.

I crack. 'Yeah.'

Outside, the guy drags his dog in the direction I'm intended for, which forces me to go the opposite way, circling the block and stalling in a side street until he's out of sight.

After two minutes of waiting at the appointed corner, expecting the police, I see Jasper step out of the building. She waves and walks over, nothing furtive in her manner at all. When she's still a few feet away, she calls out, 'You did just fine. Struck the right tone. How did you find it?'

'I didn't like walking out on her.'

'When do you let go of a body at the Mercy?'

'We'd transfer her to the morgue, who would transfer her to the funeral home.'

'And then? Everyone has to be alone at some point. This is what she wanted, how she wanted it.'

We're walking side by side at arm's length from each other and there's no hint of further feedback to come or any document-stamping to be done. Our entire contribution to that woman's peaceful exit was accepting her iced tea, eating her mother's biscuits and sitting on her bed.

'I didn't know there was payment involved,' I say.

'There can be. You and I share it with the group. This is volunteer work. If there's money it's distributed in a kind of honour system.'

'Is that legal?'

'Nothing we do is legal.'

'Is it ethical?'

'We don't ask for these gifts. People leave them to us.' Her hand goes to her pocket. She looks around before pulling out a thick fold of hundreds. She counts it as she talks. 'Twenty-two hundred. Very generous.' She recounts the bills as she divides it up. 'We'll each get seven hundred and the group will get eight. How does that sound?'

'It feels wrong somehow.'

'Tell me: what did the Mercy charge for your service?'

A fair question. 'Only accounting knows for sure.'

Jasper shakes her head. 'There you go.' She holds out my money. 'If you have difficulty accepting it, we can turn your portion over to the group.'

'No, I'll take my share,' I say.

For the first time since we met, for the first time all day I suspect, she glows, as if she's just won a bet with herself.

———

Lon doesn't answer his phone. Simon does. Lon's driving. I'm walking past the shuttered convention centre (*Sexpo!* next weekend) and they're already an hour away on the freeway. The apology I offer is based on Viv's mystery vacation of her own and 'changes' at my job. Simon tells me he understands.

'Where are you headed?'

'Don't know.'

'Should I try and catch up with you when you do?'

'Let's leave it for now.'

'I'm sorry,' I say again.

'We know,' he says, as if they've discovered a basic truth about me. I hang up and call Giulia.

'Twice!' she says. 'I am blessed. What is it this time?'

'I need forgiveness. I took Lon and Simon for granted.'

'Again, interesting choice calling me. Depending on the circumstances, I may not give it. Tell them you're sorry.'

'I did.'

'Well, I can't talk. I'm late to meet Dave. My only advice for you: don't be an arsehole. How's that? And call me again soon. Next time do it for no reason at all, like just to find out how I am.'

'You can call me too.'

'Nope. It's still your responsibility. Consider it penance.'

As soon as the phone is back in my pocket, it rings again. I hope that it's Lon, that they want me to take the next bus to meet them, that we'll spend a romantic weekend together, that I'll relax into it and live happily ever after.

It's Trish.

'Have you had any contact with your mother?'

'No. I told Joan that.'

'Do you know where she might be?'

170

'No idea. When she does this, it's her adventure.'

'There is a way that we can find her, as I believe Joan told you.'

This half-invitation dangles there, bringing a game-show quality to the conversation. Find out where Viv went or hold out for something else, which could turn out to be a pair of odd socks. The good son would choose Door Number One. Viv's son wouldn't. She turned off her phone for a reason. 'Do you mean the microchip?'

'Yes. It's a standard precaution we take with our residents—'

'—that she formally rejected.'

'Clearly there was miscommunication on this point. I've already filed an incident report. The procedure is so routine with new admissions that I can only think the doctor must have overlooked her paperwork, which is clear about her wishes. Part of the reason I'm calling you is to officially apologise. A written apology has also been sent to your mother, with information on how to have the chip removed and how to lodge a complaint. If you're of a mind to, I definitely encourage you to file your thoughts with us.'

'Whenever she's back, if she wants to give you her feelings, she will.'

'I'm sure of that. Meantime, I believe we're fortunate that we have the capacity to find her.'

'She's not missing. You discharged her. She's not your responsibility. And she's been clear with me that she's not mine.'

A slow breath. 'Actually, that chip is our property, which makes her whereabouts our responsibility,' Trish says.

'You're joking. Go get it out of her.'

'Because she's no longer a resident, we can't. You're her next of kin. You have to authorise the trace.'

'What?'

'The chip belongs to Willow Wood but we can't track it because it's inside a non-resident.'

'And this is your idea of privacy?'

'It's murky, I admit.'

'I'm not signing off on it.'

'We disagree on this, clearly. May I put this situation into a particular context?'

'Go right ahead.'

I hear her close her door. 'The day your mother left us, she told me she would never come back here. I told her that was fine, that it was what all of us were hoping for, that the deposit was just insurance for a few months. She assured me she wouldn't come back, because when she does relapse, you will get her right into the program at the Mercy.'

My insides shift. So much for Viv's discretion.

'What is your concern exactly?' I ask. 'That I didn't wait for her to relapse, that I got her admitted to the Mercy and had her euthanised this week?'

'That's not what I mean at all.'

And anyway, I want to tell her, *that was my old job. She wouldn't need special favours to get in where I work now*. What I say is: 'Then I don't understand this particular context you're putting it in.'

'Please. I actually voted for 961. I believe it should be a valid option for all.'

'It's great to hear that you're so supportive.'

'Evan. You have to understand how this rings alarms, especially with her missing like this.'

'She's not missing. Either you're accusing me of killing her or you're not. Which is it?'

'I'm sorry. I haven't expressed myself well.'

'No. You have.'

I hang up and try Viv. It goes to voicemail.

Guess I'm free for the weekend.

———

I find myself at the multiplex on Barkley Street, in a matinee.

A woman is biking across Russia—she's oblivious and healthy and, despite the known risks in her path, not specifically suicidal. A dust storm, some dodgy rice eaten in the home of a generous farming family, and three flat tyres in a row don't slow her down. A little ingenuity with electrical tape and she keeps going on her way.

Through my pocket, a bright blue J lights up my phone.

I slip out of the nearly empty cinema to take the call in the foyer. It's Jasper, the male one, with the offer of another visit.

'Busy time of year?'

'Yes,' he says.

Sixty-six-year-old social worker, recently retired because of worsening MS. Apparently his marriage hadn't been good for a decade plus. His forced retirement and decline in motor skills didn't improve things. Unlike Sanford, he would have liked her to stay. After twenty-two years together and no kids (couldn't), they divorced two years ago. At the time, she said she would still help out. In fact, she hasn't. The man could live another ten years like this, but he has no reason to. He wants to die today. Upshot: Am I free this afternoon?

Instilled with Mercy safeguards, I ask a series of questions. Jasper has no specifics on how disabled he is, if he's got friends, if he's got money, or if he's utilised all his social worker skills to see how he might eke out some meaning from his life. I keep to myself my need to make a psychosocial assessment. Instead, I say sure, skip the rest of the movie, and give the man a call. Since this organisation is so artisanal in its methods, my only intention is to have a chat.

There's music on in the background, piano. The guy rests the phone on a table while he opens a beer. 'I've got a system for doing this.' There's a minute of fumbling before I hear the pop and the fizz. Once he's back on the phone, he gives me some of the data I'm after, taking his time with it, lingering on his father's early death (mesothelioma), his wife blindsiding him with the divorce, and the disease. The story is told without tears, as though it were an inventory of clogs and rust and poor upkeep for a plumber to address. The only thing left is for me to come sit next to him while he takes it all apart. 'See you real soon,' he said. 'The door's unlocked. Let yourself in.'

From the cinema to his place involves one bus across the city and another down towards the train station. His place is a middle-income construction from the 1970s, a dingy box of white bricks with frayed edges. It overlooks a courtyard that's bald except for a few sturdy city trees. Entering the building, I briefly look into the glass eye of a security camera. It's a big building. No one's around on a Saturday afternoon. I could be anyone.

His apartment door is open.

'Hello?'

Nothing. The hallway is in need of a paint job. A framed poster of a museum painting—an open window, murky light falling on the glum scene of a man rocking one crying child in his arms while stirring a pot on the stove to feed another.

'Hello?'

In the next room, Louis Armstrong is blowing 'St James Infirmary'. I know it from one of Simon's playlists.

The place feels empty, as if robbers just left and forgot to take the stereo. In fact, I'm so sure he's already dead that when I come around the corner into the living room and see his body stretched out in the red leather recliner and the front of his head blown away from one side, I experience a brief pulse of satisfaction. That's right before running to the kitchen sink to throw up.

I keep my mouth close to the plughole to minimise splash. There's a cut-through window from the kitchen to the living room, enabling me, between bouts, to confirm what I saw. My first view was correct, except the recliner is beige. There are two more episodes of vomiting—the first represents the rest of the popcorn, still identifiable; then breakfast cereal, which has had a few hours to become pink and sludgy. I turn on both taps and wash it all away with my hands rather than use the sponge sitting neatly next to the tap.

There's a moment of silence and then the song starts again. The piano plinking amid the foggy noise of a nightclub eighty years ago. Some man's voice announces the song, then the trumpet starts all over again. Even if you're not suicidal, the music is grim. This must have been on repeat for the past hour.

I gag one more time over the drain. All that comes up is stomach acid.

Next to the sink in a little plastic baggie is the Nembutal. That was only his backup plan. Why did he bother with me?

But this wasn't about me. He couldn't wait.

I think about leaving, walking through the living room again and past what's left of him. It makes me push my face back into the sink, retching up nothing at all, holding my throat to keep quiet so the neighbours won't hear.

Very glad I didn't have the nachos at the movie.

I give the sink another clean, take five breaths, and head out to survey the room.

He dressed for today. Jeans with a pressed crease and an unrumpled denim shirt. His body looks flatter than the cushions he's lying on. His legs are splayed wide from the impact, with a piss sunset across his crotch. There's a wheelchair next to his chair.

I look at the head. A flesh toupee sits askew, resting against the top of the recliner. There's that, and a clean-shaven chin. That's all. Around him, meat and bone shrapnel has sprayed wide across the dark blue shag carpet, with a few flecks extending to the doorway. Another step forward and my feet would be in it. The gun is on the floor, just out of reach of his limp hand.

I am standing, transfixed by this scene. His last view, the picture window, looks across the courtyard to an identical building that lines up so evenly with this one I could believe there's a dead body in the opposite apartment.

The phone is on a table next to the recliner, with the half-drunk beer beside it. He told me how he'd made sure he would be found before 'the smell gets too strong'. An old friend, a paramedic who could be trusted not to flip out at the sight of a body, will be swinging by for an early visit tomorrow morning. Hope he's not expecting breakfast. The recommended eighteen-hour limit before planned discovery doesn't apply to a death from a seriously open wound.

The song starts again. *So cool, so sweet, so fair.* The song is firmly linked for me to Simon, who lectured us on its importance to Louis Armstrong's career and made us listen to every note of every version. Now what I'll think of and not be able to mention is a four-room apartment, cluttered with the junk the ex-wife didn't want, and a mangled corpse on a red and white recliner. He hung up the phone, heard the trumpet solo of doom, and reached for the gun.

A sealed envelope lies across the wide mouth of a repurposed mustard jar on the coffee table. *Sorry Mike!* is written on the front in shaky letters, suggesting more pep than in the usual suicide note. Decorum keeps me from opening it to see how you explain this scene to an old friend.

Thanks to the merciful powers that be, I am not expected to wash him. And that there's no family to console, no documentation to sign. The ex-wife will find out and integrate the information. Maybe he was a bastard. Maybe she was.

Poor Mike.

The sum total of this guy's treasures, he took the time to tell me, will go to a distant nephew who's just been through a divorce himself and is struggling with it. They were never close. He'll get a phone call, a registered letter. The money should help him out of a hole, he told me.

I let myself look at his head again. There's the hint of an eye.

To stave off my madness and sadness or the appearance of an irate neighbour, I power off the stereo with my knuckle.

Did anyone hear the gunshot? Are the police on their way?

It isn't until I go back to the kitchen to retrieve the Nembutal that I see the money. There are yellow tiles and an avocado fridge and oven, so the fat stack of fifties by the sink could have easily been missed. They are kept together by a post-it marked *Jasper*. A potentially damning loose end. I pocket it all, give an apologetic 'Goodbye' to the remains lying in the recliner, and go.

The female Jasper answers when I call. She offers to help me reflect on what's happened. I attempt to decline. My plan was to slip back into the next showing of the same movie, somewhere around Siberia, but she doesn't care. She insists on a teahouse midway between our locations. I need the support, it seems.

A wall of spotless, nearly empty glass shelves imparts an Asian flavour to a distinctly Caucasian establishment. Jasper's more relaxed today and orders a pot of Dragon Wing tea for us to share. On behalf of the organisation, she accepts five hundred dollars, half the cash he left, with a murmur of approval. She tucks it into a belt under her blouse as she glances around the cafe.

'Try not to take it hard about him jumping the gun,' she says, entirely without humour. She puts her hand on her chest. 'In here, he knew you were coming. That's where the goodness is.'

'Really, I'm okay. I've seen worse. I did a short stint in Emergency.' I didn't like it.

'Yes,' she says, glancing past me to an austere assortment of square teacakes. Apparently, the debrief is over. This meeting was just to collect the cash before I had too long to sit with it. I don't mention the Nembutal.

The tea arrives in a blue-and-white porcelain set. The steam smells like old pants.

'Who doesn't get your help?' I ask.

'We will talk to anybody. We're not in the business of rejection.'

'You're not in a business at all.' I eye her money belt.

'What are you asking?'

'For example, a man calls up. Middle of life and dreams are all gone. Nothing fatal, but he's lost his marriage, his kid, lost his job. Maybe he's moving back in with his parents. He's lost the plot. Lost the point. Lost.'

'That's situational. Our people self-select. Your man wouldn't contact us.' She smiles, showing teeth. 'Suicide, even the best-reasoned ones, causes ripples. The man you saw this afternoon didn't have anyone to fall back on.'

'So are people without anyone to fall back on more appropriate?'

'That's not what I said.' I'm ruining her tea.

'The man I just left was situational.'

'He had an active disease process that would not qualify for 961.'

'He was also sad.'

'Well, the man you described is a different case. He would not be for us, and if he called, we would tell him so.'

'To him, that might seem like one more rejection. One more reason to drive off a road.'

'What are you talking about?' she asks, suddenly giving me her full attention.

'Nothing. A hypothetical.'

The waiter comes back. Jasper orders a pistachio friand in a tone that suggests our dialogue is over. Despite a profoundly empty stomach, I don't order anything, though I'm not sure who I'm punishing.

Jasper's disdain for a man with my father's simple despair is not even what's troubling me. It's that Nettie was right about me. The dead man short-changed me on an essential level. The end result of this afternoon was what he wanted, but not what I wanted. I went to his apartment to talk, to support, and he only wanted me to make sure he was dead.

Nettie's aunt would be content that his goal was met, hop on her bicycle and pedal to the next stop.

Nausea. I want to leave.

Jasper asks a passing waiter for more hot water. Her top lip splits when she speaks, revealing a deep red line of blood tentatively held in by a thin film of skin that seems opaque in the red lantern light. She either doesn't feel it or it doesn't concern her, because she gives the waiter the same businesslike smile she gave me.

When he goes, she says, 'Frankly, it's a relief to have you with your experience and your questions. What usually happens is we

178

get volunteers who come in a thousand percent motivated and get absolutely rattled by their first death. I can tell you're going to be all right. I've got a sense about people.'

—

The person I would like to discuss Jasper's Path with is Viv. She would have questions about their porous filter for new 'friends' and their pay-what-you-wish business model. But she's not answering her phone and she's not home. I assume she's maintaining her blood pressure, or Trish would have called. The postcard says *I won't be gone long and you can get yourself settled elsewhere.* Finding this elsewhere should be high on my to-do list, but until she reappears, I will stay here. Without her, employment, or even Lon and Simon, I don't think I can put down a deposit on anything. I stock the refrigerator with bacon and eggs—for Saturday night dinner and Sunday breakfast. Changing the sheets gives me a last whiff of her violet perfume and tucking in the clean ones makes me feel right at home.

—

Lon finally answers his phone on Sunday night. At first he's monosyllabic, but he can't maintain it. I apologise some more, tell him my boss commandeered me on Friday. That there are funding struggles with my project.

'Come work with me,' he says. 'It's time you left that awful place.'

The money from the two Jasper jobs is stacked on the coffee table in front of me. 'No.'

'Then you should have been in the car with us,' he says. He told me they ended up in a cabin next to a campground where a school group was rehearsing *A Midsummer Night's Dream* by a lake. There were mosquitos. 'We had enough of a good time, but we were both pouting that you weren't there.'

I'm quiet. I've said I'm sorry three times already. As effective as apologising can be, limits are necessary.

'Anything from Viv?' Lon asks.

'Nope.'

'Aren't you even curious?'

'Yes, but she can do what she wants.'

'What is it with you two? Do you get points for neglecting each other?'

'Something like that.'

'So I suppose Simon and I should feel totally flattered you forgot about us.'

'I'm sorry,' I say again without thinking.

'We had that cabin to ourselves and didn't even have sex,' he says.

'That's my fault too?'

'Kind of.'

It's easy to picture them in a square wooden room, with shutters on the windows, crickets and moonlight outside. Theatrical teens frolicking nearby. And Lon and Simon, stretched out on the double bed, alone, wondering how they're expected to fuck, just the two of them.

I look at the stack of cash again. 'What if we take a room at Rabu for a few hours?'

'Don't you want to line up some new couple to keep you entertained?'

'No. I want a proper date. If we can get a room tonight, let's do it.'

After a muffled conversation with Simon and a laugh, he comes back on. 'We're touched. We accept your apology.'

―

The clerk at Rabu has an early-primate hair pattern that's been uniformly clipped with the number-one attachment over his head, down his neck, under his t-shirt and, one suspects, to his shoulders.

'You boys expecting anyone else tonight?'

I look left at Simon and right at Lon and tell the man *no*.

'Enjoy yourselves,' he says, handing over the key card.

We get up to our floor in time to hear a woman in the next room achieve epic completion. It takes an excruciating minute but we wait in the hallway until she gets there. Our mutual jealousy of the duration and power of female orgasms leads to a moment of silence before I swipe the card and open the door.

As the purist among us, Simon takes the first step in, breathing deeply. 'I get apple pie spice.'

'Better than the possible alternatives here,' Lon says, closing his eyes. 'There's more. I can sense the people who came before us.'

He waits a beat, until Simon says, 'Yes, we got it.'

Simon sneers at the way the bathroom wall leaves a corner of the room unusable. A pair of upholstered beige-and-blue-checked chairs are backed against the wall. 'Does anyone come here to sit?'

The murky lighting dulls a gash on the headboard. I pull back the paisley bedspread to inspect the white sheets. 'No specks, no stains. The field appears secure.'

Lon turns on the sound system. Bossa nova. 'At least they've got the music right.' He unpacks champagne from his backpack and rummages through the minibar. 'They only provide us with two glasses, naturally. How we are oppressed!' He goes to the bathroom and returns with a plastic cup.

I let myself fall back onto the mattress and try not to think about the woman on her bed with her dolls, the man in his red chair. That's not what this room is for.

Simon, standing near my legs, unbuttons his orange shirt. Lon gives him a look. 'Not yet.'

'Why not? I'm just getting comfortable.'

Lon, distributing glasses, tilts his head in my direction. 'The gentleman has paid for four hours here. Talk. Foreplay.'

Simon slinks out of his shirt, then tosses it onto my face. A whiff of the armpits activates my pleasure centres.

With one hand, he unbuttons his pants. They drop to the floor, too fast for a proper striptease, but the pear bulging in his white briefs and the museum-quality manliness of his legs make up for it.

Lon nudges Simon to speak.

'Now?' Simon leans over me, pinning my shoulders against the bed in an instant. I always forget how strong he is. 'Before anything happens, we need you to hear this: Lon and I talked about you this weekend. As you can imagine. Then we talked about you, in a different way, on the way over here. We want you to know, whatever you've got going on, at work, with your mum, we want you to stay over with us more often. We officially like having you around.'

I look down, notice a shift in the front of his underwear. The declaration of liking me caused blood to flow.

Lon pops the cork.

'Thank you,' I tell him. 'I like being had.'

Simon stands back up, turns sideways to show it off. 'Just wanted you to know how we feel.'

'Thank you,' I say again.

'"Thank you",' Lon mocks, as he pours champagne into two glasses and the plastic cup. 'Is that all you've got?'

'No.' I take the cup and raise it, tallying my previous and recent lies to them against how good they've been to me. 'Let's drink to it.'

'To what?' Lon asks, fishing.

Simon intervenes. 'Flux,' he says, raising his glass towards me. 'What you're in the middle of.'

'Flux,' I agree.

'Romantic.' Lon adds, 'Don't ever fucking stand us up again.'

I sit up so we can entwine our arms three ways to drink. It's awkward, but we get it done. Our faces stay close even afterwards.

Simon asks Lon, 'Did you bring the cashews?'

'No, did you?'

'So much for appetisers.'

With the first round down, an uncertain, datelike pause sets in. Lon pours another round, then strips. No underwear. With his arms folded and his half-hard dick draped coyly against one thigh, he leans against the wall at a flattering angle and just waits. He puts on his easy-going call boy face: *Aren't we here to have some fun?* All that has to happen is for me to invite him onto the bed.

Simon, who has wandered over to the desk, opens each drawer. 'Did they really need a writing table in here?'

Lon and I chide in unison, 'Simon.'

'Critiquing the room gives me scope to fully appreciate beauty.' He puts down his glass and jumps onto the bed next to me, takes my head in his hands and kisses me. I kiss back. He lets me overpower him and push him over onto the mattress, until I'm above him.

Lon reaches from behind me to take off my shirt. Simon works on my pants. They undress me with amazing speed and no resistance. I feel naked.

We are all on the bed. Lon smells like soap. I can see the scene at their place an hour ago: Lon saying they should shower first, Simon saying *No, let's just go*, Lon insisting, Simon waiting for him. It doesn't matter; in a few minutes we'll all smell like each other.

Simon scoops us into a circle, putting one hand on my neck and one on Lon's, holding us in his fond grip, like prizes. Lon attacks, kissing me. Undeterred, Simon takes the southern route.

There's a tricky balance of attractions when sleeping with couples, especially once you're acquainted with each other's skills and strengths. Tonight, enlivened by being at a hotel, it is a free-for-all at first, but leading to our trademarked daisy chain of blow jobs. Still, the lust feels lustier on a strange bed. Simon, usually the quiet one, and even with his mouth full, manages to grunt with porny gusto.

I catch sight of the three of us in the gold-flecked mirror on the ceiling—heads bobbing, palms kneading thighs, legs pushing for new positions. The view slows me down. Look at us. Even here, so careful with our positioning, so eager to please. Not one true pig among us. Lon's technique always seems to lead the way, skilfully matching friction with pace. He manages us both very well and we let ourselves be managed.

Simon and Lon notice my upward gaze and it slows them down too. Lon smiles at the mirror. 'Five dollars says there's a camera behind it feeding direct to the front desk.'

'Then let's keep his attention on us,' I say, forgetting my manners and climbing over them to grab both of their cocks and jam them into my mouth. There's a laugh at my clumsiness, a readjustment of arms around thighs, pulling harder than before. And then, up at the top end of the bed, the two of them give me sweet reciprocity.

Nursing journals frequently advise that a clinician with a challenging workload must make time for periods of self-care. This right here, no matter how it looks from above, is what they're talking about: a king-sized bed, the solidity of muscles, of arms and legs, their faces, each a bit lost in the current activity, all moving as one. And an indulgence of dicks.

'I want to fuck somebody,' Lon says, which means we're moving to the main event.

'Me too,' I quickly add, joining in our informal game of *Not It* that Simon always seems to lose.

After a bit of unobtrusive lubing with the gel they packed, Simon takes possession of the centre of the bed, gets up on his hands and knees—with his big shoulders squared and out, legs spread, arse tilted slightly upwards—and presents himself in the most manly, regal way I have ever seen. I need no more encouragement and get right there behind him, prodding and teasing and prodding and sliding home. He is audibly grateful, even saying my name. In another moment, I'm being prepped by Lon. His slight curvature seems to have been designed for this position and as soon as I am skewered I become Lucky Pierre. The practitioner—and the one practised upon—is both powerless and central to the act. Forget forgiveness. I'm where I'm supposed to be right now, between them. Thought stops.

Simon is propped up on one hand, jacking himself with an increasing tempo, and I reach around to stop him, putting both his hands over his head, which lands us forward, onto the mattress. The back half of him pumps harder. Lon's arms tighten around me and he lets himself fall, crushing me excellently. There's kissing. I can't seem to hold them close enough or drive any harder.

No one is in control. The motion tilts the tower on its side, with hands still on the hips in front of us, plugs still in sockets.

'Let's stay here for a while,' Lon says, breathing heavily and redistributing pillows so we can enjoy the ceiling view of the ebb and flow of brinkmanship. He slows it right down, threading his arms through mine till all four of our arms encircle Simon's furry chest. I have nothing to add. My throat gives out a guttural wheeze.

Lon revs into me, pushing me into Simon. He goes faster, making me do the same.

I try to hold still between them, but Simon's arse seems to yank me into forward motion. 'Slow,' is all I can say.

'No,' he tells me. He doesn't usually make demands, but now he pulls himself off me and rolls Lon and me over, so Lon is on his back and I'm on my back on Lon. Simon sits down on me, facing me, so he can stick his thick tongue down my throat. 'There,' he says, resuming speed.

I alternate between grinding up into him and falling back onto Lon as if he was a mechanical dildo.

Simon is jerking off, two-handed now, and I couldn't stop him if I wanted to. 'I'm close,' he says.

'I'm closer,' I manage.

Which is all Lon needs to hear.

Three money shots later, we separate onto our backs, just breathing. 'Not as loud as next door, but still,' he says.

Simon gives a long, appreciative, 'Ahh,' then says, 'I call the shower.' He wins that game too.

Lon and I are left alone, gazing at the mirror above. My mouth is open. Like Iris, dead in her bed. Like Viv, wherever she is tonight. Lon wraps an arm around my neck, almost cutting off my windpipe to get close and give me an extra kiss. He whispers in my ear, so close his stubble tickles, 'Do you know I love you?'

I pretend I'm too busy relaxing in the afterglow to have heard, shutting my eyes. How could he say that? I've had my back to him this whole time.

He rocks me until I open my eyes. He gets his face next to mine to say it once more in a regular voice, his skin shining bright in anticipation of words from me that don't come.

His expression fades a little. 'Sorry,' he says. 'It just came out.'

———

We try a pho place two blocks away that Simon likes, which brings the incandescent light of reality back onto us, along with the taste of chilli oil and coriander. A taxi back to their flat acknowledges the evening as a kind of date night. There's no smooth way for me not to go inside with them.

After I climb into my middle position in their bed, thinking resumes. That *I love you*. It's my fault. I should have taken Lon's suggestion and tried to find some strange tonight.

But this can be stopped. Whatever we've done physically has surely run its course. Tonight will be the end of it. The three of us will never get into bed together again. A few more excuses from me or a few more casual snubs and they'll give up on me. Or, better, I'll tell them what I've been doing with my days. I suspect that will be enough for them.

I cross my arms behind my head to survey this room for the last time. Simon takes it as a cue and cuddles up to my armpit. Lon is folding down the sheet to his exact specifications.

There's no need for a dramatic split. The next time I'm asked to sleep over, I'll politely decline. Just friends. With boundaries, not benefits. I won't even have to stay with my mother. With the next paycheque, I'll regain my independence.

''Night,' I say.

''Night.'

''Night.'

Peace of mind never arrives, starting with the fact that there is no next paycheque.

I'll pick up a few shifts at the Mercy.

I'll take Viv up on her offer of payback. Whenever she resurfaces.

I'll rent my own place.

This cycle of thought is repeated until 4 am, when I slide out of bed and take my phone to the living room. The little Tibetan carpet next to the terrarium has begun to feel like my early morning office.

I read nursing blogs—soothing stuff that breaks the cycle—losing myself in a recounting of the thankless miseries of a diabetes educator. *I spend hours coming up with meal plans for these people, which they ignore completely and still make the time to come back to see me.* I don't blame them. They want to stay oblivious and healthy at the same time. So many hopeless cases.

———

I come home and do nothing. I don't look for apartments or nursing shifts. I don't pick up when Lon calls. Viv doesn't call me. I am almost worried about the entire state of affairs, but it turns out that the cinema on Barkley doesn't check tickets if you go straight from one movie to another. I live on nachos.

On Wednesday, Jasper pulls through for distraction. 'This one may be a good fit,' the male one says. 'Not far off official protocol and not likely to have a gun.'

Old lady, recently widowed, with cardiac problems, colon cancer and new, painful bone metastases. Plenty of them, with sharp pains that she's describing to these non-clinicians as being ten out of ten in severity. The bad news is that because she's eighty-six, the cancer is moving slowly. The doctors give her eighteen to twenty-four months. Comfort measures aren't cutting it. There's no family she's interested in or interested in her. Her friends have all died or live in nursing homes. She's travelled for work, seen the world. 'I've had my turn.'

To spare her neighbours, she's taken a hotel room a little way out of the city at an anonymous resort. She's done her research. The place is old enough not to have cameras in the hallways, and the maids operate in pairs, so the discovery of her body won't be too upsetting.

On the phone with me, she's equally thoughtful. 'There are people going every which way through the lobby. No one will know who you are or where you're headed.'

We arrange for my 5 pm arrival. 'Do you have an idea of what you'll be doing until then?' I ask. I am not taking two buses and walking half a mile to find another corpse.

'I'll have my lunch and sit by the window here. I'll wait for you.'

———

The place is vaguely historical, early 1990s Tudor with a Ye Olde kind of sign over the restaurant that promises the best burger. For the elevator ride up to the Sunset floor, I am joined by a pair of tennis seniors, carrying their racquets in matching cases and wrangling a posse of similarly accessorised grandchildren. Once sporty grandma has shepherded them towards the front, she goes to work on me. 'You're indoors, you know. There's no need for the sunglasses.' She flashes a winning smile at her charges.

'Too true,' I say, jiggling them up and down while not actually removing them.

At the third floor the family piles off to a lecture about the rudeness of that man.

I'm all right with her disdain. The paramedics will be wheeling the body past her in the lobby and she'll turn to her husband and say, 'I knew there was something about that boy I didn't trust.' She'll put her hand straight up to be interviewed and the only detail she'll remember will be the sunglasses.

In shaded silence, I finish the ride up.

A used breakfast tray is the sole sign of human presence in the long hallway. Someone left their bacon.

The door to the corner suite is propped open with a pale blue chair cushion.

'Hello?' I call from the doorway.

Before I can re-experience the trauma of my previous unlocked door, a voice comes from deep inside. 'Is that you, Jasper?'

'Yes.'

'Come in. Close the door after you. I'll be right there.'

This suite occupies a corner turret, with an interlocking woodwork-patterned wallpaper along the ceiling, rounded windows everywhere, all looking out on the lake and parkland below. Past the boundary line of woods and over the far fence, I can see an idyllically curved meadow against a blue sky. Beyond that, the inevitable emblem of princely splendour, a golf course.

A grand desk is laid out neatly with a leather blotter and what looks like a farewell letter, with a thick envelope for Jasper right beside it. Occupying the centre of the opposite wall is a four-poster king-sized bed with gauze curtains blowing around, perfect for lying in state. The only people to suffer here will be the maids, and they probably see more dead bodies than I do.

She comes out of the bathroom, spryer than I would have expected, looking down as she buttons a cuff on her blouse, apologising for not greeting me at the door, blaming it on the hot water not being in a hurry to reach the top floor, and coming to a full stop when she sees my face and I see hers.

It's Myrna, with a fresh blond dye job.

She takes a step back and puts her hands to her mouth. 'I don't believe this.'

'Neither do I.'

'It was Evan, wasn't it?'

Bonus, she remembers my name. 'Yes.'

'Do you moonlight for these people?'

'You could say that.'

'Small world. You could have saved me a lot of trouble if you had told me that when we last met.'

'I didn't know you had cancer. That was never mentioned,' I say.

'Well, I do. Now, never mind who we are and what's happened before. You're here, and truthfully, I'm willing to put the past behind us because I know you can get the job done. I took my pain pills this morning. I took the anti-emetic half an hour ago. I'm as ready as I'm going to be.' She points to the note and envelope on the desk. 'For your organisation. You do good. The ATM only gave me hundreds. No one can trace those, can they?'

'No.'

'I wasn't certain. Now. Why don't you go make me a three-thousand-dollar drink?'

The glass, bottled water and Nembutal are lined up on the wooden bar cart. There's also a decanter of something that looks like sherry. I take advantage of the presence of a full ice bucket to cool down her glass, to dull the taste. I pick up the packet and give it a shake.

'I tested it with the kit your people suggest. Ten grams in there. They say you never know what you're getting.'

'No, you don't.' I dump the ice, pour in some water and swirl in the powder with a teaspoon. This woman doesn't need sarcasm, she needs support. 'That sounds impossibly hard—losing Leo and being sick yourself.'

'Thank you for understanding.'

It's an outrage that she has to thank me for this. What court would convict her for wanting to join him a few months before her time? Yes, her prognosis is too long for 961 guidelines, but who cares? 'I'm very glad I can help you now. I had no idea.'

'Don't worry. I wasn't your patient. You people didn't need to know. I took my treatments at St Anthony's so Leo wouldn't worry. And, pardon me for saying so, but Leo's glass seemed fuller.'

'Don't you worry. I can add water but it just makes more of it. If you can tolerate it at this strength, you can have some sherry right after.'

'Good to know.'

I mash the last clump to invisibility.

'Ready?' she asks.

'Ready.'

'Away we fly,' she says, taking it from my hand while the mixture is still spinning. With no ceremony or speeches, just a few gagging gulps, she drinks, then holds the empty glass out to me. 'The sherry, please.'

I pour her a shot. She accepts the puny offering with a wrinkled nose, and swishes it through her cheeks before swallowing and putting the glass back on the desk.

'Sweet boy, thank you for sitting with me for this. Seeing Leo go like he did, nice and quiet after all those miserable treatments— everyone should witness that, to see how easy it can be. I've seen so much worse. Ooh.' Her hands go to her head. 'It must be the sherry.'

'Do you want to sit?'

'Not until I have to.' She puffs in and out a few times, stretching her arms out. 'Should we have a bit of music?'

For a moment I imagine she'll flip on the same bossa nova station that they have at Rabu, further confusing my sex life. Instead she walks to the closet by the door and retrieves a violin case, which she lays on the bed and opens. The violin is the colour of almond skins, and fitted into the dark green velvet lining of the case like a newborn.

'You sit,' she tells me, pointing to one of a pair of high-backed easy chairs by the window. Button pillows on the seats and gold fringing. I turn one around so I'm facing her.

'How long do I have?' she asks.

'A few minutes, five, ten.'

'Ten,' she decides. 'How about Saint-Saëns?'

'What?'

'Saint-Saëns. Born in Paris, died in Algiers. Concerto in B minor. First movement.'

'Any special significance?'

'Yes. It's the one I've been practising. And it's less than ten minutes. Let's see how far I get. I don't know it perfectly. I'll just play it as it feels.'

Her hand tucks the violin above her clavicle, her face steadies and she begins. Suddenly there is a concert going on in here. 'The rooms on either side are empty,' she assures me, before I can even have a nervous thought.

The violin opens low and heavy, following a tune that's more menacing than melodic, which is then interrupted by a light-hearted variation of itself. This continues, the weighty alternating with the dreamy, elaborating in both directions at once.

The piece lightens further with some plucking, so light that Myrna smiles. She stops in the middle of a phrase. Holding the violin away from her and the bow against her chest, as if she was about to play the buttons on her blouse, she says, 'May I trust you with a secret?'

'Of course.'

'I don't have cancer.'

'What?'

'Healthy as a horse. Except that now I've swallowed that stuff.'

'No,' I say. 'We have to get you out of here.'

'I'm not finished playing the piece.'

It's been less than three minutes. In the hospital, I could call a code. Where we are, though, is at least a ten-minute drive from any facility that could intervene. She watches me realise all this.

'This is so fucked up.'

She taps me with the bow to chastise me for my language.

I say, 'Maybe we can get you help here?'

'What help? I drank the drink you made for me.'

She's right. There's nobody I could tell this story to. 'I wouldn't have done it.'

'It's illegal either way. I'm staying where I am.'

'You've involved me. I'm responsible.'

'No. You're innocent.' She looks victorious at her logic.

'This isn't what I came here to do,' I say.

'No? What did you come here for?' She frowns. 'You people think you can zoom in on skates to tell me when it's my turn to die. I'm a contented individual, not depressed, not suicidal. I'm taking control. I'm . . .' She looks at the ceiling as if she has all the time in the world to choose the right word. '—bereft is the right way to put it. Bereft. Leo is dead. The sight of old friends who are now that much older does not gladden my heart. So it's this ending, which is rational—or spend another evening alone, waiting for worse. No thank you. How about I sit down?'

She's got minutes left and I'm arguing with her.

'Yes, yes.' I jump up, desperately servile, dragging the other chair so it's adjacent to mine. She drops into it comfortably, placing the violin and bow on her lap.

'Sit down,' she tells me.

I do.

'I'm sorry to have upset you. I wouldn't have mentioned the truth to anyone else. You knew Leo, so I figured I could tell you. If it's any consolation, I would have done this anyway, alone. I wanted someone here.'

'It's all right, I understand,' I say, trying to.

'I was one of three sisters—I'm the last. My mother always told us to leave parties early.' She swallows twice, her fingers at her throat. 'I got the drug. You're only keeping me company. That's all you people do anyway.' She lowers her hand to her chest. 'I'm feeling woozy. In my tummy. Is that normal?'

'You might be getting tired,' I say.

'No, I'm expecting that. This is different.' She burps ominously, stands up and gingerly walks over to put the violin back in its case, steadying herself on furniture as she goes.

'Let me know if it gets more uncomfortable.' I try not to think about the torrent of trouble if she doesn't die.

'You'll be the first I tell.'

My fingers pat the spare packet of Nembutal in my shirt pocket.

She burps again and settles back into the chair. 'Maybe that's better.' Another burp. 'My peers get it. Not the God-botherers; no, the ones who have had enough doctors' visits. They're more open. You, you're at an age where your body still does what you expect of it.'

'Oblivious and healthy,' I offer.

'That's it!' She holds out one hand to me, which I take. Fingerprints be damned. 'So you see that this, right now, isn't the frightening part. Come closer,' she says, reaching further up my wrist to yank me closer.

I kneel next to her, awaiting cardiac failure. Hers or mine.

She pushes the corners of my lips up with her thumbs. 'Please smile for me. That's what you're here for. A young man's smile and all it doesn't know. I might have asked Lambros here instead of you. He's the social worker at our place. He would have been first choice if it had been legal to even broach the topic with him out loud. He and I have a history. A young one like you, good-looking. Married a girl he met on a bus—a short ride across the city, it was enough for them to know. Sat down with me the week after Leo was gone and asked what I was going to do now. He knew how Leo went. He never asked me, like the other idiots there did, if I was taking a class or booking a holiday to take my mind off things. He knew what I was planning and I knew he knew, we just couldn't discuss it. We were simpatico. An idiot would say we were married in another life or some nonsense like that. Whatever the case, I wasn't going to risk his employment. When I was leaving this morning—I told them I was bringing the violin into the city for a tuning and staying away for the night—I saw Lambros dashing through the dining room. There had been a death: fancy that. I don't think he even saw me going. He'll be fine.' She's assuring me. 'Just give me one smile, please, that's all I'm asking of you.'

I do, but it's a complicated one.

'I've been talking so much. Did Leo hang around this long? I don't—' The whoosh comes for her. She's losing focus. Her nails, opalescent and recently done, scratch lightly against the fabric of the chair, back and forth. She stares at the upholstered arm. 'Seems so sad now, every last thread of this . . . You ought to know—'

There's a gurgle, an abrupt unravelling of her neck muscles, the same ones that braced her violin for years. Her lungs relax what's left of the sentence she'll never finish. Whatever it is I ought to know escapes as '*pff*'.

All she has to do is finish the job, and over the next ten seconds she does, glazing to unconsciousness. I keep watch, ready for a deep autonomic gasp for oxygen that would roar her back, however briefly. It doesn't come.

Instead, her head slowly drops forward; then, after another bubble escapes her lips, the rest of her rolls forward, chin into chest, her forehead tilting towards her lap. She's unbalanced in the chair, sliding onto the edge of the cushion. My arm shoots out across her as though we're braking too fast at a light, but it doesn't stop the slide. Thinking of the nursing rule drilled into me by a dozen physios, *You can't catch a falling body*, I take my hand away and let her fall as she would if I weren't here. She jellies south, slipping off the cushion and landing on her knees. For a moment she teeters, upright, as if this will be her final pose. Then, with nothing to stop her, the muscles let go. She face-plants onto the carpet, the full weight of her falling body cracking her nose against the ground and forcing the last air out through her mouth.

Another *pff*.

I'm appalled to be part of this. I feel almost as sick as I did at the gunshot wound.

In another minute, she's stopped breathing. Her nose is flat. Her eyes will be blackening soon. Leo won't even recognise her.

The room looks like a perfect suicide scene. The body on the floor, the note on the desk.

I do what I'm here to do. I put the thick envelope in my pocket. I check the hall, which is thankfully still empty except for the breakfast trays. I shut the door behind me and go, taking out my sunglasses as I reach the elevators.

Should I have carried her to the bed with her broken nose? What would Lambros have done?

If there's a turndown service, the maids will find her tonight. Otherwise, not until the morning. Either way, her face will be so bruised from her fall and position that an open casket will be out of the question.

Wasn't there a niece somewhere? She'll get a phone call.

The charming cobblestone driveway from the hotel is long and lined with caring and observant staff. I call Giulia with the goal of acting natural as I pass this gauntlet—and of course to find out how she is.

In love, it turns out. She's finally told him so, after keeping him waiting for nearly a year. He's glad she took her time, though she assures him it is a word and not a condition, that the implementation will take some work. The fact that he's still hanging around after her lecture shows that he's willing to try. The conversation drifts to me, and since I've reached a leafy suburban street, I tell all. She strongly advises me to stop breaking the law, and to start answering Lon's calls. Also, she suggests I scope out the treasure chest to see if Viv has taken her passport. That would be reason to worry.

On the train ride home, I picture Lambros getting the news and not being as fine as Myrna assumed. Did he really know that this was the subtext of their conversations? Would he be relieved to know that she was already unconscious when she hit the carpet? Would he wish she'd stopped him this morning to say goodbye? Even if she didn't want it, was there more he could have done?

I go straight to the treasure chest. When I shake it, I can hear the sound of some stones and papers shuffling back and forth. The lock looks extremely pickable, though the lid might break in the process. I stare into the keyhole and remember Viv's twenty-year-old fatwa on my even touching this: *Locks have reasons all their own.*

Plan B.

Trish is so very relieved to hear my voice. 'I'll set up the trace right now. You can authorise this over the phone.'

Within minutes, I learn that Viv's location has been the same for the past forty-eight hours—that's all they can track—the town of Mead. It's a hiking mecca in the mountains three hours away. The beach was a lie.

The street view of her current spot shows a faded yellow rectangular motel with a row of evenly spaced log-cabin-style doors. There's a nominal lawn with a bright spinning kiddy platform that is probably no longer legal and two painted horsies on springs. Beyond that, ten parking spaces.

Viv's phone remains off. Even though she's alive, she's still not in the mood.

I call the Treeline Lodge. She's there.

The manager, who isn't the owner but might as well be because he's been behind the counter for so damn long, tells me, 'Checked in over a week ago. She took up every flyer we have on the local walks. The Chocolate Room, and the parachute people too. I saw her heading over to the restaurant across the street the first day she was here. Haven't heard a peep from her since.'

'Has anyone seen her?'

'Wouldn't know about the others. It's mainly me here. Wait, that's wrong—she did have a conversation with the housekeeper on the second morning. Asked her not to bother with the room while she's here.'

'Did she give a reason?'

'Said she'd keep the place clean herself. Promised her a big tip either way. My girl reported it all back to me because she's the honest type. We're at capacity most of the season, and this cleaner we've got says to me that since she doesn't have to do your mother's room, are there any other jobs I need done? Not like the locals, I'll tell you that. Czechoslovakian. She's after a husband and citizenship, in whatever order she can get, but they work like slaves. Do you believe it?'

'No.' I tell him I'm coming today.

'I could slip a note under her door to let her know. Make sure she's here to greet you.'

'That's all right. I'll surprise her.' I don't want her doing a runner.

'Is this going to be a giant drama?'

'No giant drama. I promise.'

I call Jasper, who proposes a hotel lobby for the meeting. No debrief this time. I just give her half the money and I go.

———

A small platoon of retirees, loaded up with daypacks on their backs and binoculars around their necks, have already taken over the seats near the front of the bus when I get on. In the rear, a grim middle-aged couple, attending to an oversized and apparently intellectually stunted teenage daughter, have spread themselves across four seats. They're across the aisle from the bathroom, possibly with good reason. I claim a pair of seats in the middle of the bus and stretch out as if I might sleep.

Once we've tunnelled our way out of the city and past the gauntlet of lower-tier shopping centres, we get to the rolling hills, which dip and crest in uneven rows all the way to the baking horizon.

A bread factory slams into close view, right next to the highway, red bricks blocking out everything else. Old-timey signage flies past, suggesting that inside there's a single baker hard at work, sinking his round fists into a mountainous ball of dough.

At the sight of the logo, I go *pff*.

The *pff* that ended Myrna's last lecture, the *pff* when her face hit the carpet.

The factory disappears, replaced by a nondescript refinery pumping out dirty smoke. Probably necessary for me to enjoy my standard of living.

Standard of living. The phrase makes no sense. Ask Myrna.

A trifecta of fast-food outlets, quaintly joined together under one corporate gable. *Pff*.

Near the front of the bus, one of the older men braces himself between the rows of seats to distribute sandwiches. He loses his balance, falling over an armrest with a hand landing on a woman's shoulder. She props him back up, laughing.

Pff.

The girl in the back row gets loud and incoherent, demanding a red wristwatch her mother forgot to pack.

Pff.

This trip.

Pff.

At the bus station I did follow Giulia's advice on one count by finally calling Lon back. I told him I was going to find Viv. He played it cool, told me to let them know when I get back.

Giulia's circumspect approach with Viv could have been the way to go, making sure she's at least in the country without violating her independence like this—and without giving Trish any satisfaction. But this doesn't break any locks. And so I find myself on an unrequested mercy mission for which I will most likely receive the opposite of gratitude. At this time tomorrow I will be stretched across these same seats, *pff*-ing at the other side of the road.

Summer has flattened the entire palette, drying out most of the greens, turning the soil to dust, and drawing a thick wall of haze down over everything. For a good half-minute we drive past an endless Christmas-tree farm. Each row of plantings is taller than the last, proceeding from the plastic-protected saplings, to the metal-staked teenagers, to the tall and the free. And, for several rows after them, in between, the inevitable fallow ground.

My operating theory has long been that, owing to prolonged exposure to my mother's unsteady enthusiasms, and the scarcity of imprinted memories left by my father—absent even when he was present, Viv likes to say—my genetic expression of fearlessness versus fear should skew my mother's way. If this were true, I would have bought a ticket for a different bus, going to the beach or the airport, where I could pull a Viv of my very own and leave all the good people behind.

But I didn't. And no one made me get on this bus, least of all Viv. I'm not here to prove my innocence to Trish or my motherlove to Lon. Maybe this is another escape—from my underground altruism, from sending out résumés for dull and legal shifts in another ward at the Mercy, from defining whatever it is Lon and Simon and I are up to.

If I can just see that she's all right, I will get on the next bus home.

Of course she will take this as proof that there is no free will and only parental influence, that I've got too much of Claude in me—I've got his grey goggles on and I'm worried.

Or we blame the Cuba Libres and I don't know any better.

In any case, I'll be there in half an hour.

One lane veers off to join a freeway and our road turns east towards the mountains. The roadside scenery scales down from the recognisable chain stores and car yards to the shabby one-of-a-kind places that made this nation great. An off-brand petrol station with a broken sign. A miniature golf course with a chipped blue octopus, its long tentacles cupping each of the eighteen holes. It looks easy.

I see Myrna, dead, her nose flattened against the carpet. Her face lingers outside the tinted bus window. Behind her, the octopus recedes into the landscape, keeping its goofy eyes on me. *Pff.*

———

The manager is watering daisies, but puts the plastic can down when he sees me, to bring me into the office with all the furtiveness of a spy.

'Perfect timing,' he whispers. 'About an hour ago, I walked over there to look at her rental car. There's a thin layer of dust on it. Could be from going into the park, but since it's here in the middle of fine weather, I thought it could be from staying still, like there's something wrong. So I knocked on the door. I don't hear anything. I was getting to think about coming back here for the master key when she finally answered. Not opening up, though, staying right in her room. Told me she was not presentable, but that she was okay. I made up some story about having to lay eyes on the room every few days—which the owners do prefer, although I don't believe she's in there tearing the place apart. She told me, sure, I was welcome to have a look, and then managed to put me off anyhow. Since I figured you were on your way, not a problem. I asked if I could bring over some kidney bean soup. I know the soup schedule across the road. Today is kidney bean. She agreed to that one, said to put it on her tab and to knock and leave it by the door.'

From beneath the counter he brings up a well-set tray with two packets of crackers, a cardboard cup of soup with the top still on, and a Coke bottle with a few cornflowers poking out. 'So when I said your turning up was great timing, I meant *perfect* timing.' He slides the tray over to me and shoos me down the concrete path towards Viv's door.

My knock is followed by a long pause and paper rustling.

'Is that the soup?'

'It's the soup and your son.'

'Evan. Everly.'

'Do you want to open up?'

'What are you doing here?'

'I'll tell you when you open up.'

'I can't. This doorknob. It's too round.'

'Bad day?'

'Yes. My hands. Who told you I was here?'

'No one. If you can't open the door, how were you planning to get the soup?'

'I want the soup.'

'How were you planning to get it if it was outside?'

'Don't fight me. It's been a slow morning.'

'I'll see if I can get a key.'

'Stop. I don't want more of his questions. We can figure this out. What are you here for?'

'I'm here to see how you are.'

'I'm glorious.'

'When was the last time you left the room?'

She gives me silence.

'I'm getting the key.'

'Did you bring anyone with you?'

'Like who?'

'Henchmen. I feel like this is a raid.'

'It's just me and the soup.'

'Tell me how you got here.'

'Bus.'

'I mean how you found me.'

'Not until I see you.'

'Then no.'

Time passes.

'I'm getting the key,' I tell her. 'We can talk, face to face.'

'You say.'

'You can have the soup.'

'Is it canned or real?'

I lift the lid. There's no point in lying. 'Looks canned, with extra greens floating in it for effect.'

'That's what I deserve. This room's a pigsty.'

'I'm getting the key.'

'I'll be here.'

'I know.'

The manager's been monitoring us from outside his office. He rushes over, holding out the key.

'I think she's just tired,' I tell him.

It's a bad scene in there. Viv's sitting in sweatpants in a vinyl chair that's been dragged to the centre of the room, roughly equidistant from the door, the bathroom and the television. Food wrappers, clothing and magazines are spread out in a smaller arm's-length orbit around her. There's a smear of blood from her left temple to her ear and a few more drops of blood encrusted on her t-shirt, as well as some dark brown food stains. She smiles. The front teeth that were replaced after the fall down the stairs, gleam. The others don't.

I put the soup tray down on the night table on the far side of the bed, the only clear surface in the room, and then go back and lean in for a hug, which she tolerates.

'What do you think?' she asks. 'This room is good for my purposes. The air-conditioning has one setting—freezing. I shut it off because the temperature has been mild today, but the windows are too heavy to open.'

'You're bleeding.'

She touches the side of her head. 'That's dry. It's from the other day. You should have seen me. Not when I slipped, but the rest of it. I found a shortcut along a creek bed.' She holds out her hands, illustrating the leaping with her fists. 'Rock to rock to rock. And the last one was slippery.'

'And now you're here?'

'I overdid it for two days. I've been resting since. So peaceful at this place. No demands. Let's see that soup.'

Full concentration is required for her to steady the cup with her hands. She sniffs the plastic lid. 'Smells all right.'

'Do you want me to take that off for you?'

She nods. I take off the lid and give the cup back to her. She sips from it quickly.

'What have you been doing for food?'

She tilts her head towards a pile of menus on a phone table. 'They all deliver. There's decent Indian here. Imagine.'

'And since when can't you turn the knob?'

'A towel worked last night. I was motivated: fried clams. Not that we're anywhere near the ocean. Frozen, but they hit the spot.'

'Maybe it wasn't so good for you to go off the grid.'

'I didn't get far enough. How did you find me?'

'It's unimportant.'

'Oh,' she says, returning her focus to the soup.

I pull back the curtains and open the window. The manager is still lurking at the edge of the walkway. I wave for him to stand down.

'Look at that stunning afternoon,' she says, sipping the soup.

Across the street is a row of shops, with awnings, flower pots in front, an even strip of blue agapanthus separating the pavement from the road. Behind the shops, a wall of forest going up to the hills.

'Some beach,' I say.

'I changed my mind. I can still do that.'

'I know,' I say. 'How did you even find this place?'

'Don't you remember? We stayed here before. With Claude. You were too young.'

'Right here?'

'Right here,' she says. 'Just for one night, to get us organised. Then we camped in the park for the rest of the week. We hiked every day. You and your father caught two fish.'

I have a quick vision of us together, in shorts and sun visors, scrambling after a fish that's flopping all over the bottom of a painted rowboat. An invented memory.

'And you wanted to re-create this trip on your own?' I ask.

'I wanted to see what it would be like now. There's a tent and a sleeping bag in the car. I was going to go to the beach after this.'

'No casinos?'

'Why do I need to go to those places anymore? I want to be outside.'

'Anything else on the itinerary?'

'No itinerary.' She laughs a little. 'Which turns out to be for the best, doesn't it? Your father made a whole list. I brought it with me.' She points to a yellowed piece of paper unfolded on the coffee table. It's my father's writing—a sober list of camping supplies. 'I didn't make it that far.'

'You kept his list all these years?'

'In the little chest. I thought it could be useful someday. If I were feeling more able-bodied, it would be.'

'Why didn't you ask me to come with you?'

'You don't even remember this place. It has nothing to do with you.'

'It absolutely does,' I say in the calmest voice I can manage.

'Did you come here to argue?' After three false starts she hurls herself forward, resting her wrists on the arms of the chair, and pushing up onto her feet. 'Come. Let's go have a look at the park before the sun goes down.'

She uses her palms to hitch up the elastic band of her pants, outlining the shape of an incontinence pad. She sees me see it. 'I'm wearing a fresh one, if it's any of your business. Car keys are in my purse.' Holding onto the back of the chair, the desk and the wall, she trudges towards the door.

'Ah, I brought this for you.' I offer a white tablet, a steroid, from the bottom of my pocket. I put it in her palm.

Recognising an old friend, she swallows it down with a sip from an open bottle of apple juice that was sitting on the desk. 'That will give me some oomph.'

It takes her a long moment to get started again, but she does. Slowly she leaves the room, hugging the wall on either side of the doorway, lowering herself down the small step to the paved path outside, one foot at a time.

There's a long paved walkway around the playground to the car. Viv takes the shortcut, despite the uneven ground, pretending she's patting the rocking horses on their heads as she uses them to stay upright.

'You played on these once,' she tells me, as if it's nothing. The horses, though, with their come-hither eyelashes and their toothy grins, give me a nod of recognition in the breeze.

At the car, Viv lets herself collapse onto the bonnet with an exhausted thump. She laughs. 'Do you mind if I don't drive?'

'No problem.'

She props herself along the passenger side of the car until she reaches the door. I open it for her. With a conscientious turn to aim her butt towards the seat, she lowers herself in, dragging in her legs one at a time.

When I get to the driver's side, she's still struggling with her seatbelt. 'These fingers—'

I click it and straighten the strap across her chest.

'Good. Good to be outside.' She peers up into the rear-view mirror. 'You could have had me wash my face.' She manages to yank the door closed. 'Forget it. Drive.'

—

Conversation sticks to the roads we're on and the magnificent sunlight beaming down on them. An old apple orchard covered with lichen, a pair of jet skiers ruining the view of a lake, the irony of an entire family of trail walkers eating potato chips by the side of the road. Each sign we pass is read out loud, with special commentary given to towns with funny names. There will be no discussion of frailty or a call to Marais. She directs every turn as if she's lived there for years, advising me how to signal, how to drive into the park, and how to buy a day pass.

I drop her off where she tells me to, at the start of the trail. She gets out of the car quicker than she got in, and slams the door. By the time I park and meet up with her, she has made the dozen steps to the main board with the map of the trails.

'Claude had us take the Beech Tops Trail,' she says. It's a ring of mountain ridges that circles the park, graded as moderate and taking three to four days. There's a lake in one corner of the loop, where Dad and I must have caught the fish. I imagine their orphaned spawn, long dead.

Viv puts her finger in the middle of the green expanse on the edge of the map. 'That's where we camped. Just the three of us. Oh well. Let's try the Discovery Loop. Says it takes an hour, so let's give me two.'

The families with kids young enough for this walk have already left for the day. This trail is paved and level, winding around a dozen blue markers that explain what makes this forest special. Viv finds her pace here, taking time to read each sign aloud, more for a rest than out of genuine interest.

The sun slips behind a ridge and the temperature drops a little. The grass at the bottom of the hill has gone the dark green of long hot summer.

'Do you remember any of this trip?' she asks.

'No.'

'See?'

'At least I went fishing with Dad.'

'And what good is that to you now?' She moves to the centre of the trail, either to edge me out or to seek solitude for her walk. I stay a few paces behind. As pleased with myself as I am for making the trip here, she's only letting me accompany her because she is so much weaker than before. She would be happier alone.

The woods make their own silence, only broken by a flock of birds gathering on branches nearby to discuss supper. Viv stops where the trail touches a turnoff to a dirt track that dips down around a large boulder and disappears.

'Won't know unless we try,' I say.

She peers at the rocky path. 'I may need a hand getting back. I *will* need a hand.'

'I can offer that.'

'You should have shown up the other day. I was faster.'

'I wasn't invited.'

'You weren't invited today. Was it the rental car people that tracked me down?'

'No.'

The track gets steeper, distracting her, making her hold onto every branch. Her grip is better, though, as she precariously swings from one tree to the next as she makes her way down the hill.

An old man coming up from below using walking poles steps off the track for her to pass. 'You two'll be the last ones there,' he tells her.

She smiles, not taking her eyes off the track, as if one wrong word and this winning streak will be over.

The path levels off at a valley—a small patch of lush meadow. She looks back, breathless, at what she's done.

'Is the tent in the car?' I ask.

'Yes. Why?'

'Do you want to stay here tonight?'

She closes her eyes. 'You're humouring me.'

'Let me. I'll get it and bring it here. And some food. You can camp.'

'No,' she says. 'It was an absurd plan.'

'It's not. I'll go back to the motel. You've got the strength now. You can have a night here.'

A branch snaps at the edge of the meadow. We both look up in time to see the back of a rabbit running away.

'No. You won't be able to tolerate that fool of a manager there. We'll stay together,' Viv says. 'There's a camping store on the main street. Pick up another sleeping bag.'

'That means sharing a tent. Isn't that a little close for you?'

'You caught me feeling maternal.'

'Okay. You scout for a site and I'll get what we need.'

'Are you aware that the official campsite is up by the parking area?' she asks.

'You can find us a better deal out here, I'm sure.'

She steps off the trail to rest against a tree and lets me switch on her phone so I can find her when I come back. 'What if I have a fall while you're gone?'

'What if you do?'

'I'll either get back up or I'll stay down.'

———

The boot of the car has been stocked with most of the necessaries for an overnighter, including Coke, rum and lime—straight from Dad's list. There's no ice, but it will do.

Two stops along the town's main street provide the rest—a sleeping bag, a roast chicken and an extra cup for my Cuba Libre.

Outside the chicken place, I call Trish and then Lon. 'She's her old self,' I tell them both.

No need for specifics.

———

By the time I follow the trail back down to the valley, a wind starts coming through and the temperature dips further. No sign of Viv.

The third time I call she manages to answer the phone. There's the sound of her dropping and retrieving it, but eventually she's able to speak, almost breathless with excitement. The meadow was too damp for overnight. She found a level clearing just up from it. She can hear the wind through the trees. A dragonfly landed on her elbow. I should take my time.

Once I'm in the meadow I call to her, following her voice through a density of twiggy bushes. She's sitting on the ground with her back against a beech, her knees pulled up to her chest, peacefully festooned with leaves and twigs from her efforts.

I brush her off and wrap her in her jacket. She's proud of the site. No rocks, no roots, and there's a trickle of waterfall somewhere close by.

I pitch the tent while she watches. 'Last time it was you sitting around while Claude and I set up camp. You know you're on your way out when your children start doing things for you.'

'Cocktail?'

'Why not?'

She's able to hold her drink with one hand. The steroid is working. I don't mention it. We wrap ourselves in sleeping bags and sit in respectful, wordless communion with the night coming on. I'm glad to be here, but for her sake, I wish she were by herself.

The birds have given over their part in the evening chorus to the crickets and the frogs. Just as the wind started, it stops. The trees and even the sound of the creek fade to quiet.

I forgot paper plates, so we cover ourselves with napkins and eat the chicken over the foil bag between us. A last blackbird at the base of a rock hops over to watch us sternly.

Viv returns the look. 'That one is going to narc us out to the ranger.' The bird flies away. 'Even if it does, my opinion is that this was worth it.' She grips a piece of chicken in her fist like a child, holding it away from her mouth to say, 'Everybody at the campground wishes they were right here with us.'

I wake up to the flicker of summer lightning. Another flash exposes the inside of the tent. There's just enough light to see that Viv is on her side, facing me. 'Good morning,' I say. 'Smells like roast chicken in here.'

She grunts. 'It's three am.'

'Is that the sound of rain or waterfall?' I ask.

'Don't know.'

More silent lightning. I unzip the flap to look out at the sky. 'No rain coming,' I say. 'A few stars. Now that you've told me I've been here before, I'm filling myself up with false memories of the three of us. When we were here was there a meteor shower?'

'I don't remember.'

'What if I do?'

'Can you cut it out?' she says.

'What?'

'Pretending everything is hunky-dory.'

'What? It's summer lightning. Are you mad because I'm here?'

'I wish. I'm mad because I've peed.'

'Oh.'

'No warning even,' she says.

'Well, we can blame the sound of the creek.'

'Just stop.'

'I'm sorry.'

'Whatever energy it was that got me down here is gone.'

'I don't have another pill. I didn't know how you'd be or what you'd want.'

'Did you happen to bring a spare pad?'

'No,' I say.

'Me neither. I didn't think. Claude would have.' She puts her hands over her face. 'I hate this. Not just the pad. Needing you. I hate it. I can't pretend it's going to change. This is how it's going to be.'

Fake cheer won't help. 'I don't mind,' I tell her.

'I do, and I still get a vote,' she says. 'I'm not falling back to sleep, wet like this.'

'I'll keep you company.'

With a twist she manages to turn herself to face the vaulted roof of the tent. 'Okay, keep me company.'

'Give me a topic.'

'Tell me how you found me.'

'How about a different topic?' I say.

'No, I like this one. How?'

'All right. It was Willow Wood.'

She holds up her hands, mystified. 'I didn't leave them a clue.'

'They microchipped you. On admission.'

'They didn't. We had that whole conference about it.'

'They did it anyway.'

She gasps. 'Under my skin? That is such a profound violation.'

'It is. They're very sorry. Admin error, they say.'

'It wasn't an error.' She rubs her hands over her upper arms to find the chip. 'I don't feel a thing.'

'They inject deeper than that.'

She slaps at her arms. 'Get it out of me.'

I put my hand over hers to calm her, which only makes her claw at herself harder. 'If it's any comfort,' I say, 'Trish couldn't legally track you until I gave my approval.'

She goes still. 'So then you gave them *your* approval?'

'I wanted to know where you were.'

As much as is possible in a two-person tent, she backs away from me. 'Why on earth?'

'Because you're my mother. Because you'd gone off without warning.'

'But I left you that note.'

'It took me a few days to even find it. When I got here you couldn't even open the door by yourself.'

'That's my problem, isn't it?'

'Is it so bad that I came?'

211

'Yes, it is. Very bad.' She pushes her head back against the ground and twitches her feet. 'Is there some line I forgot to sign to keep me from being branded and watched so you all know where I am, or if I'm hydrated, or if I'm playing too close to my limit?'

'I'm sorry I came. I should have just believed what you wrote on the postcard.'

She says nothing.

We can go right now. I can help her up the hill. We've left places in the middle of the night before, packing up much more stuff than this.

'You know Claude left a note,' she says.

'You said he didn't.'

'It came by mail, a day after the accident.'

The alternate histories I've fabricated suddenly roll out in all directions—the quick decision on a sad night; the hidden dark side of himself that he couldn't bear; the money trouble he had to protect us from. Or this one, from when I was six: he possessed a map to a secret, wonderful place, a map that Bad People killed him for. For an instant I wonder if he was foolish enough to send the precious map through the mail to her.

'I guess we can stop calling it an accident then,' I say.

Viv laughs a little.

More lightning. 'Ooh,' she says. 'Dramatic.'

In the dim light, I see her close her eyes.

'Wait. Is that the whole story?' I ask.

She opens them. 'Claude was a very depressed individual. It wasn't a note I was about to put aside for you.'

'Why are you telling me this?'

'He had a few words for you. He said, "I hope Evan can find something—anything—and stick with it and be happy with it."'

'That's his wisdom?'

Viv rolls back on to her side. 'That's not nothing. God knows he never managed it.' She nods her head at me. 'And I'm not so sure about you, either.'

'Meaning?'

'Meaning I've no clue why you've hunted me down like this. You should be out saving the world or saving yourself. What about graduate school, for instance? Willow Wood still has the deposit, you can use that money for something worthwhile.'

There's a pause for digestion of the fact that that deposit will be needed again, soon.

'I wanted to be here,' I say. 'With you. For you. If you need it. If you'll accept it.'

Viv reaches up and taps my chin. 'That's Claude talking. That hanging on. That didn't work out too well for him, did it?'

Dad is suddenly crammed into this tent with us. Our sad family.

'You ought to leave me here,' she says, tracing her other hand back and forth along the top of the tent. 'At least it's quiet.'

'Trish would be real fine with that.'

'Trish. Abandoning me to the insects and the weather would be preferable to sending me back there. That's my nightmare. I bet Trish has a care plan on file for when I get back. With any luck, they'll change me twice a shift.'

'Better than here.'

'Clean and dry. That's the baseline. They'll park me in front of the TV seven hours a day. The best thing you'll be able to say about me is that I don't have bedsores. Kill me now.'

'You won't go back there. You're not helpless. Let me take you home and we'll see how it goes.'

'Sounds fun.'

'I want to.'

In the darkness of the tent, her eyes glistening with what I may be mistaking for gratitude, she says, 'Why on earth would you want any part of that? I promise you, this is not the part where I suddenly start to shine.'

HEROICS

VIV SAID AS little as possible for the long slog back up the hill to the car, even less for the ride back to the hotel, and then home and the slow climb up the stairs to her apartment, where she declined more steroids and their stupid illusions and just let me help her into bed.

Three days later we were in Marais's office. After tinkering with her implant, making her endure another round of tests ('Pick up the fork. Bring it to your mouth') and locking her in position for a new set of scans, he closed the door and admitted to Viv, with a regretful sloping of his bushy brows, that he was out of ideas.

'Life is going to get harder. Plan for that. It may be slow. It may happen quickly. We don't know.'

'Does she get a choice?' I asked. No one laughed.

'Unfortunately, no,' Marais said.

Viv, her movements and thoughts and voice fully bogged, whether from the recent deterioration, from the morning of tests or from this news, said to him, 'So, you're breaking up with me?'

'There's no mincing words with you, Vivian, is there?'

'I'm not saying what's really on my mind.'

Since the visit to Marais, Viv has left the building once—to go with me to the bank to make me a signatory on her accounts again. Other than that, contact with the outside world has been minimal.

To keep the OT away she claimed a head cold.

Trish said she'd drop by. Viv put that off too. When the well-meaning calls from Willow Wood became too intrusive, she emailed her request for a copy of the disclaimer she'd signed declining the insertion of a granny tracker. That bought her a few days' respite.

The apartment is filling up with cleaning supplies and incontinence products. Her whole life is confined to the triangle between the couch, her bed and the bathroom.

In the morning, I orient her and get her moving. Mainly she needs the initial push, vital items laid out for her—sweatpants and t-shirt; bowl, spoon and mug—and some supplies in the fridge. Regular steroids provide the energy required to make her own lunch and use the telephone.

She says she doesn't have any interest in the internet or online games. 'I wouldn't even trust myself.'

In the evening, after I've got her back to bed, I take the cushions off the couch and make it up with sheets. Sleep has become a spectrum kind of thing around here. Some nights she'll make it to the bathroom and need help getting back to bed. Or she'll be in the hallway, standing there and not knowing why. Some nights it's hard to say if either of us have slept.

After she's dictated the day's shopping list, she reminds me not to plan my life around her. But she's practising thankfulness. She appreciates every fork I hand her and makes me come to her for a kiss before I go out the door.

I finally register with the Mercy, assure them I'm psychologically recovered from the traumas of the job with Nettie, and list my availability for working in Renal, Orthopaedics or Respiratory. That work is mechanical and painless. The patients come and they go, with minimal emotional drama.

The second time I turn up to work on the Renal ward, Lena is there, amused to see me. A patient is being hooked up right in front of her. 'What brings you here?' she asks.

'I'm here to assist with patient transfers and management during rush hour,' I say.

Not the details she was after. 'Welcome aboard,' she says.

We barely see each other again during that shift, but the next time we work together, she takes me aside after handover and whispers to me, 'Come to me with any questions about this ward. Do not trust Michelle under any circumstances.' I feel welcomed. We never discuss Nettie or the program, none of it.

I make myself a regular on the other wards too. Saying yes to a few shifts pays the bills and keeps the Mercy offering me more. That's the extent of my self-care: I don't take any assignments in Psychiatry, Oncology or Palliative. I don't call the Jaspers and they don't call me. We seem to be taking a breather. Or there's an autumnal lull in planned deaths. Whatever the case, there's work at the Mercy, and that's enough. Fourteen more years and there'll be a fat pension waiting for me. Ha ha.

If I'm away for a chunk of time that roughly corresponds to business hours, Viv accepts that I've been at the hospital. When I don't get a shift, I maintain my mental health by reading in the park until the end of a theoretical workday. Nursing journals—as dry and emotionless as I can find them—to keep up my skills for when I go back to full-time.

Or, I'll see movies, usually thrillers with an emotional hook. A black-ops assassin who's only in the game because her first husband was killed. A newlywed's amnesia that can only be resolved by killing the bad guy and saving the government. A race against a ticking bomb to find a kidnapped child in the middle of a country on the verge of civil war. I begin keeping a tally of old or dying characters. The few that are there aren't big players. They may be able to recall a key code, and once they do, the movie discards them. If the character is sick and curable, it's usually a kid desperate for a kidney or a liver. If it's an adult, they inevitably want a heart. The kids usually get what they need in time. The adults, only sometimes. In the end, there's the payoff—a reunion, a romance, a newborn crying amid the carnage of an alien battlefield. These stories never did anything for me before, but now I can sit in a nearly empty afternoon cinema and cry right through the credits. Something about the hope in those scenes. Something about Viv being so sick that she's letting me take care of her.

Giulia says it's anticipatory mourning.

One night Viv tries to teach me five-card draw, the game my father started her on. We play side by side, with a couch cushion between us as a tabletop. She takes control of both our hands to tell me how the game works, but freezes before we get far.

Viv is my excuse for not sleeping over with Lon and Simon. Truthfully, sex—solo, duo or triad—has not been high on my to-do list. Still, Lon offers to look in on Viv on his days off. She turns that down too, along with his plans to get other help in here—at least some rehab for her, some cleaning for me. Viv doesn't want it and neither do I.

—

On a side street not far from my preferred megaplex is an organic cafe. The place is staffed by a commune of fresh-faced adults, dazedly cooking with miso and inventing combinations of juices. They serve up every dish with eye contact so intense it's practically narcotic. At the cash register, their grizzled leader watches his flock with steady attention. They all live together in a building close by. It's easy to speculate about his rough restrictions on their education, their limited contact with the outside world, and his lurid nightly demands. There's also a potential child labour question, particularly with regard to one young girl who clears the tables. In fact, they all look happy, healthy and beyond oblivious. They have no unscripted moments ahead. Hence the painless gaze.

When delivering my sprout salad one afternoon, a woman wearing the same grey smock as her brethren, with French plaits up in a bun, asks me if I'm all right. At first I think she's too quick to be assessing my satisfaction with the salad, but then realise that my cheeks are still damp from the movie I just saw. The last scene was a street corner reunion between an old woman and a young boy, each five years older than they were in the first scene—before war broke out, before the boy went into hiding and the old woman risked her life to save her son, before everyone else in their lives died (including the boy's parents and her son). Despite literally impossible odds, and with unlikely physical stamina, they each crawl out of the rubble towards the ruins of the same grocery store where she used to give him treats—glimpsed in flashback, for the forgetful. Together, they are broken and yet emotionally whole.

'A sad movie,' I explain to my stoned waitress.

She nods. 'Would you want to come back after six? You could hear what we're really about.'

She knows a mark when she sees one. For a genuine moment I imagine coming back after six for the full indoctrination—lining up by our bunk beds at night, saying prayers, pulling back our covers in unison, bedding down sinlessly, and waking up feeling balanced and sure of our responsibilities and able to cooperate all day long, maintaining an even buzz of productivity and deference to a greater good than our own selfish needs.

I look at the waitress. Her eyes might as well be marbles.

'No, thanks. But I will try the carrot cake.'

———

I'm on a bench in the park one afternoon, reading about fungating tumours, when Nettie jogs up. Blue leggings, blue shirt, and an expression that's impossible to decipher. She comes to a stop in front of me with a solemn bow. 'I've been looking for you here for a week.'

'You know how to reach me.'

'This is for face to face,' she says.

I close the journal and fold my hands, braced for it. 'Are you recording this?'

'No. It's Sanford.' My mind runs fast to some ugly scenarios before she says, 'You're in the will.' My mind goes to some spectacular places before she clarifies. 'Specifically, your job. He's funded it for five years. The funding only comes if you're in the position.'

'What?'

'I am offering you your job back. Your last job. Assisting.'

'That makes zero sense. He would have had to have added me after our first meeting. I didn't even impress him.'

'Well, he saw potential.'

'Do you want me back there? Is this because HR blocked you from hiring my replacement?'

'They're not hurrying it along, I'll say that. But I've soul-searched over this. You wouldn't have been there for him if you didn't have the heart for the work. And that's necessary. As Sanford was privileged enough to discover.'

'Thank you.'

'You're welcome,' she says. Her expression tells me nothing about what the outcome of this benchside visit might mean to her. Why should it? It's only a job.

'My answer is that I'm not sure. I've been taking odd shifts at the Mercy.'

'I know.'

'And I've been helping out with Jasper's Path.'

She's unmoved. 'Makes sense. I did my time with them.'

I'm so grateful for the confession that I don't bother trying to act surprised. 'Oh,' is the best I can do.

'They were too far out on the frontier for me. I shudder to think what they're up to now. Are they free-form enough for you?'

'Yes and no. I've done some visits, but . . . complicated. My mum's home now, worse than she was, and needing me more. She doesn't want to go back to Willow Wood.'

'And how's Evan doing?' Nettie asks.

'Okay. Thanks.'

'Life,' she says, putting a kindly hand on my shoulder. 'Sounds like you have enough to think about. The job with me is yours if you want it, and not just because you're already paid for.'

'Good to know.'

'See how you feel. Last I heard, the Jasper's Path position doesn't come with benefits.'

She holds up her hands in a two-gun salute, gives me a smile, and jogs back in the direction she came from, leaving me only with a possibility.

I preferred the brief moment when I thought I'd inherited a million dollars, free and clear.

———

That night, Lon rings from downstairs. In the fish-eye of the security camera, he holds up a blue enamel casserole dish. 'I've got a curry here that won't take no for an answer.'

'Lon's coming up,' I tell Viv, who gives a short-range shrug as I buzz him in.

I survey the place, tidying madly. A pop inspection by a nurse can reveal a thousand breaches. For several weeks we've resisted outsiders, slumping into a mutually agreeable level of squalor, with most activity centring around the coffee table in front of the couch. Tonight we've shared a bowl of gnocchi, which have proven, one by one, way too ambitious for her to swallow. The pasta sits half eaten with a fork sticking out of it. A sippy cup of red wine is lodged between two couch cushions.

Family Ties is on TV. Neither of us is watching. Viv's eyes brighten at my panic in anticipation of Lon.

He's at the door. She raises her hand an inch from her lap to point to my shirt. A sauce stain.

Lon brings the cheer. 'Finally: admittance.' He notices my shirt and doesn't say anything, going directly to Viv, who remains statue-like on the sofa for his embrace. 'I would have come earlier, but your son prefers to compartmentalise.'

Having him here makes our situation real. When he lets go, she falls back against the cushion.

She nods as he talks about the weather, Willow Wood and being allowed into the apartment, but it's not clear if she's listening. It's not clear if he is either. He berates us for having already eaten dinner by 7 pm and goes to the kitchen to clear space among the takeaway containers in the refrigerator for the casserole dish. He barks out reheating instructions for the curry and tells us not to use too sweet a chutney with it.

When he returns to Viv's side, he pushes away a nearby wastepaper basket of chewed-up gnocchi in tissues so he can squat down next to her. 'Now. How are things?'

'The way that they look.'

Lon's kindness doesn't falter. 'Do you need anything?'

'No nursing, please.' She points a weak finger in my direction. 'He's got that covered.'

'I come in peace. Just to offer my services to both of you.'

'This isn't difficult,' she says.

'That's good to hear. You're definitely missed. I keep getting requests.'

She isn't interested. 'Trish isn't allowed to come. You are. Not her.'

'I'm not talking about staff. I'm talking about residents. Evie, for one. She keeps asking where you've gone to and I keep telling her you went for a hike.' Lon is so peppy it's heartbreaking. 'She'll be happy to hear I've seen you.'

Viv looks confused. 'Seen what?'

'Seen you.'

She looks down, taking in her position on the couch, the pillows propping her up, the protective cushioning under her legs, the cotton blanket she's wrapped around herself to avoid a chill. 'You mean me rotting in place here?' A satisfied edge accompanies the self-deprecation, owning it. 'Tell the office and the others there they can stop checking up. They can turn off their surveillance monitors. I will be taking no more unauthorised hikes.'

'Not right now, but who knows? Give it time, a little exercise, maybe?'

She's thinking *Idiot*.

To prevent further intimations of Viv's impending improvement, I butt in. 'She's had reviews and scans. They checked all the leads. This is where things are at.'

Undeterred, he asks her, 'Did you at least have fun while you were on the run?'

Viv gives me a look of unexpected and unprecedented love. 'We did. Tell everyone that.'

Lon leans back into the couch, equally fond. 'Exactly what I would expect.' He offers me his hand. I take it and accept a squeeze.

Viv turns away from us to the TV. 'I don't ask personal questions,' she says. We let go of each other.

'This is a social call, for both of you,' says Lon. 'I am representing Simon and me.'

'Myself,' Viv corrects.

He doesn't care. 'We offer our various services, to both of you, should you need them.'

Viv says, eyes still on the TV, 'That's nice of you. Thank Simon too. To be clear, if anybody at your place of work decrees that I have to go back, I have a plan in place.' Her head tilts towards me. 'He's been in training for this for months. He's going to kill me first.'

Lon's face goes still.

As does mine.

'We're taking it one day at a time,' I say, suddenly sunny and hopeful.

'I'm not going to any hospital. No heroics,' she tells Lon, as if I can't be trusted. 'And I'll die before I go back to my cell at your place.' Her face is expressionless, but she's more present than she's been at any time since our night in the tent. 'That's my clearly stated wish. Do you hear me?'

Lon looks to me and I look down, pretending none of this is happening.

Viv goes on, to both of us, 'I will get worse.'

'Mum, there are no guarantees,' I say, becoming the idiot. 'We don't know if it will come to that.'

Lon tries to take her hand, but she pulls away, until he insists, wrapping her fingers in his. 'Can I ask, as a friend, is there anything I can do for you tonight? Let me tidy up the kitchen?'

'Not a thing, darling,' she says. 'We're thriving here. We'll eat your curry. Thanks so much for dropping by.'

'There's more where that came from. And not just curry. If you need anything to make things easier for you, we can—'

Viv opens her eyes wide, showing that her full attention is on the TV.

He takes the hint, lets go of her hand and stands up. 'I guess I'll go then.' The TV erupts in canned laughter. The three of us watch Alex Keaton screwing up scrambled eggs for his family.

'Goodnight, Viv.'

With effort, she tilts her face slightly to accept a kiss on the cheek. 'Goodnight.'

I follow Lon to the door. 'You see why I don't get an evening off,' I tell him.

'I see where you get it from.'

'Get what?'

He stops. 'Let's be civil and call it wilfulness. This no-help, no-contact thing. It's getting pretty Grey Gardens in here.'

'I think we're doing a good job.'

'The death talk? Is that constant?'

'It comes up,' I say. Minimise, minimise, minimise.

'It scares me. For you.'

'She's depressed about her situation, understandably.'

Lon gets in my face. 'Have you said you would help her do that?'

'In the abstract. The way people talk. You know.'

'No. I don't know. Fill me in. When she said you were in training for this, did she mean your job?' He takes a step back for a better view of me. To watch me lie. He puts his hands on his hips and waits. Trish must have told him.

'She's not a hundred percent herself,' I say.

He grunts as though he's been kicked, then gives a defeated smile. 'Evan. Please tell me something that's not a story.'

All I'm craving is to go home with him, no questions asked, curl up on their couch between them with a sippy cup of wine and just watch *Family Ties* until my mother is dead.

'Please,' he says. 'I *know*. Just talk to me.'

Instead of trying to figure out what it is he knows, or asking him for anything, even a hug, I tell him, 'We're okay here. Really.'

Taking pity on me, he breaks the eye contact and grips the front door. 'Okay, all right. If your idea is to keep her here, at least tell me what you're doing to stabilise the situation. Because this—' he waves his hand at the living room '—is not sustainable, not without someone going to hospital or prison.'

'Give me options.'

'For one, accept that you can't do this on your own. You have to be realistic. Decide what's safe, what you can get help with. You can get services in. And, you seem to keep forgetting, Simon and I exist.'

'Thank you.'

'"Thank you"?'

'Sorry.'

'Evan, I don't know how you feel about us. We take you seriously. We love you. You're in the middle of something impossible here and you think you've got nowhere to turn. It's not the case.'

'And what's two?'

'Two?'

'You were giving me options.'

'Sorry. There is no two.' His cheeks flush. He's not waiting for a confession or the right words or even a connection. 'That's the sum total of your options: accept that you're not on your own.'

'Thanks.'

That's one thanks too many. He shakes his head at me, the way he does at Simon. 'Why do you make me try so hard?'

'Because I love you too?'

He gives me a disappointed smile. 'You'll have to do better than that. Goodnight. Call us sometime. Enjoy the curry.'

I watch him from the landing; he's still shaking his head as he goes down the stairs. I have the urge to go to the laptop and write up my reflection on it—something about being powerless and central and not knowing the right words to save myself—but Viv is weakly calling me from the couch.

She is keeling forward from the edge of the cushion, resting both hands on the coffee table as if she's about to stand. No progress beyond that seems possible tonight.

'Headed somewhere?' I ask.

'What? No. I've decided. For dinner tonight I want French toast.'

'We already had dinner. Gnocchi.'

This is news. She turns her head up towards me as best she can. 'Look at you. You're going to cry. If it's that damn important, we can have the gnocchi.'

I rub my face with my hand. 'I'm not going to cry. You had your dinner. It's in front of you.'

She peers down into the bowl and laughs. 'Well, how do you like this?' She picks up the fork and aims it at the bowl.

'I wish you hadn't said I would kill you.'

'You haven't told him about your job? What a weirdo you are,' she says. 'Don't worry, I kept it vague.'

'You really didn't.'

'The point is that you passed,' she says, trying to stab the gnocchi without much success. 'You let me know you'll be ready when I need you.'

'When did I do that?'

'When you told him it might never come to that. We both know it will come to that. Once I can't get off this couch or can't talk,

228

I want to be gone.' She waves her arm wide with finality. 'No bed baths, thank you very much. I know when it's time to fold.'

'I understand.' I grab the hand that's holding the fork and help her catch some pasta.

'Thank you,' she says. 'You scratched your chin when you were talking to Lon. That's your tell. You were lying. He probably knew it too. He's a smart boy. Go get the treasure chest.'

'What?'

'You know. My chest. Do I really have to tell you where it is?'

No. I bring it to her and, with poor coordination, she starts pressing on the hinges.

'Doesn't it need a key?'

'I lost that years ago.' She holds one hand out towards the kitchen. 'Get the paring knife.'

I do. Not even in my sneakiest teenage years did I ever think I would be granted a viewing. She shows me how to angle the knife along the rim until the fake gold lid pops open.

I peer into this forbidden zone. The sight of a few expired passports brings a twinge of intrigue, that they might be for other identities she's had. Inside is a mess of jewellery, a pair of dangling pearl earrings, a few unset hunks of polished turquoise, folded documents and a familiar-looking small plastic baggie of white powder. In fact, it looks very much like the one that I stashed at the back of the knife drawer for a very rainy day.

'I bought Nembutal,' she tells me, proud. 'They deliver right to the door.'

'Amazing.'

She slowly hands it to me. 'So you know where it is. And you may as well have this,' she says, pulling out a small book, from under the papers, with hand-stitched binding. 'Your baby book.'

I open the faded blue cover. Glued to its faded pages are a faded ultrasound, ink blots of my little feet and hands. A birth announcement with an address I don't even know. An archival lock of my hair. Chinese horoscope. A cash-register receipt for their first box of nappies, with a heart drawn in pencil around the price. A picture of me wrapped up in a white blanket and sucking on my fist in my father's arms.

'People used to keep these,' Viv tells me. 'As a keepsake. Keep's sake? Before Facebook.'

'I didn't know this existed.'

'How could you? It was in the chest. I think you're supposed to get it when I die, but here it is. This was your father's thing more than mine.'

I sniff the book for a whiff of him, but it just smells old.

'He added to it until you could walk, and then we were too busy running after you. If you're going to get sentimental about it, look at it later on. I want to talk about the Nembutal.'

I hold the book against my chest. 'Go ahead, you crazy crazy lady.'

'I know I can't get past your fussy program unless I'm terminal, so having this will make things easy for you, when you have to do it.'

'I have to do it?'

'You'll do it. I know you well enough by now.' She stops and pictures the scene we're both picturing. 'With two suicides for parents, I wouldn't like your odds. Nevertheless, you're up to this.'

'Am I?'

'I'm your mother. I know what you're about. You know I'll haunt you if you don't take care of me like I want. Now, put the Nembutal in the kitchen drawer so we both know where it is, and put your little book away for now and let me eat my dinner in peace.'

———

There's not much more evidence of Dad in the book, other than that he started it and then—sometime after my first word, which was *Mama*—he stopped. I fall asleep with it next to me on the couch. In the morning I stare at the photo of his arms around me, trying to understand why he didn't find this little baby enough to be happy about that he could have stuck around.

The days continue downward, with no more pretend discussions about rehab or even much conversation.

I don't call Lon or Simon. I don't call Nettie. I don't even call Giulia.

This afternoon's movie is about a piano teacher who is or isn't a paedophile, trying to clear his name by finding the real paedophile (who, in silhouette at least, seems to look just like him), so that he can go back to giving one-on-one lessons in his old Victorian mansion. It's okay.

The movie's almost over when the J flashes on my phone. The cinema is nearly empty so I answer in a whisper. It's a Jasper I've never heard from before. He's chipper, prodding me about my time at the Mercy ('They're only doing forty percent of the work that needs doing') and about the guy who shot himself ('Violence is not the answer!'). The reason he's calling: he has a friend for me to visit. I take the details in the hallway. The brief is brief: a woman, thirty-two, melanoma, recurrence in liver and bone. There's enough of a family history for her to believe that the brain is next. No partner. The woman's family isn't close, except for the mother, who's been her main support. There's tension there. The drugs and discovery have been organised, she's written her farewell. How does later this afternoon sound?

'Impulsive.'

'For you, maybe. We've been talking with her since way before the cancer came back, twenty-two months. She's a long-time friend. I was going to be there but I have to get in to see my doctor this afternoon about a personal situation. And this woman is set on going at the same time. Says she doesn't care if you've never spoken before. And the situation I need checked out cannot wait. Don't ask.'

I don't. I take the phone number and address and head back into the dark.

The identity of the actual paedophile is left blurred enough so we're never sure if there's a bad man lurking or if it's the piano teacher's dark side. Either ending works for me. The last shot is of a pair of hands guiding a student up the scales. No tears required, just creepy doubt. I leave before the credits, and make first contact with the client.

'Well, thank fuck,' she says. 'Half an hour?'

'Whenever you need me.'

'Cool.'

———

It's a brick villa, at least fifteen years past new, sitting in the middle of a row of five. There are one-storey columns in front of the gated front doors, painted stone planters on each porch, and bushy hedges curving around the garbage bin.

The woman is tinted yellow from jaundice but looks younger than her age. A few years of being told what to do by doctors and being softly handled by nurses would keep anyone youthful. The magenta camisole with the matching shawl and pumps makes her look even more pampered and protected from reality.

'Glad you're here. They said we haven't talked before, but I think we must have. I'm sure I've talked to every last one of you. That doesn't matter now, obviously.' She laughs a little. 'I took the anti-emetic when you called. I wanted you here for the Nembutal, not for company, to make sure it works.'

'Whatever you want.' I say, touching the spare packet of Nembutal in my pocket as a talisman.

'Cool.'

The walls are covered floor-to-ceiling with framed paintings, meticulously painted copies. 'They're all mine,' she says, pointing to the largest of them. Her specialty is impressionist vases of flowers. 'Art history major, as if anyone cares. A field that's also terminal. If I'd known I was pulling this short straw, I would have gone for

232

it, become a legit forger. Bet you hear that all the time. Would've, should've, could've.'

I recognise a painting of a silvery tree in the hall. 'That's a van Gogh,' she says, her shawl slipping from her wrist, revealing a ladder of scars up her arm.

The living room has an easel set up next to a computer monitor. 'Don't be too impressed. In the end, it's half skill, half maths. They all have homes lined up, for after. Friends. The thing is, is that my mother gets none of them.'

A family meeting and a tweaking of meds—I'm picking up a strong sense of psych meds here—would have been a useful strategy before letting the death conversation progress. Not sure how Jasper's Path handles that. At least she looks sick. Maybe she's on steroids today.

She wants to light some candles, put on her death playlist, and hop in the bathtub, which she's filling right now. If all goes to plan, she'll dose, get in the water, conk out in a few minutes, and drown. She's totally stoked by her own creativity on this plan. 'Has anyone ever used that as backup before? I've looked and looked and never seen it.'

'Not that I've heard.'

Two dozen pale roses stand in a plain vase. Once she's in the tub she's going to tear off the petals and sprinkle them on the water. 'So I've got something to look at at the end.'

'You've thought of everything.'

'I've had to.'

For the next ten minutes she sits on the couch with a makeup bag and does her face. 'This is for me. I swear, it's the one thing I'm going to totally long for when I'm dead.'

She shuts the compacts, liners and lipsticks, throws the cotton puffs to her side, stands up and does a turn to show me the final product. She looks like a sick woman wearing makeup. 'Don't worry. I know my body is going to look like shit by the time Mum finds me.'

No clue as to what the mother's crimes were, but she will be made to suffer.

A nearly forgotten last project: burn a dozen red spiral-bound notebooks—her childhood diaries—in the kitchen sink. She opens the window to fan the smoke out. 'This is hard, erasing myself but that's what I've got to do. Wouldn't have been able to do this last year. But I had to discuss it, *unpack* it. And your mob there forced me to *deal*, to *know* why I'm taking back my life from God. Lying back and letting them pump their drugs into me, letting my mother scream at all the nurses—that would have been normal as normal gets. That would have been the easy way out. Not me, I insist on taking the longest road.'

When the pages are a smoky black pile, she turns the sprayer attachment on them until they turn into a soggy black pile. She scoops it out, mushing it in her fingers, double-bags it and puts it in the trash, leaving flakes of soot still floating in the air.

There's one brief wipe of the kitchen counter with a tea towel before getting down to business. She pours in the water, the Nembutal, and drinks it in one gulp. 'Foul. I'm taking a spoonful of sugar unless you tell me I can't.'

There've been few pauses for me to make a contribution. There's no point starting now. I shake my head.

She crunches the sugar in her mouth, and hands me a fifty for my visit. 'I tried to get to the bank yesterday to get more, but there was so much to do. Sorry.'

I assure her that she should not be thinking about money now.

'Thanks for saying so.' She picks up her iPod player and casts a glance from the hall into the bathroom. 'So it will be lights off in here, except for the candles. The music will be loud. I'll yell if I get into trouble. After half an hour, make sure the job is done. That's all. I'm not going to worry about my decency with you having a look. You're gay anyway, which completely figures. And anyway, I'll be covered in rose petals. Thanks for coming out for this.'

'Sure.'

With a kiss on the cheek you would give as you leave a party, she goes into the bathroom.

For thirty minutes I listen to Nirvana playing through the door. What else would she have done if she had known she was getting the short straw? What made her think she was getting the long one? Alongside her rage at her mother, her disappointment with whatever she didn't get or do, are these forgeries of drawing rooms and their flowers—oblivious and healthy. If only she had known. She would have raged the whole time. She would have painted something else, something fierce and sick.

At the appointed minute, I check the bathroom. Her body is floating in the tub, camisole and hands drifting within their own small currents. Her fingers are spread, collecting petals. No checking the pulses here. Her head is underwater. Her eyes are half open. Still life.

The tub was an effective fail-safe, I'll give her that, and more picturesque than the shotgun approach, from my perspective, but I'm not her mother. Tomorrow she'll walk in, calling her daughter's name, look in the living room, the bedroom, then here. At least with the head blown off she wouldn't have to look into her daughter's expressionless eyes. She could imagine an intruder, an afternoon of gun-cleaning gone wrong. Instead, she'll get this view.

Correction: this view plus twelve hours of bloat. Her daughter's corpse should be on its way to filling the tub by then.

Iris and her daughters raising a toast, I can understand. Myrna cutting Lambros out of the discussion, I can understand. Even the man in the recliner, setting up his friend to discover half a head had an urgency to it. This woman in the bathtub, though, she'll be leaving her mother the most violent last word of all.

A bubble escapes from some orifice, giving rise to a soft plink that breaks through the petals. The five votives are perched in an unholy pentagram around the edge of the tub. A few more hours and they will have burned all the way down.

Viv is not in her usual position on the couch.

The carpet in the bedroom is dark with water trickling out from beneath the closed bathroom door. As I open it, I picture the scene I just left.

My mother is naked, on her knees, with her torso slumped over into the tub. Her bare bony arse faces the doorway, her legs splayed apart on the floor that's half an inch underwater. A thin stream of shit runs down one inner thigh. Her arms are deep in the tub, which is still running over. I hurry around to turn off the tap and see that her eyes are wide open, just above the water, either terrified or excited. Her mouth is agape too, as if she just woke up to an alarm.

'Mum!' I lift her away from scalding and drowning and prop her against the side of the tub. 'Mum!'

Her arms, shoulders and chest are red from the water. She shuts her eyes, at being moved against her will. There's a pool of foamy spittle on her chin. Even as I prop her torso against the wall to assess the burns and keep her upright, inside herself she is struggling, trying to move, concentrating on the tub, trying to get back there. And she's not going anywhere.

'Mum?'

Nothing.

'What's your name?' I throw a towel across her body. 'Can you say your name?'

I grab more towels and put them down to sop up the water on the floor.

Her expression stays neutral, not even trying to communicate.

'Where are we right now?'

She takes a breath and swallows a few times before whispering, 'Bed—' She swallows again, to give the sentence another try. Nothing comes. 'Bedti—'

'It's not bedtime yet,' I say. 'It's not even seven o'clock. I've just come home. Can you tell me where we are?'

'Fight,' she says. Her mouth is wide. The effort involved in getting the words out is the same as shouting. She's still trying to move at the same time. She can't. I can tell that in her mind she's screaming at me.

I run warm water out of the shower nozzle. With one knee, I keep her body against the edge of the tub so I can direct the spray over her chest and arms, which are dappled with brightening red welts. 'You've had a burn. I want to cool it down.'

She opens her mouth to drink. I let her slide down against the side of the tub, with the water pouring off her chest and pooling out over the small dam of towels around her. What I'm looking at is bare and slack and red like meat in a butcher's window.

A good night's sleep won't fix this.

Two thoughts, in rapid succession. First, the Nembutal, all of it, is in the kitchen drawer. And then: we don't have the anti-emetic.

I could give it to her slowly enough to make sure she keeps it down. If that doesn't work, there's always the second dose. In half an hour, I can report that she was dead when I got home. A cerebral accident, which it probably is.

Unless one of the medics gets curious, in which case I'm deregistered and imprisoned, all for following her wishes. Or we could each take one dose and hope for the best.

Who would find us? I have a vision of Lon holding another casserole up to the downstairs camera until he gives up and gets the police to open the apartment. What if she survives and I don't?

Out of ideas, as Marais would say.

With my free hand I reach for my phone and call for an ambulance.

Viv's head rocks from side to side, hypnotised by the flow of the water onto her as I give the operator a calm and clinical description of the situation. Near the end of the call, my mother looks at me, as though she's just understood what I've been saying. I confirm the address with the operator, while Viv shakes her head, *no*.

The paramedic says the burns are minor, second degree. She applies some cream that seems to relax Viv, who closes her eyes. As the woman tends to the skin, she makes the mandatory five attempts to interrogate my mother about what happened. Viv still isn't speaking, so the questions are redirected to me.

When she's done, the paramedic takes me into the bedroom. 'How long has she been like this?'

'She's in shock.'

'Your mother is aphasic. When was the last time you two had a clear conversation?'

'This morning.' She talked about cleaning out the refrigerator.

'We have to bring her in.'

'It's just a few burns. Is that necessary?'

'Yes.'

'She's not going to like that.'

'Isn't it hard to say what she's liking right now?'

'She has Parkinson's. She's had dips like this before.'

The woman remains unmoved by my negotiations. 'Here's my view: her burns, your absence when they happened, her inability to give me her side of the story, tell me the overall safety of the home environment is inadequate for her condition. You called, you're concerned—that's good, but on paper it's looking like neglect, or worse. I'm not going to document each part of that, but for my peace of mind, I'd like to bring her in and have her situation reviewed. Any objections?'

I'm directed to collect her regular medications and any power-of-attorney forms and advance directives. While they wrap and strap Viv to take her down the stairs, I grab all of the above.

On the ride to the Mercy, Viv's eyes bolt open and then half shut, going fixed for about five seconds, accompanied by complete rigidity, double incontinence and bubbling at the mouth. From my strapped-in seat by the side door, I reach out to rest my hands on her. I lean forward and put my head on the side of the stretcher, against her calves.

238

At least we're going to the hospital, I think, as if that's a good thing. She dozes, or something, until we reach the emergency entrance.

———

After a cursory clean-up, followed by a speedy CT scan that tells us she hasn't had a stroke, there's a slow few hours of waiting in an eight-cot holding room. Finally, an intern sweeps open our curtain to make the bold move of giving Viv four hundred milligrams of ibuprofen for her burn pain. With some guidance, she's able to hold the pills on her tongue. Getting the water into her and getting them swallowed, however, is a joint effort.

The intern stands by the head of the bed, reading notes from his screen. 'I want to keep her overnight and monitor her.'

I stay by her side for hours. There are no changes. She remains the most placid person in the room, striking in her refusal to succumb to the chaos and have another seizure, as if good behaviour will get her out of here.

Behind the next curtain, a woman's quavering voice says, 'I love you.'

A younger man replies, 'I love you.'

Again with the *I love you*s. Surely by the time you've brought someone into an emergency room, love can be assumed. This isn't a confession. Maybe it's an apology, or insurance against whatever else may happen when the test results come back. In the consulting room, where I've heard it the most, it simply means *goodbye and good luck*. The words are more of a mantra than anything else—for the speaker more than the recipient. Like singing in the dark when you're scared.

Then there's Lon, on the bed under the mirror, telling me the same. His dick was still hard, so it barely counts. It felt real enough, though.

I want to pull open the curtain and ask this couple what they mean.

Viv just stays as she is, eyes closed, perfectly blank. She wouldn't tolerate anything as bland and unimaginative as *I love you*.

'You've been a hell of a guidance counsellor,' I tell her.

She snores.

———

In the middle of the night, the intern comes back to ask what's new. The question seems more academic than concerned. The intrigue of Viv's abrupt deterioration has clearly enticed him. In fact, he's been thinking: since Viv was attempting to take a bath, which a woman with previously reasonable insight, like Viv, would not have been doing, the episode must have occurred *before* she got to the tub, and possibly worsened once she was there. When he mentions the idea of admitting Viv for further tests until we can really figure things out, her face suddenly registers awareness, in the form of brief eyes-wide panic. He doesn't change his tone or subject.

I remind him about the implant, which brings up a range of complicating factors that are out of his skill set and jurisdiction. It also limits the tests he can order. Robbed of potential sleuthing fun, his attention wanes. He confers with the nurse and they agree to let Viv go in the morning.

Viv floats back to sleep.

In a final gesture of futility before giving up, he orders a urine screen, something I could do with my password if it seemed necessary. He starts to write up a prescription for a broad-spectrum antibiotic, 'in case there's an infection brewing in there. She can still swallow, can't she?'

'She took the ibuprofen,' I remind him.

'Right.'

'If you're giving her the antibiotics anyway, why bother with the test?'

He smiles. 'I recognise you. You're on staff here, aren't you?'

'Yes.'

'Then you'll know where to take this,' he says, handing me the prescription.

The first punchline of this admission comes around five in the morning, when the intern's final verdict is delivered, through the ward nurse. Viv will go to rehab.

The nurse lets one finger of one of her hands touch my mother's wrist. 'A little rehab can do a lot,' she says, tapping her finger there, before she leaves.

Viv blinks at the curtain, still swishing from the departure, and says, 'Bullshit,' each consonant loud and clear.

I laugh, but then search her eyes to see if she means it or if it's a residual tic of her somatic nervous system.

———

I use Marais's personal phone number, which he generously provided before we'd even paid for the implant. It's Sunday morning but he is polite, and so sorry to hear about her decline. He repeats approximately, what he told us two weeks ago: he's broken up with her.

'If you want me to come and see her, I can. I'm not going to put her through more tests. My feeling is that what follows from her may be rapid.'

'How rapid?'

'We only know the direction, not the precise angle.'

'Are we talking years, months or weeks?'

He pauses. 'You know I can't say. She's strong. Months? A year, maybe?'

I hang up and repeat it all to Viv, whose eyes seem to be following my chin. 'Is that rapid enough for you, Mum?'

No response.

At 10 am, the discharge planner opens the curtains to deliver the second punchline: seems the usual rehab that the Mercy feeds to is at capacity. However, there's a very nice facility with similar rehab equipment and staff that the discharge planner has heard has better food and a bed that it turns out they're holding just for Viv. The place is called Willow Wood.

My mother's face doesn't change.

The discharge planner advises, 'If I were you, I'd jump on it.'

'My mother doesn't want to go there.'

The woman reaches across the bottom of the bed to give Viv a consoling foot massage. 'I get it, sister, believe me. But it's better than staying here. I've put plenty of people over there who have settled right in.'

On Viv's behalf, I think: what *sisterhood*?

'Is there any other place she could go?' I ask.

'Not this week and not with her level of cover.'

'What about taking her back home, where she wants to be? I'm a nurse. I can get a hospital bed.'

'You want to take this lady home?' It's as though I suggested taking Viv on a balloon ride over wine country.

'It's what she wants. Does she get a say in this?' I put one hand on the advance directive in my pocket, ready to draw if necessary. 'We've been managing there.'

'With her like this?'

Viv's head tilts sideways then jerks back up. A glistening of spit collects at the base of her mouth. 'Slee—?' she says.

'It's morning,' I tell her. 'We're figuring out what happens next. Then I'll let you rest.'

'This must be a tough moment for both of you,' the woman says.

'Thanks. I wasn't sure.'

'It is tough and you don't want tougher. Are you a nurse and a physio too? Do you have a mechanical hoist to lift her up? Do you have the staff to spell you? Because she's twenty-four hours right now. My promise: she will feel better and she will do better in a facility—any facility—than home with you scrambling to try to do it all. What you've been getting away with up till now, you can't get away with anymore.'

Our attention shifts back to the patient, as if she might cast a tie-breaking vote. The spit dribbles and I have a vision of trying to roll her from side to side to change her, and trying to drag her up the bed every time she slides down.

The discharge planner straightens the sheet across my mother's feet, stroking one foot almost tenderly. 'I'm sorry to put pressure on him, doll. He loves you. You see a lot in this job and sometimes you can tell when things are going to work and when they're not. Can you give it one shot?'

In a pleading sort of way, I mirror the request to Viv, squeezing my fingers around her other foot. With a spastic turn, she kicks both legs out, knocking our hands away.

———

As soon as the general manager of Willow Wood realises that Viv is a returning customer, she absolutely insists that my mother's adjustment period will be made rippleless if she's admitted to the familiar sights, sounds and smells of the nursing wing, and calls me on my own phone to tell me so.

Within the privacy of a curtained room, I find my most measured tone to lobby on Viv's behalf for the rehab bed, until the woman feels sorry for the patient's deluded son and relents, granting Viv its use for at least today and tonight. Hanging over this pointless favour is the threat of a full functional assessment and case conference on Monday afternoon. After that, they'll decide where she truly belongs.

'Great news,' I tell Viv, and explain the first part of the plan.

Her eyebrows rise and fall once, most likely because she knows it's futile: ten minutes after they talk to Marais she'll be deported back to the nursing wing.

At least this gives me a day to work with.

———

The transfer ambulance wades slowly out from the Mercy into the midday traffic. No siren is required. The cargo is lined up in the back: Viv, dozing and strapped into an upright position; next to her, an old man in a hospital gown looking giddily confused. Every time the van hits a bump, he giggles.

The paramedic sitting near the head of my mother's stretcher has the distant gaze of a low-level worker intending to finish advanced medical training soon with the main goal of qualifying for far more interesting assignments than the one in front of her. The paramedic squatting near the patients' feet looks like she'd rather be working on her tan. They both seem dazedly glad to be close to the end of their shift. The old man's more switched-on wife sits next to him. She's wearing an evening dress—they had a long Saturday night, too—wearily raising her smile each time he raises his.

The old man decides to break the ice, starting with my mother. 'So, let me understand: are we all going the same way?'

Viv doesn't even blink.

The second-in-charge at least knows a good joke when she hears one. She pulls up his loose black socks, which have drooped around his scaly calves. 'We certainly are.'

My phone hums. J.

The would-be doctor tells me, 'Take the call. We've got a while.'

I answer. It's the most recent Jasper. 'Hey there,' he says. 'Never heard from you yesterday. No surprises, I hope?'

'The visit was uneventful.' Was I supposed to ask about his doctor's appointment? 'No surprises.'

The old man covers his mouth with both hands at the hilarity.

Jasper says, 'You know, before yesterday she and I had a lot of time to bond. Up and down a lot, that one. Was she relaxed?'

In the back of a slow-moving, otherwise silent ambulance, I struggle to come up with the right description. A woman in a tub, under the water, makeup getting washed away. Was she relaxed? 'Not with her mother,' I say.

'Well, that relationship: it's complicated.'

'Yes.'

'You see lots of mothers and daughters. Look at your friend Nettie, for one. When she brought her mother to us, she was at the end of her rope. She had given the old lady exquisite care for years, but that didn't stop the dementia from getting worse and worse—her mother was paranoid, biting. It couldn't go on. In the end, Nettie gave her a fine death.'

Nettie said her mother stopped drinking one day and just faded away. I must have missed the first part of that story, when she slipped her the Nembutal. *Exquisite care.* Every time she asked me how Viv was doing, was she assessing me for signs of impending matricide? Or was she grooming me for it? I tell Jasper, 'Yes. You see lots of variety.'

Viv is drifting off again, as though she's just had another seizure. 'Thanks for checking in,' I tell Jasper.

'Ah, one thing. What sort of contribution will we be recording there?'

'She gave me fifty dollars.'

'Five oh?'

'Yes.'

He laughs. 'Are you being serious? Her family is quite well-off.'

'She said she ran out of time to get to the bank.'

'She certainly took long enough getting to yesterday. Are you being serious? Fifty dollars.'

'Yes.'

'Real surprised. Real surprised.' He sounds like he believes me but is only now gaining a full appreciation of her. 'To be honest, she talked up a big gift, several times. Held it out to others here too, when all the while we were giving her a lot of our time. A lot. Frankly, I'm disappointed.'

'I can hear that. Do you think she arranged for more money to come later?'

'We're cash only. She was well aware.'

'Oh well. It's hard to know what was going through her mind.'

Everyone except the would-be doctor must have stopped listening in on my call, but I'm convinced she knows exactly who and what I'm talking about. Maybe they had to pick up the woman's bloated body, right after the mother called this morning.

Our van starts beeping as we back up to the receiving bay at Willow Wood. 'I need to go,' I tell Jasper.

'I knew she was half-crazy from the beginning. Should have listened to my gut. Moving on. A quick one: availability? We have a good friend who is looking for a visit next Saturday. There'll be a big family brunch in the morning and then the family will leave. Crushing story here: retired professor of history, already had two strokes, hands barely function, mostly blind at eighty-one—'

The back doors are opened by two personal care attendants. The relatively cool afternoon air rushes in, along with exhaust fumes banking up around us. The medics jump out and start unlatching Viv's stretcher.

Jasper continues. '. . . friends are long dead, and he's firmly against institutionalisation. A long life of the mind behind him and now he's contending with this.'

They lower Viv out of the van. The stretcher's legs drop down beneath her, hitting the pavement hard. Her hands flap from the motion as she's transferred to a wheelchair and strapped in.

Nettie gave her mother a fine death.

'I can't,' I tell Jasper.

The journey to Viv's room provides impressive optics, though it's hard to tell if she's noticing. The orderly who's pushing her announces the sights as we pass them: 'Stationary bikes, spa pool, light dumbbells, six Pilates machines.' Even I'm beginning to believe she'll be using them before long.

As she's wheeled around a corner, she stares in the direction of a motivational poster. The star is a blond kitten on a white lacy pillow licking her paw. Black border, bold white caption: *Tell Her She's a Tiger and Watch What Happens!*

This was the sort of poster that Viv banned at every one of her schools. If she saw one taped up in a hallway, she would tear it down and find the culprit, waving the offending item and saying, 'No one actually likes a cheerleader.'

I step ahead of the wheelchair to check Viv's face for a bitter glint, and point out the kitty to her. 'Penny for your thoughts?'

Not even a twitch. Her mouth hangs open. Her eyes continue to track the cat, as if trying to comprehend.

My chest empties. My head empties. She's not bouncing back from this one.

For the past eighteen hours, I've been lying to myself that it's generalised disgust keeping her stony, but now only a specific test for electrical evidence of her revulsion at that poster could convince me she's still in there.

Our small procession continues through the treatment area. A team of student physios, each hugging a red inflatable exercise ball, part ways to let us pass. They're fresh and ready for their afternoon rounds.

Whenever they get around to meeting my mother, they won't be able to get her to hold a spoon.

The apartment smells swampy when I open the front door. The bedroom carpet is soggy under my feet. The bed is still pushed against the far wall so they could get the stretcher through. I climb past it to open the window. At least the place can air.

In the kitchen, there's a brown banana on the counter and half of a roast chicken in the plastic tray it came in. I need to eat, but won't. Instead, I sit on the counter, with my legs dangling over the Nembutal/knife drawer.

I call Giulia. 'She wants me to kill her. Would have wanted me to. I mean, I have power of attorney, which lets me make choices for her.'

Giulia lets out a garage mechanic's whistle. 'Is this the legal way or your fancy freelance way?'

'The second.'

Another long whistle. 'Oh, crap. So, that power-of-attorney cover is more theoretical.'

'Yeah. It's for my peace of mind.'

'Right.' For the first time I can remember, she's quiet.

'I had to tell somebody.'

'Okay, easy. You've got at least two futures. Here's what I have for you on them. Aside from whatever it would mean to look after her, invest in caring for her—I'm talking about your soul, not to mention your time, energy and money, when you don't even know if she's all there—the carbon footprint of a woman in her condition, getting full nursing care and taking up a bed in a facility, it's enormous. Jumbo-jet enormous. That's a lot of wasted energy—for herself and for you—and dead against her wishes, I'm fairly certain. Nevertheless, I will also tell you that after my father died, even though he was sicker than sick and ready to go, and even though in the end it was a nurse mistaking him for the guy in the next bed that killed him, I spent the next year crying my way through the city and apologising to him for things I might have done to save him. I still do. So, I'm just saying that killing your mother, ready as you both are for this, expect an aftermath.'

'Wish you were here,' I say.

'We can come next week.'

'We?'

'*Oui*.'

'Wow.'

'Don't worry, Dave can walk around while we talk or sit with Viv. Or feed her the drugs. Whatever you want.'

'Good.'

She sighs. 'I can see your little head, needing a haircut, peering over the top bunk, looking down to check if I'm awake yet.'

'You were always asleep.'

'I guess I wasn't then, was I? Can you stay with Lon and Simon the next few nights?'

'I can't tell them what I'm thinking about with Viv.'

'Human contact is all. Sleep in the middle. Sleep on the couch. You need it.'

'Maybe.'

'And, final words of wisdom: If you do what your mother's asked you to do, do it well. Prison would not agree with you. I don't think it's like the porn.'

'Thanks for the tip.'

A few hours later, a fire engine going by wakes me. I'm on the couch and the kitchen light is still on. I strip and, squishing over the soggy carpet, relocate to my mother's bed, but there is no more sleep in this future.

———

Trish calls me before nine on Monday morning to tell me that Viv is being transferred to the high-care part of the nursing wing.

'They promised us she had until the end of the day,' I say. 'Have they even assessed her?'

'They don't need to. She's not appropriate for rehab. And they want the bed. A young guy is coming across this morning. Car accident. I apologise. She's deteriorated so fast. I've already had a chat with Dr Marais, who agreed with the move.'

'This is exactly what she doesn't want.'

'She's doing well, though. With a little help, she had a spoonful of porridge.'

'Did you get any response from her?'

'She may re-emerge a bit, once she's settled in.'

'Wait.' It's worse than Viv imagined. 'Is she going to the dementia ward?'

'Because of her cognitive state and her limited capacity for communication—'

'Please!' I say. 'Let me bring her home. We were doing well here.'

'The staff over there are trained for—'

'I don't care about the staff.'

'I understand where you're coming from, but the deposit was left here for a reason and I'm afraid this is the reason.'

I put one lucky Nembutal in my pocket and go.

———

Today, Trish is wearing a garland of red and orange plastic leaves around her neck. Autumn must really be here. Her dress matches, with dangling open sleeves that would preclude any serious nursing. If she weren't sitting at a metal desk under a fluorescent lamp, she would look like she was on her way to a sacrifice.

When she sees me, she turns efficient in a pre-emptive defence against incoming filial rage. It's misplaced, I'll admit it, but I'm bringing it.

She smiles. 'Have you been to see your mother yet?'

'This is against her wishes and you know it.'

'I do.' She gives the moment another moment. And then another. It's air that I don't feel like filling. 'Evan, she's here. She's safe. I'd like you to give us a couple of days to see if we—'

'You know she didn't want to end up like this.'

'You're free to stay in her room as much as you want. There are no restrictions on visiting hours. We will do the heavy lifting you were doing at home. You get to have the contact. That is the best that we,' she circles her finger between us, 'have for her.'

'She had other plans. Last week she bought Nembutal for herself.'

The placating comes to a screeching halt. Trish lifts the garland over her head and drops it on her keyboard. In a lower, less-assured tone, she asks, 'Why are you telling me this?'

'To show you how serious she was.'

'I know your mother. I know how serious she was.' She puts her head in her hands for a long minute, before pushing back from her desk and standing up. This new mode doesn't feel professionally kind or even chummy. She ushers me out of her office. 'Come. Let's go see Viv.'

Two sets of key codes are needed. When we get through the doors, it's pastels and greys, tidier than a regular ward, because the patients are bed-bound and there are few visitors cluttering up the place. The air is scented with a top note of lavender oil. I try to shut off my receptors to what may lie beneath. The only human element is music—golden oldies piped in through the speakers—and the occasional murmur of a voice filtering out from a room. No discernible words. No screaming or crying.

'You see?' Trish says. 'The standard of care here is among the best in the state.'

Two nurses walk briskly past us towards a corner room, following the sound of someone weakly banging on a metal bar. One is carrying a file, the other a kidney dish with a syringe in it. They move smoothly. No hurry.

'Are the nurses on benzos here too?'

Trish doesn't respond. She grabs Viv's file from the station as we pass it and leads me to the far side of the ward, where the only sound is Tony Bennett. He's everywhere.

Viv is in a small single bed with railings. She's tiny and asleep, with pillows shoved in to aim her towards the opaque window that doesn't open. The TV hanging high over her bed is thankfully off. Trish closes the door behind us.

'Mum.' I rub the skin, already slack, on the inside of her wrist. Reflexively, she makes an awkward fist, pulling her hand away and opening her eyes, not with alarm but with sleepy curiosity. There's zero recognition. She looks at Trish and then closes her eyes.

'What's she on?' I ask.

Trish opens the file and shows me. Nothing. A little cream for her burns.

'Impressive,' I say. 'So this is what her brain's done to her.'

Trish uses the controller to raise the head of the bed. Viv's eyes open again at the change in altitude. Trish picks up a cup of water from the bedside table. There's a bent straw sticking out of it that she aims at Viv's lips, which open on cue and remember how to suck.

'She's fortunate her insurance covers high care,' says Trish. 'By the time it's our turn do you think there'll be places like this?'

'Approximately how long would you want to live here?'

Trish leans close to Viv and strokes her shoulder. In a soothing voice, she says, 'Evan tells me you bought Nembutal so you could kill yourself when you got too sick.'

Viv stops sucking on the straw. Her eyebrows go up.

Trish goes on, 'He says you would rather die than stay here with us taking care of you. Is that true, Viv?'

Viv's eyebrows go up again, her cheeks balloon and her lips shut, as if she's going to say a word that begins with a *b* or a *p*. Then the whole apparatus relaxes. Whatever the thought was, it's vanished.

'If she's trying to say anything it's *please*,' I say,

'You may well be right.' Trish kisses my mother's forehead. Viv looks up at the ceiling to see where the kiss came from. 'At least she's not in pain.' Trish keeps staring at Viv's face, which is slack again, while she says to me, 'You can do it right here, you know.'

'What do you mean?'

Viv's light breathing turns jagged. Trish rubs her sternum to wake her again. 'We're talking about you, Viv, and I want you to try to listen. If this is what you want, I need you to blink once for me.' Viv shuts her eyes tight, then farts, which sparks an infant's innocent smile. Trish, who I'm sure has been exposed to far worse, repeats herself. 'Blink if you understand me.' Viv just stares.

Trish asks me, 'Do you think she's comprehending? I don't.'

'If she is, she can't do anything about it.'

Trish fixes her gaze on me and then on the sink in the corner of the room. She straightens up, keeping a hand on Viv, and tells me, 'It's actually better that she came in. You don't want this happening in your home. If she's here, in her bed, it will look like another seizure. You won't have to answer questions. And there won't be an autopsy, unless you order one. If this is what you want, what you think she wants, do it sooner rather than later. She was just admitted following a deteriorating incident, and a catastrophic change won't raise attention now.'

'Thank you,' I say.

'Don't you dare. I'm only trusting you with this because you have experience. You are taking full responsibility and risk. If it comes to it, I will deny this conversation to a jury.'

I ask, 'Can you get me twenty milligrams of metoclopramide?'

Trish isn't fazed. She nods and leaves the room. And here we are, with permission, even though it's just a wink and a nod. I can take care of my mother right here.

Viv has dozed off again. 'I'm sorry, Mum. I couldn't keep you out of this place,' I say. Afterwards, she'll be nearly as responsive, but still, and colourless and dead.

Trish returns and hands me the tablets, which I pocket. 'How long does it take?' she asks.

'Twenty minutes at the most.'

She does a few internal calculations. 'Night-time could be better, but I won't be here. Getting the certification then could be harder, depending on how many doctors we have. Afternoon handover is between two-thirty and three. No one will be around then and you will get your documentation signed off easier. I'll do what I can to make sure.'

The clock on the wall reads 11.20. Underneath is a whiteboard with the day's minimal schedule written out. Three meals and the movie *Easter Parade* being screened in the sunroom at four.

'Staff will alert me as soon as they know,' Trish says. 'I'll come right away, to offer condolences and get things moving. You'll have to find a funeral home and arrange burial or cremation plans. Are you ready for that?'

'She wants cremation. Her ashes will be my responsibility.'

Trish puts my mother's file under her arm. 'How do you think you're going to be?' she asks me.

'I've done it before.'

'She isn't your patient.'

'This is what she wanted. Knowing that helps.'

Trish gives me a sceptical nod. 'Sooner may be better than later for you too.'

She leans over to give Viv another kiss. 'You are a wonderful woman,' she says and turns away quickly for the door.

I stop her. 'Has this happened here before?' I ask.

A weary look. 'Yes, it's happened here. It's happened for centuries. As right as it may be, and as much as I may one day be begging for it, this is not why I became a nurse. I don't want to know another thing about it.'

And she leaves me with Viv, who's asleep, head turned at an odd angle, breathing shallowly into her shoulder.

11.25.

Nettie should be at her desk right now.

The walkway to the Mercy is alive with the oblivious and healthy, whizzing past on their bikes, jogging in happy tandem. The cars motoring underneath are the same, transporting their tender packages to productive business meetings, plentiful food co-ops and wine-clinking house closings. No one is terminal or even frail. Another dozen healthy babies are being born. Viv—and she would agree if she could—doesn't matter much to any of it.

I spot Nettie even before I reach the elevators. She's in the cafeteria, reading a newspaper in the middle of a long table. A cluster of Chinese nurses are sitting around one end, two seats away from her. Nettie speaks Mandarin, but as a second language, which makes it more of a party trick for them than a bond, and this means she sits alone. I tap the edge of her newspaper. She doesn't startle.

'Do you have a shift today?' she asks.

'No. I was looking for you.'

'Really?' Her expression brightens slightly: surely I've come to accept the job.

She nods me into the empty seat across from her.

'I need to ask you something.'

'Anything.'

I check out the smaller nearby tables. A man, younger than me, hooked up to his chemo and picking at a donut. Two dazed nurses drinking their coffees in silence.

Nettie leans over and softly says, 'I'm not recording if you aren't.' She smiles.

'I'm not.' Deep breath. 'My question is about your mother.'

The happy-to-see-me face dissolves. 'That's fair. Ask away.'

'How did you do it?'

'Oh. Is this about Viv?'

'Yes. We're there.'

She closes her eyes for a long moment. 'I'm sorry to hear that.'

'How did you do it?'

Nettie pauses, looking confused, until she figures out what I mean. 'I didn't.' She looks more bemused than wrongly accused. 'Did they tell you I did?'

'They said you gave her a fine death.'

She understands. 'Yes, but I couldn't have done it. I'd fed her and washed her for years, the way she took care of her mother. I was the sick one, sticking with it for so long. I couldn't work, couldn't think outside of her bedroom.'

'But you did go to Jasper,' I say.

'They helped me find the Nembutal, yes. I didn't give it to her. Her sister did. She wanted to do it.'

'The nurse?'

'Yes. She had retired by then. They had been close their whole lives, shared a bed until they were ten. Even after my mother stopped speaking, they were practically telepathic. My aunt gave her more confident care than I ever did. She didn't think twice about it. Could have been giving her an aspirin.' Nettie gives a grunt and a mild laugh. 'I'm sure she didn't lose a minute of sleep.'

255

She can see my body language is all wrong. My arms are folded, I'm hunching forward, sweaty. 'I'm sorry,' she says. 'What it was like for my aunt is not what it would have been like for me or what it would be like for you. I have no wisdom to give you here. I'm sorry. I really am.'

'Thanks anyway.'

Nettie reaches across the table to put her hands on mine. 'I'll take this visit to mean you haven't made up your mind about the job yet.'

'Correct.'

———

12.50.

Viv is asleep with her mouth open.

'So, Mum, Trish has given the greenish light for the matter we discussed earlier. The goods are in my pocket. Other news. Nettie couldn't do this for her mother, but because you raised me right—or let's just say, because you raised me—I can.'

Loud exhale.

'We have two hours to wrap this up. An age for you, since you've been here too long already, but as you may have heard, we have to hang out until handover. Any final words for me? Let me have them now.'

I tug at her hand for a response. 'Nothing? I keep thinking about what Dad said. Or what he wrote. Or what you said he wrote. If I'm going to break the family curse, I have to figure this one out. "Find something and stick with it and be happy with it." How might it have been to hear that when I was younger? In your professional opinion, would it have outweighed the chaotic home influences? Not that I have any right to complain now. As you've told many a teenager, "you can blame your parents for the first fifteen years. After that, it's on you."'

Viv swallows and coughs.

For an instant I think I've reached her by quoting her to herself. Wrong. Her eyes stay shut. Her tongue just lolls in and out a few times, puffy and dry.

'I can take a hint.' No ruminating. I hold the cup of water close, drawing the end of the straw across her cheek to activate a response. 'Here you go. Practice for later.' She slowly sucks at the tip of the straw until the water flows hesitatingly up to her mouth. Viv's eyebrows go up as the water goes down.

'Exquisite,' I say. Like the care Nettie gave her mother for years. 13.02.

'Since you don't want to talk, what do you say to a nap? It's hard to believe but I haven't been sleeping well. Let's scooch you over.'

I put one hand on her hip and one against her shoulder to slide her across the bed. She steels herself against me like a goat, grinning at the struggle. The guardrail is there to catch her on the other side, so I push hard until I win. She gives up, winded from the effort. Her feet are still in the centre of the bed and I straighten them, smoothing out her hospital gown and tucking the starched sheet back in around her. She watches the ceiling as I climb in next to her.

'Yes, I understand that you're not keen on the physical closeness. Tough. How many more times will I get to do this?'

From the hallway speakers, a woman with a blond-sounding voice is singing cheerily in tune with some merry-go-round kind of music.

Viv's resistance is gone. I hold still to see what she'll do with me right next to her. Over the next five minutes she moves across the mattress banking up against me, with her forehead resting against mine, face to face.

———

'Sir. Hey, sir!' In the doorway there's a man in an apron. 'Is she going to eat her lunch?'

I blink myself awake and sit up. A beige tray of food is on the tray table next to us. It wasn't there before. Mum shifts away from me. 2.08.

'Sorry to bother you, but I've got to clear,' he says.

I tell him, 'We didn't have a chance with it.'

He comes into the room and investigates the tray, lifting the plastic cover off the main course with a gloved hand to reveal large round slices of pale meat with gravy a tone darker on top. Nearby, a soft pile of greens, a pile of mashed whites, and some red relish.

'It was turkey dinner,' he says. 'They came in to feed it to her and seeing you two out like that probably gave up. Can I take it?'

I'm thinking about my alibi. 'Leave it and I'll see if I can get some into her.'

'Sure.' He takes a step out into the hallway to the roller rack and comes back to the bedside. 'If that's cold, try her on this.' He puts a can of Ensure on the tray and rolls the whole table closer so I can reach it from the bed.

At 2.11, I deliver the anti-emetic to her in a spoonful of pureed cranberry. She chews robotically, eventually remembering to swallow. She opens up for a second bite, which she doesn't get. As soon as the spoon is away from her lips, her mouth forgets the project and goes limp.

Halfway there.

A tiny nurse sticks her head into the room. 'Everybody's awake in here?' She's on her way down the hall, holding one hand on the side of the doorway as a brake. 'That your mother?'

'Yes.'

2.15.

'Good boy,' she says.

To prove it, I bring a scant second spoonful of cranberries to Viv's mouth, which opens for it, accepts and chews.

'You must be Evan.'

'Yes.'

This is enough to draw her into the room. 'I'm Meena. I looked after your mother before. Too bad. Life just isn't fair. Nice woman. Feisty,' she says with a wicked smile.

Somewhere deep in my mother's remnant brain, she is raging, *Feisty is another word for impotent. Go fuck yourself.*

'Mind if I have a peek and see if she's dry?'

258

I get off the bed to clear her path. Meena digs under my mother's sheets—without applying hand sanitiser, I notice—and reaches between the folds of her gown for a clear view of her pad. 'All clean,' she says, giving Viv, who's still moving her mouth around the second spoonful of cranberries, a pat on the shoulder for good behaviour. 'I'm on tomorrow. Maybe see you then.'

'See you then.' I add, 'My mother may still be sleepy. Would you mind closing the door on your way out?'

'Can do.'

2.22.

The little bulge of Nembutal is intact in my pocket. I take it to the basin and slice through the tiny square of tape with my fingernail to open it. A mint-green plastic mug sits on the shelf. I half fill it with water and pour in the powder, stirring it with a dull knife from the lunch tray.

Viv blinks at the wall. Her mouth opens and closes.

A quick double knock at the door is followed by Lon entering, perspiring from the trot over from low-care, his lanyard still swinging on his chest. 'Hey. I just found out.'

2.27.

'Thanks for coming,' I say.

He squeezes sanitiser onto his hands and rubs it in while I slide the green mug into the most hidden corner of the basin. Lon leans over the bed, his face close to Viv's. She puts on a faint smile, one I've never seen before, as though she's been told to act nice for company.

'Viv, I am so sorry,' he says to her.

'Did Trish tell you we were here?' I ask. She must have. She sent him here to intervene.

'No. I saw Viv's name on the bed list. Since I hadn't heard from you I was afraid she was here on her own, so I ran over.' He stays by her side, holding his other arm out for me. I walk into his almost absent-minded embrace.

'Sorry,' I say.

'Don't be,' he says. 'Stroke?'

259

'Seizure. A wrecking ball. Friday.'

'Friday.' He doesn't look away from her, but tells me, hurt. 'You should have called us.'

'It's been crazy,' I say. 'This was on the cards for a long time. She knew. I knew. It's practically a relief.'

'You look real relieved.'

Viv breathes out noisily.

'Can you do this?' he asks me.

In an instant, I attempt to triangulate the view from where he's standing to the sink, to determine if he can see the cup of Nembutal. Maybe he can. 'Can I do what?'

He pauses over my confusion, then catches what must be a very particular tension in my face. 'Can you visit her and sit with her until she dies a natural death? She will, you know. She's in the right place. You've got us for backup.'

'She doesn't know we're here.'

'You know she's here. Isn't it enough that she seems tranquil?'

I can hear *Hell no* echoing through her brain.

2.31.

Eyeing the clock, I ask him, 'Handover?'

'I can slide in without anyone noticing. Will you be here tonight?'

'I can't even picture the rest of today,' I say, trying to. Getting her to drink a bitter cup of Nembutal and keep it down. I'll alternate it with cranberry sauce. I'll climb into bed next to her while she dies, managing my distress until I inform the staff of what's happened. Then I get to let it out. Go through the motions with Trish, convince Lon that one final blessed seizure came right after he left the room. Plan a small funeral and call a few of her favourite students to give them the time and place. And what to do with her ashes.

'Stay,' Lon says. 'I'll swing by after my shift, pick you up, we'll get you fed tonight, whatever you need.' He holds Viv's shoulder, speaking loudly to reach her. 'Will you let us take care of him tonight?' He turns to me. 'See? She's cool with it. Either way, I'm coming back later and taking you home.' He glances at the meal tray. 'You should give up on the lunch and just get the Ensure into her.' He kisses Viv on the cheek.

'Yeah,' I say.

'And here's more high-tech care you can give her,' he says, walking over to the basin, grabbing a pale purple container from the ledge and tossing it to me. The cup must not have registered. I catch the bottle. It's lotion, the source of the ward's lavender smell. 'Put some on her. Make her happy.'

'I will. See you later.'

'See you later. You can do *this*,' he says, staring me down to be sure his meaning is clear.

'Got it,' I say, as he goes. I close the door after him and tell Viv, 'See? I can do this. We can do this.'

A glimpse of that fake smile again. Gas.

2.33.

'Can you hear the music, Mum? The DJs or the algorithm running the station has gone contemporary, or at least come as far as Joni. They're playing your song. "Both Sides, Now". You loved it once, all world-weary and wise. What was she—twenty-two? Already she knew everything. I want you to picture her standing outside by the door here. Still young. That washed-out blond hair swinging around. She's wearing a black turtleneck minidress. The guitar's hanging off her neck on a woven strap. A Mexican pattern you'd like, with some fat piece of turquoise set in the middle of it. Singing just for your send-off soundtrack.'

Viv's eyelids open to half-mast, then shut. Her breathing lapses into a steady *ssss*. Not only tranquil, but sturdy. Strong. Her skin is well perfused with blood. She's breathing. Warm. Still alive.

Months, Marais said. *A year, maybe.*

Joni finishes and a light xylophone starts up, slow and almost tuneless, going nowhere, with no vocals, no direction, to keep the natives distracted during handover.

2.36.

I pull back the sheet to look at Viv's prized feet one last time. I'll wash her body after. I'll ask one of the nurses to help me.

Viv would probably appreciate it now, but that's not how it's done. Besides, staff will need to see me cry.

I squeeze some of the lotion onto my palms, warm it up, then work on one foot at a time. Her body relaxes. When I massage it up past her ankles, thumbing into her calves that will never walk again, her eyes open a little and she gives a contented *jhjhjh* sound.

'It's like you've died and gone to a spa, isn't it?'

She keeps going, jutting her chin towards the feeling, getting louder. The rougher I get with her legs, the louder she gets. The last of the lotion is massaged into those sacred feet of hers and she's revving. When she's dead she won't feel this.

I take my hands off her and she's still going.

Find something and be happy with it.

I wipe the remaining lotion off on my arms. She's *jhjhjh*-ing softly. 2.39.

I take the cup of Nembutal to her bedside, put the straw in it, and hold it close to her, slipping a hand behind her warm back so she can sit up. The touch of my hand starts her purring louder again.

The cup is in front of her face. The straw is just out of reach of her mouth. 'Mum. This is Nembutal. If you drink it, your heart will stop and you will die. Is this what you want?'

She stops, jerks her hand up to her face, pokes her fingers against her cheek.

'The choice is yours.'

I give her back a squeeze to keep her up in a drinking position. This starts her going again. It doesn't matter that it's not a massage. The touch is enough. The corners of her mouth even hint at a smile.

'The choice is mine then.'

I put the cup down next to the turkey dinner. I take her hands in mine, rocking them back and forth in front of her. The touch is enough.

'What do you think about that?' I bring my face close to hers. All I get in return is a vague expression of wonder.

2.43.

'What about Trish? She's looking out for you. What do you think of her?' I bounce Viv's hands higher.

That gets a long *jhjhjhjh*.

'Lon's going to come get me later. Can I have a sleepover?' Another *jhjhjhjh*.

I speed up and she gets louder.

I slow down and she gets quieter.

'What about this room? Do the pastels work for you? If they officially admit you to the ward, family are allowed to make decorating requests. We could paint the walls turquoise so bright it would make your eyes hurt. You wouldn't even see the clock.' As long as I keep her hands moving, the serene moaning keeps up. 'Or bring in your jungle painting from home even.' She's still making her sound. 'What? No comment on that? You said this place was your nightmare.'

Her eyebrows lift slightly: *that was then*.

I stop moving.

After several seconds, she stops her sounds. Her attention feels different from when I grabbed her hands. Not merely tranquil—some part of her is present for me. And soothed. A minute passes and her attention disperses, shifting to the metal bedrail next to her, which she stares at like she's never seen such a thing.

I squeeze again and her head tilts towards the pressure. A half-hearted *jhjh*. It even sounds a tiny bit critical.

'Is that all I get?' I ask.

She says nothing, which is her sly way of saying *yep*.

'Then that's enough for me.' I let go of her hands. 'Looks like our minds are made up.'

2.46.

I pick up the cup of Nembutal, take it over to the basin and pour it into the drain.

By the time I get back to the bed she's looking at the bedrail again.

'Do you forgive me?' I ask.

My mother blinks, which means yes or it means no or it means her eyes are dry.

I climb back in next to her. She rouses at the intrusion while inching her body towards the new weight on her mattress, curving against me again, keeping her eyes open this time. I watch her too. Her mouth relaxes. Her hospital breath fills the small space between us.

'Nothing a little mouthwash couldn't fix? Or should I just collect your perfumes and bring them in.'

She almost nods.

'Don't worry, I know you like to have a hedge. There's a spare dose waiting at home. For when I run out of exquisite care or when you stop purring.'

I break her gaze to reach over to the tray table for the Ensure. 'Here it is then, your mortal fear.' She looks at the can. 'Coffee latte. At least it's not strawberry. *That* would be cruel.'

I pop it open and take a swig. 'Not the best, not the worst. It's what's here. If you don't like it, you can give it to me.'

I put in a new straw and hold the tip of it in front of her mouth. She closes her eyes to concentrate but she knows exactly what to do, pursing her lips together and pushing them forward for a sip.

ACKNOWLEDGEMENTS

OVER THE YEARS that I have worked as a palliative care nurse, despairing patients or fearful carers have occasionally asked me if something might be done to speed things up. My first answer is short and legal, some softened variant of *No*. Then I reorient the discussion to pain management and specific burdens to see if there are any other measures that can ease their distress. We can almost always improve a situation. When we can't, and when the topic comes up again, part of me wishes I could say, *Sure, just let me get the drugs for you*. But another part of me is glad that task is not within my job description. This is when I am relieved to have another outlet.

At the start of this process, the Australia Council provided a generous grant that allowed me to change my nursing/writing ratio so I could begin to plan a book about a dying assistant. (My original proposal to them was for another subject, so any objections you may have, please don't take them to the Australia Council.) More recently, Varuna provided me with space and three rainy weeks in the Blue Mountains to write the last scenes. I am grateful to both for their help.

It feels necessary for a nurse who writes to be clear that no patient details were used in the writing of this book. That said, I wouldn't have written this book if so many patients hadn't left their mark on me. Thanks goes to all of them as well as to my amazing and supportive nursing colleagues.

Also: Abigail Asher, SJ Finn, Krissy Kneen, Jennifer Morgan, Nicola Redhouse and Sharon Block were and are necessary readers; Lisa Jacobson offered some late but critical wisdom; Nicola Barr revealed herself to be not only a fierce agent, but a whip smart editor. Additional deep-tissue work was performed by the cheerful and yet direct efforts of my publisher Robert Watkins, the extraordinary Clara Finlay and the wonderful Kate Stevens. I'm also so very grateful for the passion shown by the team at Hachette Australia, including, but not remotely limited to, Jessica Skipper, Tom Saras, Andrew Cattanach, Daniel Pilkington and Nathan Grice. Finally, thanks to Corry DeNeef, for wisdom and love.